THE NEW HOUSE AT THE CHALET SCHOOL

THE CHALET SCHOOL SERIES
By E. M. BRENT-DYER
in order of publication

THE NEW HOUSE
AT THE
CHALET SCHOOL

ELINOR M. BRENT-DYER

W. & R. CHAMBERS LTD
LONDON & EDINBURGH

Latest Reprint 1963

Printed in Great Britain
by T. and A. CONSTABLE LTD., Hopetoun Street,
Printers to the University of Edinburgh

DEDICATED TO

GERALDINE AND EILEEN CUDDON

WITH LOVE FROM

ELINOR

CONTENTS

THE NEW HOUSE AT THE
CHALET SCHOOL

CHAPTER I

THE NEW ARRANGEMENTS

'WELL, Jo! So here you are. Have you had a good holiday?'

The tall, dark girl who had just entered the front door at the Chalet School dropped her suitcase and gripped the hand Matron was offering her. 'Hello, Matey! Jolly to see you again! Yes; we've had a very good week, thank you.'

'That's good hearing!—No; leave your case there—or rather put it to one side, or someone will fall over it. Mademoiselle wants you as soon as you come. She's in the study now, so you'd better run along at once.'

Jo Bettany raised her eyebrows. 'What—before I take my things upstairs?'

'Yes,' replied Matron briefly, turning to go to the other end of the house, whence she could hear the voices of those girls who had accompanied Jo down from the Sonnalpe, where they had been spending their brief spring holiday.

'Oh, all right, then. Don't let anyone bag my special bed, will you?'

'That will be all right.' And Matron vanished with the air of a busy woman, while Jo, after glancing at herself in a nearby mirror to be sure that she was

9

quite tidy, went along the passage to a door and knocked.

A quiet voice spoke at once : ' Entrez ! '

Jo went into the sunny room, where flowers, books, and a glorious view of the Tiern See, the lake near which the school was situated, made it really charming. At the desk in the window sat a plain but pleasant-faced woman, unmistakably French, who smiled as the Head Girl made her curtsey. This was Mademoiselle Lepâttre, the acting-Head of the Chalet School which she and Jo's sister, once Madge Bettany, now Mrs Russell of the Sonnalpe, had started five years before on the shores of the loveliest lake in the Austrian Tyrol. When Miss Bettany became Mrs Russell, Mademoiselle had taken over the direction of the school, while the late Head of it still retained a deep interest in it, both financially and otherwise.

' Bon jour, Mademoiselle,' said Joey, advancing to receive the double kiss she always expected on such occasions. ' You have enjoyed your holiday ? Yes ? And we also. It has been very pleasant.'

' I am glad to hear it. And now, mon enfant, seat yourself. There is much to tell you, and but little time for it.'

Jo sat down wonderingly. What in the world did this mean ? Why must Mademoiselle speak to her *at once* ? As a rule she settled in before she reported herself. She fixed curious black eyes on the Head's face and waited.

Mademoiselle looked at her. ' You know, of course, my Jo, that this term we open our new house ? '

Jo nodded. ' Yes, Mademoiselle. Madge told me so.'

' Ah, but she has not told all,' said Mademoiselle slowly. ' As you know, our middles will be over there.

Not all of them, for the very youngest will go to Le Petit Chalet. We are making that the junior house, and will have all the little ones there.'

'But I thought they were full up there,' protested Jo, dropping into English in her surprise.

'That was true. But for the future there will be no class-rooms there or at the middle house. All will be over here in the Chalet, for only the seniors will live here.'

Jo thought this over. 'I see. It's a good plan. But what will happen in the winter, Mademoiselle?'

'We are arranging for that. We are building covered passages which will communicate with all three houses. During the summer holidays, which, as you know, will be very long this year, they will be erected, and when winter comes it will be quite easy for all to come to the school, whether we have storms or not.'

'That will be jolly,' said Jo appreciatively. Then she laughed. 'Do you know, Mademoiselle, you're making me quite sorry I'm leaving this term—sorrier than I was, I mean. I should like to be in all this new business.'

'Well, at least you will be in it for this term,' said Mademoiselle, with a smile. 'But I have yet more to say. Have you ever thought who will take charge over at the new house?'

'I thought Miss Wilson was to be Head,' said Jo, rather startled.

'She will be Head, yes; also Miss Stewart and Miss Nalder will be with her, as well as our new Matron. But we must have prefects there too.'

Jo had been lounging in her chair; but now she sat bolt upright, for she began to guess what was coming. 'Mademoiselle! You mean——'

'Yes, my Jo. For the future, our Head Girl will always be over at the middle house. She will have other prefects with her, of course. We all, I think, recognise that the middles are the girls who most need the prefects. And though the Quintette '—Mademoiselle gave a little smile—' will be broken up this term, still, as I think you know, they are not responsible for *all* the sin among the middles. Elsie Carr and Margia Stevens are now seniors, and will remain here. But Evadne Lannis, Cornelia Flower, and Ilonka Barkocz, with Maria Marani, are to be seniors at the new house. I trust they will rise to their responsibilities, and now put away their childish mischief.'

Jo remained silent, chiefly because she felt too stunned to speak. She was to leave the Chalet, which had been almost Home to her for five years, and go over to the new house ! And what did Mademoiselle know about the Quintette ? And who on earth were the other prefects to be ? Her three greatest friends were Frieda Mensch, Marie von Eschenau, and Simone Lecoutier, the last named being Mademoiselle's young cousin. They four had come up the school side by side, and though she had friends among the other prefects, these were nearest to her. Were they to be separated now ? But Mademoiselle was speaking again, and the Head Girl gave her full attention to the words.

'We have considered the matter very carefully, and we think it wisest to place the four strongest prefects above the middles. You are Head Girl ; Frieda is Second Prefect ; Marie is Games Prefect ; and Simone is your friend, all of you. It is you four who will be there, and you must be prepared to be greatly responsible for the good order. Miss Wilson and her colleagues cannot be over there all the time, nor even most of the time. So we shall look to you four to see that rules are obeyed, and that all goes as it ought.' Here Mademoiselle's tone altered, and she looked straight at the Head Girl. 'I know that it is much to demand of you, my Jo. But the school has given you much, and now it asks for this in return.'

'But—do you mean that we shan't go back to the Green dormitory again ?' gasped Jo, whose ideas were all at sea. 'But—I've only been there and in the Yellow, except for one term in the Violet. I simply can't take it in, Mademoiselle !'

'Suppose we go over to the new house for a little and see your room and the prefects' room there,' proposed Mademoiselle. 'If you will bring your case and settle your possessions, then it may help you to realise it better. Matron has already sent over those you left here the week before last. I think you will like your room when you see it,' she added persuasively.

'My room ? *Not* a dormitory ?' asked Jo, following her from the room.

'No. As prefects, you four will each have a room. Naturally, as Head Girl yours is, in many ways, the best. But we have tried to make all four pretty, as I hope you will agree. Simone likes hers very well— she is there already. When Marie and Frieda come you will show them theirs, n'est-ce pas ? And I hope you will all like the privacy you gain thus.'

'It's very good of you, Mademoiselle,' said Jo, as she picked up her case and opened the front-door for the Head, 'but it seems such a change I can't believe it.'

'But you will soon,' Mademoiselle assured her, as she turned into the path that led round the house.

' This is the way the prefects will come, Jo, except the one on duty. Each of you will have a morning in turn when you will bring the middles over for work. Also you will take them back for Mittagessen. When we have our passages built, there will be no need for this. But for this one term, when you must cross the field, it will be necessary for one prefect to be in charge ; and the girls must march properly, and in good order.'

' Yes, Mademoiselle,' assented Jo.

They turned off the path, and went down the flower-garden, and through a wicket-gate, newly erected, and into another garden where men were hard at work, bringing what had been meadow-land into proper trim. The girls had not been permitted to see much of the new house during the previous term, for the weather had not been good. For another thing, the authorities had not been anxious to have any accidents, and the tall ladders might have been too much for some of the more wicked spirits among the middles. Now the Head Girl eyed her future abode with interest. When last she had seen it, it had been surrounded with scaffolding. That had vanished, and before her stood a large, long house, two storeys high in front, though the back had an additional floor. It was built largely of wood and plaster, like the other two houses of the school, and the plastering had been decorated with frescoes. Four casement windows ran along one side ; then came the front-door, with a big porch, and another casement. Above these ran a line of ten windows ; and above these again what proved to be a roof-garden, the flatness being broken by two ridge-shaped skylights which, as Joey found later, lighted the back cubicles of the two large dormitories at the front of the first floor.

'We will go in,' said Mademoiselle. 'Come, Joey.'

Jo followed her, and found herself in a wide, square hall, with a passage running right across it at the back, obviously leading to the ground-floor rooms ; and a wide staircase springing from the centre to the upper regions.

'We will see this part first,' said Mademoiselle, as she led the girl to the back of the hall. 'Leave your case by the stairs, and you may get it when we return.' She turned to her left and opened a door, giving a glimpse of a pretty room, with flowered curtains at the wide window, plants on the broad sill, and a canary in a large cage, piping cheerfully. 'This is the prefects' room, where you four will sit and work, and have your Kaffee und Kuchen by yourselves when you wish. See, mon chou,' and she opened a cupboard-door, 'we have provided cups and saucers for you. But you shall examine all this later. Now we must go on.'

Jo followed her out of the room and into a much larger one, with desks set in straight lines, and a mistress's platform and desk at the top of the room. 'This the study ? ' she asked. 'I suppose the middles will do prep here ? '

'Yes ; also we shall make of it a detention-room, I think. Now we come to the common-room, where you will dance, and amuse yourselves.'

Jo looked round it. Like the prefects' room it was very gay with flowers, and bright pictures hung on the walls. 'What's at the back ? ' she asked.

'The kitchens and their offices. Also your Speisesaal, for you will have meals here unless for a great occasion. This door leads out, and will be the door used by the girls. From here we shall build our passage. Now we will go along to the other end of the house.'

They duly went, and Mademoiselle pointed out the splasheries which the girls would use during the day-time.

' Where does this door lead to ? ' asked Jo, pointing to a baize-covered door at the end of the wider passage.

' That leads to the sanatorium. Come and see it,' said Mademoiselle. She took the Head Girl through, and showed her the very complete place, with cubicles for sick cases, a smaller room for suspects ; and a dainty little chamber intended for a nurse. Beyond were the bathroom, and a tiny kitchen where meals could be prepared. Jo was delighted with it all, and especially with the fact that it had its own ' front-door ' which led on to a little lawn with flower-beds, where convalescents could take the air in privacy.

' I think it's marvellous,' she declared. ' I'm going to have a week-end here if I can, I can tell you ! I suppose Jem arranged it all ? What a brain that brother-in-law of mine is ! '

' Yes,' said Mademoiselle. ' Our dear Dr Jem saw to all this. But if you are ill, Jo, I shall warn Matron to give you castor-oil. So be careful ! '

Jo chuckled. ' You couldn't utter a worse threat ! I'll be careful ! '

After this they went upstairs, where everything was as fresh and dainty as downstairs. On either side of the staircase were two big dormitories, each divided up into cubicles, one containing eighteen and the other sixteen. Behind the smaller one, and looking up the Tiern Valley, were the rooms of the three mistresses and that ordained for Frieda Mensch. Behind the other came a narrow dormitory with six cubicles. Passages ran across the ends of the long one that bisected the floor, and down these lay bathrooms and so on at the back of the house. To the front were three rooms.

' Those at the far end are for Simone and Marie,' explained Mademoiselle, ' and one larger one for two of the senior middles. Their windows all look towards the stream and the Kron Prinz Karl. But you will see those later. Come, now, and see your own room.'

She preceded Jo along the wide corridor to the end nearest the original school. ' The end room, which has two windows and looks on to the lake and also the school garden, is the Matron's room,' she said. ' Then comes the room Cornelia and Ilonka will share. And this is yours.' She threw open the door, and Jo entered her new domain.

It was a delightfully pretty room, with buttercup-yellow walls, white paint, and curtains, rugs, bed-spread, and hangings all of white besprinkled with jonquils, daffodils, and buttercups. The china on the wash-stand—no bathroom for the Head Girl now—was painted to match, and there was a little white bookcase beside the bed, with room for about a dozen books in it. A copy of the ' Garden ' Madonna hung over the bed ; and on the opposite wall was a print of Antonio Moroni's ' Tailor,' a favourite picture of Jo's. She gave an exclamation of delight, for the room was so pretty and sunshiny.

' You like it, ma petite ? ' asked Mademoiselle, with an anxious look at the clever, sensitive face.

' It's beautiful,' said Jo quietly. ' Thank you, Mademoiselle. It is one of the prettiest rooms I have ever seen.'

' Frieda's faces north, so she has orange and white,

and her flowers are marigolds and nasturtiums,' said Mademoiselle. ' Marie and Simone face east, so they are all pink. Only we have given Marie crimson roses and pink lupins and delphiniums, and Simone has fuchsias and almond-blossom.'

' What's upstairs ? ' asked Jo curiously.

' The rooms for the servants. And there are two big dormitories which we shall not use yet, and the practising-rooms. There is also a storeroom, and as the cupboards are all kept locked, we have put a piano in there. I do not wish to have naughty children mixing salt with sugar and pepper with coffee ! ' And Mademoiselle laughed. ' We have also two bedrooms for extra staff, should we need them. At present they, too, will be practising-rooms. But now I must return, or they will be seeking me, and not know where I am. Simone is in her room, and doubtless Frieda, also, will come soon. Marie I do not expect till eighteen this evening. I must leave you, my Jo.'

' Just one moment, Mademoiselle,' implored Jo. ' When do the middles turn up—here, I mean ? '

' All but Joyce Linton—she will stay with the sick mother until Monday, did you not tell me ?—will be here by seventeen o'clock,' said Mademoiselle, using the mid-European time as they always did. ' I shall not send any over here yet. Au revoir, mon chou. I shall see you at Mittagessen, which to-day you take over at the Chalet.'

Mademoiselle departed, and Jo was left standing in the middle of her new abode, still looking round it with appreciative eyes. Presently she went to her case, which she proceeded to open before she examined the chest of drawers, in which the things she had left behind when she had gone to her sister at the Sonnalpe for the ten days' spring holiday had been already put.

'It's well to be seen that Matey has done this,' she thought, as she noted the immaculate neatness. 'Well, I'd better clear out my case, I suppose, and then go along and see Simone. I wonder what she makes of all this?'

She turned her case, and began stowing away the contents with a tidiness born of the example before her, and certainly *not* natural. 'There is one thing,' she continued to herself, 'it's all been done so suddenly and unexpectedly, and we'll be in the throes of work so quickly, that I doubt if any of us will have time to miss the dear old dormy over at the Chalet. And if we do, we'll have got so accustomed to all this luxury that it won't seem quite so bad.' She laid her gloves in their case and put it into its drawer, which she closed firmly. Then she shut her suitcase and pushed it under the bed. 'There! That's done! Now to find Simone! I wonder what she thinks about all this?'

CHAPTER II

THE PREFECTS' OPINIONS

WHISTLING like a blackbird, Jo strolled along the wide corridor and turned into the narrower one at the end. Just as she finished a verse of 'Shenandoah' a door flew open, and a slight girl of eighteen, as dark as herself but unmistakably French, appeared in it. This was one of Jo's trio of friends, Simone Lecoutier.

'Joey!' she cried. 'I thought it was you when I heard the whistling! Come in and see my room. But it is so pretty!'

Joey entered a room smaller than her own, but quite as pretty, with cretonne showing sprays of delicate pink almond-blossom, and clusters of fuchsias like dainty court-ladies, with white bells under pink petals. The white rugs had fuchsias too; and Simone's pink dressing-gown hanging at the foot of the bed matched the scheme perfectly.

'Glad to see you again, Simone, petite,' said Joey, as she sank into the basket-chair by the window. 'Well, what do you think of all this? It's a shock to me, I don't mind telling you. I haven't recovered yet.'

'Nor I,' agreed Simone, sitting down on the foot of the bed. 'When Cousine Thérèse told me that we four were to be over here for this term, I was robbed of my breath—but robbed completely.'

'I'm still breathless,' declared Jo. 'And I don't know whether I quite like it. I never, in my wildest moments, imagined that I should finish my school-life in a place that wasn't the dear old Chalet. Even all this glory doesn't make it seem worth it.'

'I think perhaps it is,' said Simone slowly. 'I shall miss our dormitory and all the good times we had together—Do you remember our circus the last night of the Christmas term, my Jo?—but we are growing up, and we must expect changes. And it will be very pleasant to have our own rooms where we can be quite private.'

'There's that in it, of course,' agreed Jo. 'At the same time, I'd rather have finished where we began.'

'I wonder what Frieda and Marie will say?' mused Simone. She looked across at her friend. 'After all, Jo, it is not so bad as it might have been. We four are still together.'

'Yes; it would have been rather a blow if they'd separated us—as Elsie and Margia are separated from the rest of that gang now,' said Jo.

'But that will be for a term only,' said Simone. 'The other four will become seniors at the end of this term, and then they will go back to the Chalet. And *we* shall not be here at all—hélas!'

'*Don't!*' said Jo sharply. 'I hate the idea of leaving school. Don't rub it in, Simone.'

'But you would not wish to stay at school all your life?' queried her friend. 'After this there will be other things for us to do, Joey. For me the Sorbonne, I hope, and all the work there. Then comes teaching, and Cousine Thérèse has promised that I shall come back here. And for you there will be certainly work at the Sonnalpe. Or do you keep to the old plan, and go to Belsornia as lady-in-waiting to Elisaveta?'

Jo shook her head. 'No; not now that Sybil has

come. And Dick and Mollie come home on furlough
this summer; and when they return, they will leave
Bride behind at Die Rosen. I couldn't go away and
leave my sister with all those babies to look after.
Elisaveta can get any number of girls to maid-of-
honour her; but Madge has only me.'

'Elisaveta will be disappointed,' said Simone, with
a thought for the young Crown Princess of Belsornia,
who, three years before, had spent two happy terms
at the Chalet School as a schoolgirl.

'Elisaveta knows how we are situated,' said Jo.
'After all, she comes here for a holiday most years,
and I shall see her then. It would be much harder,
really, in Belsornia. Court etiquette produces a
certain amount of constraint, however fond of each
other you may be. And they'll be thinking of a
husband for her before long. I'd rather have it as it
is, I think.'

'And at least we are together this term,' murmured
Simone, who, five years before, had begun her school-
life with an adoration for Jo which had never lessened,
though the years had robbed it of its sentimentality,
and the adoration had become a true, healthy friendship.

'That's true. We shall be able to *enjoy* each other
far more over here than we ever did over there,' said
Jo, with a nod in the direction of the original school.
'I like the others; but we four are—well—closer,
somehow. Have you seen my abode yet? Not?
Then come on and see it now. We'll wait for the other
two to come before we invade theirs.'

The two girls left the pretty pink room and went
back to Jo's yellow one, where Simone exclaimed and
admired to the heart's content of its owner. That

done, they toured the dormitories ; peeped out of the windows at the fire-escapes which ran down the back of the house, and then went downstairs to the prefects' room, where the canary was still singing deafeningly.

' Rather a change from the bare place the first prefects had to use,' said Jo, thinking of the time, five years ago now, when the Chalet School was a new venture, and she and Simone had been among the first middles. ' It seems scarcely possible that all this richness belongs to the school we had then, does it ? '

But Simone, who had been gazing out of the window, was not heeding her. ' Here is Frieda,' she said. ' She comes with Bill. Shall we not go and welcome them ? It would be gentille, n'est-ce pas ? '

' Right ! We'll be gentille,' agreed Jo. ' Besides, I'm longing to hear about Frieda's first nephew.'

They left the room and went into the hall, just as a very tall woman with a pleasant face came in, a slightly-built, fair girl of their own age, with the apple-blossom skin and blue eyes of the north Tyrol, at her side.

' Miss Wilson ! ' cried Jo. ' Welcome to our new abode ! How are you going to like it ? '

' Thanks, Joey. I arrived two days ago,' said Miss Wilson calmly, as she shook hands with the pair. ' How is everyone at the Sonnalpe ? Good news all round ? '

' Oh, excellent ! My sister is splendid, now, and Baby is such a darling, now I've got used to her ginger locks. The other babes are very fit, too, and full of monkey-tricks. And Mrs Linton is out of danger, and Jem says that he thinks they will be able to pull her through now. But she must never live in England again, though she may go back in the summer for holidays. She is talking of building a Chalet up on the

Sonnalpe. That will make it quite possible for Gill and Joyce to finish their education here. They are staying up till Monday, but they are coming down then.—And what do you think, you people ?' And she swung round on her two friends who had been greeting each other. ' Stacie is coming down with them.'

' I am glad of that,' said Frieda, coming to kiss her. ' Poor Stacie ! She has had a whole year since the accident. How good that her back is well now ! And did you have a good time, Jo ? '

' Oh yes ! The only pity was that it was so short. And then the first day or two were rather messed up with Mrs Linton's illness. But she's over the worst now. What about you ? And what about Bernhilda and her son ? '

' Frieda laughed. ' Oh, he has a name, Joey. He was christened last week. Bernhilda has named him after his two grandpapas, so he is Stefan Kurt. He is very well—such a big, beautiful baby, and very like Bernhilda herself.'

' And Bernie ? ' demanded Jo, speaking of Frieda's elder sister, who was an old girl of the school and who had married the elder brother of the last of their quartette, Marie von Eschenau. Bernhilda and Kurt von Eschenau were rejoicing in the birth of their first child, and Frieda had spent her ten days' holiday in an orgy of baby-worship.

' Bernie is doing well, and she is so happy,' said the Tyrolean girl, smiling. ' She is longing to show you little Stefan—yes ; that is what we call him—at half-term. Papa and Mamma want you and Marie and Simone to spend it with us. The Robin also, if our dear Madame will permit it.'

Jo smiled at the mention of her little adopted sister,

Robin Humphries. 'I am sure she will. Robin is growing stronger every day now. You will see a big change in her at half-term—unless you go up to the Sonnalpe before then,' she added.

Miss Wilson, who had been listening with interest to the talk, now nodded to them. 'I must go to my room, girls.—Joey, Mademoiselle will send over such middles as have arrived in about an hour's time. Matron Besly, who is our new Matron, will bring them across.—So you three had best make the most of your time, for once they arrive, you'll be busy.'

The three girls thanked her, and she sped off upstairs, as excited over the new arrangements as any of them, despite her years of work in the school, to say nothing of her twelve years' seniority to them.

'Bill's a dear,' said Jo, looking after her. 'Well, come along upstairs, Frieda, and show us your room. Mademoiselle told us that it was orange and white, and that your flowers are marigolds and nasturtiums. Mine is yellow, and I've got jonquils, and daffs, and buttercups; and Simone's is all pink. Marie's is pink too, I understand, but they've given her crimson roses as well. Show us yours, and we'll show you ours.'

'Oh yes; do let us go! I am longing to see it all!' cried Frieda. She picked up her case, and the three went upstairs together to the pretty room with its view of the entrance to the great Tiern Pass. After they had inspected it and shown off the other two, the trio went downstairs and settled themselves in the prefects' room.

'Now we can talk,' said Jo. 'Well, what do you think about it all?'

'I suppose it is, after all, only what we should have expected,' said Frieda thoughtfully.

'I don't see that. I should have thought they'd have given the younger prefects a chance, and left us where we were. It's only for a term for all of us, and it would have meant not quite so much changing.'

'That is true,' assented Frieda. 'At the same time, Jo, we are the eldest, and we are the four chief prefects. We should be able to have more authority. And the middles *are* the middles,' she finished.

'Yes; but don't you think the others might be more in touch with people like Joyce Linton, and Mary Shaw, and all the younger middles ? I haven't yet forgotten the shock I got when Joyce Linton referred to me as " grown-up." You, and Marie, and Simone all have your hair up. As Joyce said then, it's only because I'm bobbed that mine isn't up too.' Here, Jo stopped short, and looked at them with a funny expression on her face.

They were too interested in the subject to notice, however. Frieda laughed, and lifted her hand to the masses of corn-coloured plaits that encircled her head. 'I see what you mean. But just for that reason we ought to be able to keep better order. Evvy and Lonny and Corney need a strong hand, Jo. And they are not the only ones.'

'And we are not the only ones leaving, either,' put in Simone. 'Consider, Jo ! Sophie, Carla, Eva, Vanna, and Bianca all go too. Only those who are sub-prefects will be left to take our places. Whoever had been chosen it must have meant a change next term.'

'Well, they could have sent Louise and Anne and Paula and Thora over,' said Jo stubbornly. 'I'm sure they could quell even the whole Quintette if necessary.'

' I expect Mademoiselle wishes them to have experience where the seniors are before they come to the middles,' said Frieda wisely. ' But it is now twelve o'clock, Jo, and I hear voices. The middles and our new Matron are coming. Shall we go and welcome them ? '

' I suppose we might as well,' agreed the Head Girl, rising from her seat on the window-sill. ' Mercy ! What a racket ! *That* will have to stop once term begins.'

The three left the room and went out to receive a vociferous greeting from the new arrivals, and the conversation ended for the time being. But it was resumed much later on—to be accurate, after Abendessen, as supper was always called at the Chalet School—when the fourth of their quartette, Marie von Eschenau, had arrived and settled in in her rosy room. By that time the whole School was back, with the exceptions of the two Lintons and Stacie Benson, whose second coming to the school this would be. A year ago she had arrived, full of ideas of her own importance and a decision to impress it on the School. The nett result had been a bad accident, which had kept her prisoner for three terms up at the Sonnalpe where Jo's brother-in-law, Dr James Russell, and many other devoted men and women fought the terrible plague of tuberculosis at the great Sanatorium which the doctor had established there. Stacie's own folly had brought about the accident, and she had paid heavily for it ; but now she was much better, and was to be allowed to come back to school this term, though she could not undertake a full time-table of work, nor must she play games, as Jo explained to those who had known her during her stormy first term.

The Linton girls, just now at the Sonnalpe with their mother, who had been brought back from the Valley of the Shadow of Death only ten days previously, had come to the school the term before, and had already made a mark in the school, and all the middles cheered when they heard of Mrs Linton's slow but steady progress towards recovery.

What with one thing and another there had been no time for talk, as Jo remarked when at last she and her three friends were seated comfortably in the prefects' room at the new house, enjoying chocolate and biscuits before they went to bed. This was to be one of their new privileges, Mademoiselle had informed them, and was one reason why their pretty china had been provided. They must go upstairs no later than ten, or twenty-two, as they called it here ; but no one would interfere with them so long as they did not abuse their extra liberty.

'Altogether, it seems to me that we are in clover in some ways,' said Jo, as she stirred her chocolate.

Marie von Eschenau, an exquisitely lovely girl of eighteen, looked up. 'But not in all ways ? What, then, is it that you dislike, Joey ? Tell us, Herzliebchen.'

'It's the change,' said Jo. 'I never thought of anything but that we would finish our time at the Chalet itself. I'm not altogether sure that I like all this.'

'I know what you mean,' said Simone, who was fishing in the biscuit-tin for maccaroons. 'But, Joey, we cannot remain bébées always. We must grow up——'

'Oh, do stop it ! ' groaned Jo.

The other three laughed. It was well known in

the School that Jo resented the bare idea of having
to grow up.

'But it has to come,' said Marie. 'Why not
expect it and look forward to it, Jo, instead of hating
it as you do, and being so very miserable about it ?
David and Baby Sybil will not wish for a baby aunt,
I am sure. They will want someone who can guide
them. If you stay Kindchen, you cannot do that.'

Jo's sensitive face became grave. 'I know. But,
oh ! I've had such a jolly time at school, and I can't
bear to think that it's nearly over !'

'But so had Bernhilda, and Wanda, and Gisela a
happy time,' said Frieda. 'Yet I think they would
tell you that they are very happy now, though it is a
different kind of happiness, Jo. And Grizel and
Juliet up at the Annexe, they are happy too. And
again, it is a different kind of happiness. You will
find it like that also, I am sure.'

'But Bernie and Gisela and Wanda have husbands
and babies,' protested Jo. 'I certainly don't want
any husbands. And we've heaps of babies at Die
Rosen as it is. And Grizel and Juliet are teaching ;
but there isn't anything of that kind for me to do.
I shall just stay at home, and help with the children,
and practise my singing, and so on. It does *not* appeal
to me after the full life we lead here—it seems so—so
little, somehow. It's just doing little bits of things
that aren't important.'

'You will write your book,' said Simone soothingly.

'Yes ; but it probably won't be any good,' said
Jo pessimistically.

'I think it will be *very* good,' said Simone firmly.

'And you do not know. The husband may come,'
said Marie, her lovely face touched with deeper colour.

' Then that would mean babies of your own for which you must do everything, and that is not a little thing, Jo. Your life would be very full and busy then.'

Usually Jo shied away from such talk. But somehow this great change in her school-life had made her think. Despite her protests, she felt an older girl than she had done when she left home that morning, and she answered Marie seriously, and without the irritation she generally showed at the subject.

' I don't think it's at all likely, Marie. I don't even think I want it. Somehow, I can't imagine it for myself. You and Frieda will marry, of course ; and very soon, too. And Simone will probably do so after she has taught a few years. But I simply can't imagine myself darning someone else's socks, and pouring out his coffee.'

' I hope it *will* come, all the same,' said Marie. ' It is why God created women.'

' I don't see how it can. I don't know of anyone.'

' Don't you ? ' Marie gave her a funny little smile, which made Jo look at her sharply before she turned away. ' Oh well, if it is to come, it will come. But, in the meantime, do not try to push it back, Joey.'

' And this is our first taste of complete responsibility,' added Frieda. ' There will doubtless be many nights when the Staff are over at the Chalet and we shall be left in charge as now. Jo, it is ten minutes of twenty-two. Had we not better go round the dormitories ? I know they are not asleep yet, for I have heard voices from above as we sat here.'

' I suppose you are right,' said Jo, with a sigh of relief. ' What about this crockery ? We can't put it away dirty.'

' I will wash it to-night,' said Simone. ' You three

go and see that all is well and the middles cease to talk. To-morrow night someone else will do the washing-up.'

' Yes ; we must make our lists out. And, of course, we shall have our prefects' meeting to-morrow afternoon, I hope, to fix school duties,' said Jo from the doorway.

' Will that be there or over here ? ' asked Frieda.

' Oh, over there, of course. All school business will be—er—transacted over there. But we must get permission to have the rest of the prees over here for Kaffee und Kuchen occasionally,' said Jo. ' Hello ! Is that a Rugger scrum taking place upstairs ? Come on ! We must inquire into this at once ! '

And casting behind her all questions about the future, she went leaping upstairs to the big dormitory whence came the noise that completely justified her description of it.

CHAPTER III

JO HAS TOOTHACHE

THE term was well begun, and people were now comfortably settled in. Monday morning had brought Dr Russell with the two Lintons and Stacie Benson. Gillian, the elder Linton, had gone off to the Chalet, as she was a senior; and Joyce and Stacie had come to the new house where Joyce, who had been a firebrand the previous term, showed every sign of behaving herself and working properly. She had come very near expulsion during her first term, and that, and the remembrance of her mother's terrible illness after hearing that the expulsion was supposed to have taken place, had sobered her considerably. Unfortunately, when you have most industriously slacked for the first fourteen years of your life, it is difficult to get into steady working trim at once, and many a time did Joyce feel as if it were impossible to go on.

Stacie's problem was a different one. The only child of a professor whose one thought in life had been Greek plays, and a brilliant woman-doctor, she had always loved her work, and her classics would not have disgraced a public-school boy of her own age. But other subjects had been sadly neglected, and though she had spent a goodly portion of her enforced rest in reading and studying, she still had much lost ground to recover. And she had, to a certain extent, to make good her footing among the girls. Her first term, like Joyce's, had been a disastrous one for her. Unaccustomed to school-life, she had made many enemies, and though some of the girls had got to know her better while she was up at the Sonnalpe, it was not the case with all of them, and they still looked at her askance.

' All the same,' murmured eleven-year-old Kitty Burnett to one of her special cronies, ' she does look different, now she's got rid of that awful pigtail of hers. I never would have believed that Eustacia Benson was so pretty.'

' She's Stacie now,' replied Mary Shaw. ' Anyway, I never knew her as anything else. Was she so awful, Kits ? '

' The limit,' said Kitty with conviction. ' She smacked my face once, just because I fell over her. There was a nice row about that ! '

' Are you children *ready* ? ' demanded the Head Girl's voice at that moment. ' I'm not going to wait all day for you. If you can't be ready to come now, you can just wait and come with Miss Wilson. Hurry up ; and don't stand there gossiping ! '

The pair fled before the storm. Something, they knew, must have upset Jo that morning, for she was in none too sweet a temper. When she was like this, her tongue had an edge like a razor, and they were not anxious to incur it.

Jo shut the door of the cloak-room and stalked after them. As a matter of fact, she was suffering from a dull, gnawing toothache ; but as she had no desire to pay a visit to Herr von Francius, the school dentist, she held her tongue about it, and suffered in silence. Matron Lloyd over at the Chalet would have found out about it in a moment ; but Matron Besly was new to her work, and, into the bargain, stood rather in awe of the Head Girl. Jo had not taken to her, stig-

matising her as ' a fluffy little idiot '—very strictly
to herself, however—and had been on her dignity.

' Are you not well, Jo ? ' asked Vanna di Ricci, one
of the prefects, as the Head Girl entered the Sixth form-
room ten minutes later.

' I'm all right,' said Jo shortly.

' It's more than you look,' observed Anne Seymour,
a pretty English girl of almost seventeen, who was sub-
prefect this term, and knew that she would probably
be games prefect the next. ' You're as white as chalk,
and your eyes look like saucers with those black
shadows underneath. Didn't you sleep well last
night ? '

' Of course I did—at least I slept well enough,'
returned Jo, who was innately truthful. ' You get on
with your own affairs, and let me alone.'

Frieda Mensch, who was in the room at the time,
shot a querying glance at her. What she read in the
white face told her that Jo was in pain, but after the
snub administered to Anne, she said nothing for the
moment, though she fully intended to have it out with
her friend later on.

The morning went as mornings do at school. Jo
forced herself to give her mind to her work, though
she was not very successful. Miss Leslie, the mathematics mistress, was so interested in the new work she
was doing with the Sixth, that she paid little heed to
anyone's looks. Jo had a free period next lesson,
when she shut herself up in the library and gave a
very languid attention to Spanish history. But
nemesis was not far off. The lesson after break was
science with Miss Wilson. Jo had not seen her that
morning, as the mistress had hurried to the school as
soon as she was up, to prepare the apparatus for the

Upper Fifth, and had breakfasted there, only coming back to get some books she required. But Jo knew that in the laboratory she could not hope to escape observation.

' I do look a sight,' she thought to herself, as she surveyed her reflection in the mirror in the senior splashery. ' What on earth can I do ? I loathe Herr von Francius and all his works, and he will certainly want to stop the wretched thing—he nearly always does. If it was only a yank and done with it, I shouldn't mind so much. But that horrible grinding machine of his—urrrh ! ' And she gave a little shudder.

' If you don't want Bill to see you looking like death, you'd better borrow some rouge from somewhere,' said Anne, passing at the moment. She did not mean it, and was, indeed, only trying to repay the snub of earlier in the morning. But Jo thought over the advice, and it seemed good to her.

In the acting-cupboard was a box of make-up, and she decided that she could easily slip upstairs and get what she wanted before the bell rang for the end of break. She promptly went off, and was soon at the top of the house where the cupboards were. She got the rouge safely, and then came the question of how she could use it. There was no use in returning to the splasheries. The girls would at once exclaim. And apart from that, Jo knew perfectly well that she was contemplating a forbidden thing. Only the previous term Suzanne Mercier of the Lower Fifth had got into trouble for using face-powder. What would happen if the Head Girl were convicted of using rouge, Jo could well imagine !

She looked round. She was just opposite the door

of her old dormitory. Why not go in and use the stuff there ? She meant to put on very little, for her normal colouring was pale. It ought to be easy enough. No sooner said than done. She opened the door, went in, and swiftly made up her face as artistically as she could.

Slipping the box into her pocket until she got a chance to return it to its proper place—the bell had already rung, and she dared not be late for science—she came out, shutting the door quietly behind her, and then turned to discover that she was face to face with ' Matey.'

' What on earth are you doing up here, Jo ? ' demanded that lady suspiciously. ' And why have you been into the Green dormitory ? Don't tell me,' this in scathing tones, ' that you felt a sentimental longing to see the " dear old place " again ! '

Jo was pale no longer. The colour flooded her face to the roots of her hair. At the same moment she shook her head in indignant denial of the charge, and thereby wrought her own undoing. The aching tooth gave such a stab that she cried out involuntarily, and Matron was on the alert at once.

' What's wrong with you ? ' she demanded.

' N—nothing ! '

' Don't talk nonsense ! Have you a headache ? Here ; come down to my room and let me look at you.'

' I can't, Matron. The bell's rung for the end of break, and I'm due at science,' protested Jo.

' You'll have to be late for your science, I'm afraid,' retorted Matron. ' Now come along, and don't stand there arguing. We can argue when we are in my room.' Matron knew her Jo, and guessed, from the girl's face, that something was badly wrong.

Worsted on all points, Jo meekly followed her to the pretty room, where Matron marched her to the window and looked at her searchingly. Jo's long lashes fell under that look, and she blushed again. Matron said nothing. She merely gazed with a long, comprehensive gaze. Then she turned away and seemed to be hunting for something. Jo, with that tell-tale box in her blazer-pocket, turned to the window, the tooth aching harder than ever, and looked out at the beautiful lake—the loveliest of all the Austrian lakes. The next moment she gasped and cried out, for Matron was beside her again and had rubbed a wet sponge firmly over her cheeks.

Jo squealed—she really could not help it. Matron had not been rough, but the aching cheek was so tender that the lightest touch was agony. That wiping had been the finishing stroke, and Jo dropped into a convenient chair and blinked away the tears of pain.

' So it's toothache ? ' observed the domestic tyrant of the Chalet. ' And how long has it been going on ? '

' Since last night. At least, it's ached on and off for a few days,' mumbled Jo, struggling with the sobs that were rising in her throat.

' Why didn't you tell Matron Besly ? '

Jo shut her lips firmly. She could scarcely tell Matron her candid opinion of the latest member of the Staff. Matron, however, knew all about it without that. She was not enamoured of Matron Besly, though she hoped that once the girl had settled down she might improve with experience. She turned to other matters now.

' Rouge, I suppose ? ' she said, looking at the white cheeks.

' Ye—ye-es,' mumbled Jo.

' What a coward you are about the dentist, Jo ! ' was the scornful rejoinder. ' The very idea of going to such lengths because you are afraid of a little extra pain which would finally end the suffering you have been enduring all this time ! I am ashamed of you ! '

Jo winced ; but this Spartan treatment had the good effect of making her forget her physical sufferings for a minute or two.

' Where did you get the rouge ? ' demanded Matron.

' From the make-up box,' said Jo sulkily.

' Oh ! Well, I 'm glad to know that you aren't foolish enough to start messing up your skin with such things yet. If ever you do, you 'll spoil one of your chief beauties, let me tell you. You have a beautiful, fine skin now ; but if you begin painting, you 'll ruin it. I only wish someone would tell all the silly girls who think rouge and powder desirable what they are doing to themselves. If they only knew what they will be like by the time they are forty, they would think twice before they wasted their money that way.'

' Well, I 'm not likely to waste money that way ! ' retorted Jo, stung by this.

' I should hope not ! Now open your mouth and let me see the trouble.'

Jo opened her mouth, and Matron examined it as well as she could, for it was swelling now. She nodded her head.

' There 's no help for it, Jo. It 's a bad tooth, though I hope Herr von Francius may be able to save it, but I doubt it. I 'll give you a lotion and the chilli-paste for to-day, and we 'll ring him up and make an appointment for to-morrow morning. If it still aches, you had better go to bed this afternoon. In fact,

you'd better do that in any case. You don't look as
if you had had much sleep last night.'

' I didn't,' acknowledged Jo, still sulkily. ' But it's
our tennis this afternoon, Matron. I don't want to
miss that.'

' I'm afraid that doesn't matter.' Matron was
rummaging in a closet as she spoke. ' Here you are ;
here's the chilli-paste. Rub some on at once. And
here's the lotion. I'll mix some, and bring a basin,
and you can use it here.'

' But, Matron, Miss Wilson will wonder where on
earth I am,' protested Jo.

' I'll let her know. You aren't fit for lessons, my
child, and you aren't going to try them. I don't want
you in bed so near the beginning of term. Sit there
till I come back ; and tie this flannel round your face,
if you've put on that paste.' And off bustled Matron
to get the basin and the hot water needed for the
lotion. She soon returned, having captured Evadne
Lannis on the way, and sent her to Miss Wilson with
a message. Then she superintended the washing of
the swollen mouth, till Jo felt that the taste—and it
really was vile !—of that lotion would flavour everything she ate or drank for the next fortnight. However, she was obliged to admit that between it and the
chilli-paste the pain was greatly soothed, and when
Matron left her resting in the comfortable chaise-
longue, wrapped up in a rug and with plenty of
cushions and a hot-water bottle, she speedily drowsed
off to sleep.

It was three o'clock in the afternoon—fifteen, by
mid-European time—when she woke up again, and
then she found both Matron and Mademoiselle beside
her.

'No; rest still, mon enfant,' said the Head Mistress, as the girl began to disentangle herself from the rug. 'But why have you not spoken sooner of your pain, Josephine?'

Having nothing she could say, Jo dropped her eyes and looked foolish.

'It was not right,' continued Mademoiselle with some severity. 'You have no right to play with your health, even for so small a thing as toothache. And I cannot think why you should be so childish as to dread a few moments of pain as you do,' she added, yet more severely.

'I'm sorry,' mumbled the culprit, feeling less like the Head Girl than she had done since her appointment.

'But it is always the same,' continued Mademoiselle, rubbing it in mercilessly. 'A year ago it was the same thing. Have you forgotten?'

'No, Mademoiselle.' Jo thought to herself that it was most unlikely that she ever would forget. It had been after a visit to Herr von Francius that she had returned with several of the others to find that Eustacia Benson had run away, and there had been all the worry and excitement until they found her, on top of it. No; she would not forget.

Mademoiselle, following the thread of her thoughts, softened a little. 'Well, Matron has sent downstairs for a tray for you, and when you have eaten your Mittagessen, she will take you across to the new house, and you will go to bed. Herr von Francius will see you to-morrow at eleven o'clock, so you must be up early, as the mountain railway does not open for another fortnight; you will walk down to Spärtz to catch the Kufstein-Innsbruck express. Ah, here

comes Gretel with your tray. Eat your meal, and
then go to bed. I trust you will feel better in the
morning.'

With this she withdrew, and Jo, feeling considerably better already for her long sleep, looked
eagerly towards the tray. She had eaten very little
at Frühstück, and was hungry now. So her face fell
considerably at the sight of a bowl of bread-and-milk.

' Here you are, Jo,' said Matron, bringing it to her.

' Oh, Matron, I'm *hungry*,' protested Jo, with a
grimace.

' I dare say you are. But bread-and-milk is the
best thing for you at present. The milk is soothing,
and it will slip down easily. That's a bad tooth, Jo,
and very little might make it ache again.'

Jo took up her spoon and began to eat. But before
she was half-way through the basinful, she realised
the truth of Matron's dictum. The mere act of
swallowing set the tooth aching again as badly as
ever, and it was with difficulty that she finished her
meal. Then Matron walked her over to her own
house, where she gave her fresh lotion, and applied
more chilli-paste to the rapidly-swelling cheek, before
she saw the girl into bed with a fresh hot-water bottle.

' Didn't you know that Joey Bettany was in pain ? '
she asked her colleague, when she had left the girl
drowsing again.

Matron Besly shook her head. ' No, Matron. Jo
always looks pale, and she said nothing to me. How
could I know ? ' she finished on an injured note.

' I don't believe Jo would ever acknowledge to
toothache if she thought she could brave it out,' said
the elder woman. ' She simply dreads the dentist's
instruments. It's part of her make-up, of course.

She is a sensitive, highly-strung girl, with a natural shrinking from pain, and an overplus of imagination. You will find it well to keep an eye on her. I know she's naturally pale ; but that blanched, peaky look she has to-day isn't natural. When you saw that, and those great shadows under her eyes, I can't understand why you didn't make inquiries.'

Matron Besly said nothing. She thought Jo very stupid to behave like this about a visit to the dentist, and she lacked the experience that would have enabled her to understand the finely-strung nervous system of the girl. Matron Lloyd had been at the Chalet School for three years and a term now, and she knew Jo thoroughly. She said no more ; but after advising her colleague to look in on the invalid once or twice during the afternoon, but not to disturb her if she were asleep, she went back to her own quarters, inwardly resolving to hold a teeth inspection that night, and see if anyone else stood in need of Herr von Francius' services.

' May as well make one journey of it,' she thought philosophically. ' But how like Jo ! It's time she learned a little sense about such things. I suppose I'd better put this stuff back where she got it. Rouge, indeed ! I wonder what next ! '

And over at the new house, Matron Besly, smarting under the implied rebuke she had just received, was making up her mind that Jo Bettany was a most unpleasant girl, and that she, personally, would not trouble to go out of her way for her, Head Girl or no Head Girl.

CHAPTER IV

JO MAKES A FIND

'FINISHED, Jo ? Do you feel all right ? '

Jo nodded. 'Perfectly, thank you. It was so far gone when he came to look at it, that he said it was no use trying to do anything to it, thank goodness ! So he yanked it out. I will say for him that he can extract decently. I never even felt it. Frieda, you're next, aren't you ? '

Frieda Mensch got up. 'Yes ; but I don't think I'll be long. He will file it down, and it really is only a sharp edge.' She went to the door of the waiting-room, where Matron and the fourteen people she had decided needed the attentions of Herr von Francius were sitting in solemn state. She looked back as she reached it. 'Matron says that we may go, Jo. So that will be all right.' Then she vanished to undergo her ordeal, and Jo dropped into the nearest chair.

'Thank goodness that's over ! What with getting up at six, and walking down to catch the eight-twenty train, and beginning here at ten, I feel somewhat empty. Tante Gretchen will be sure to have a really *good* meal waiting for us ! '

'To hear you talk,' said Matron, while the others grinned at each other, 'anyone would think that a good meal was an event in your life.'

'Oh well, I don't mean that exactly. Besides, I'm longing to see Bernie and her boy, and Frieda's message last night said that he was going on all right now. It was only a slight chill; but it was worrying, of course.'

'Very worrying,' agreed Matron. 'Yes; you may go. I'm sorry I can't come with you. I've always been very fond of Bernhilda.'

'Then why not come? We could park this crowd at Onkel Reise's, while we visit the baby and his proud mamma.'

Matron shook her head. 'No; Bernhilda has had a bad shock over his illness, and she ought to be kept very quiet. I warn you, Jo, that they may not let you see her. It will all depend on how she is. If she's not well, they will probably think it would be too much excitement for her—more especially as she doesn't know that you and Frieda are in Innsbruck. Of course, they may have told her over the 'phone this morning when we had gone.'

'Matron, how *could* they? There won't have been time yet. We only rang up the Mariahilf last night late when you told Frieda that she must have that edge filed down. And it would be too late to say anything to Bernie then. They may have told her this morning; but Tante Gretchen has a busy time of it early in the morning; and I don't suppose Kurt knew either, unless he ran in before he went down to the office. All the same, I do hope they'll let us go up and see them. Frieda has been worrying ever since the letter yesterday morning, and she won't be satisfied until she has seen with her own eyes that it's all right.'

'I was very glad to hear the better news last night myself,' admitted Matron, with a thought for Frieda's stricken face as she read the letter which had brought the news that her three-weeks-old nephew had been taken suddenly ill, and the shock had told badly on his young mother, her only sister. 'Frieda would have fretted badly through the night.'

'Poor old Frieda!' said a bright-haired American girl of fifteen, who was anticipating a bad time since Matron had discovered three teeth that needed attention. 'I'm sorry for myself this morning, all right. But I guess I've felt a whole heap sorrier for her.'

'Oh, you!' retorted Jo. 'If you didn't eat such quantities of sweets in the holidays, Corney, my love, it need never have happened.'

Corney made a face at her. 'Guess I take all that's going. Poppa never worries much about such things. And anyway, no one had any time for the dentist with just ten days of a holiday.'

'We'll make up for that in the summer,' said Jo. 'Nearly eleven weeks it will be. If that isn't enough holiday for you, Corney Flower, I don't know what is.'

Cornelia shot her a glance from brilliantly blue eyes, and opened her lips to say something. Then she thought better of it and closed them again. Jo had seen her, however, and her face clouded. She knew what Cornelia had been about to say—that in any case it could make no difference to her, since she was not coming back to school. 'I wish to goodness I was just Corney's age, and had two more years at least before me,' thought the Head Girl, as she lay back in her chair.

Her thoughts were broken by the return of Frieda, very pink-cheeked and bright-eyed, as though the filing had been rather more painful than she had anticipated.

'Had a bad time?' demanded Matron, with a watchful glance at her.

'It was not nice, but it did not take long,' admitted Frieda. 'May Jo and I go now, Matron?'

'Yes, if you're sure you're all right,' said Matron. 'Meet the train at sixteen, Jo; and don't do anything wild.'

Jo laughed as she got up. 'That's not very likely at the Mariahilf. Onkel Reise will bring us to the station himself, as you know. I couldn't do anything wild, even if I wanted—which I don't.'

Matron nodded, and then turned to send Cornelia in to Herr von Francius, while the two prefects waved farewell to the others, and then left the étage where the dentist lived, and came out into the quiet street. If she could have foreseen just exactly what Jo would do next, it is doubtful if their guardian would have permitted either of them out of her sight. However, fortunately for her, she could not, and the pair strolled along, chatting happily.

'We'd better take a tram to the bridge, I suppose,' said Jo doubtfully. 'It's a fairly long walk, and,' looking at her watch, 'it's nearly twelve now. What ages he must have taken! It didn't seem like it. Come along. We can tram to the Museum Strasse, anyhow, and we might walk the rest. Let's hope they'll let us see Bernie. I suppose we'll have to see her before Mittagessen?'

Frieda concurred in this idea, so the pair walked sedately along to the Brenner Strasse, where the trams run through the city, and boarded the first that came. They duly left it at the Museum Strasse, where Joey made the discovery that her watch was wrong—as usual—and it was barely eleven o'clock.

'I *thought* there must be something wrong if it

really was so late,' said Frieda. ' What has happened to it, Jo ? '

Jo held it to her ear. Then she shook her wrist and listened again. ' Seems to have stopped. Spring gone again, I suppose.'

' Did you wind it up last night ? '

' I expect so.' All the same Jo touched the key tentatively, and found, as her friend had more than half-suspected, that all that was wrong with it was that it required winding. She set it right, calmly turning the pointers backward to the correct time, despite the protests of Frieda. Then she looked round her.

' We might do a little shopping as we're so early. I've got plenty of money. Jem tipped me lavishly before we left the Sonnalpe, and I'd like to take the baby something. Hamel's shop isn't far off. Let's go there and see what we can get. We might see Herr Hamel, and give him news of Sophie.'

Frieda was quite agreeable, so they turned to cross the road, talking all the time. Like everyone who had spent even a year at the Chalet School, both girls were trilingual, speaking English, French, and German with almost equal fluency. On this occasion they happened to be speaking in English, and though Frieda's voice was very soft, Jo's notes were bell-like in their clearness, and carried on the fresh, spring air.

They had reached the other side of the wide street, and were just about to turn down towards the big draper's shop, when Jo suddenly felt a touch on her arm. She swung round, and found herself confronting a small girl of eight or nine, judged by her looks, whose thick, fair hair was bobbed all round her head, and whose blue eyes looked frightened.

'Oh, if you please—' she faltered. Then she stopped, looking ready to burst into tears.

'Hello! Where did you spring from?' exclaimed Jo.

'Please—would you come and speak to Mummy?' pleaded the child. 'She—we don't understand German, and it's so puzzling, and we can't find our way. Only, when I heard you speaking English, I—I thought you might help. She's just back there.' And she pointed towards the corner where the Museum Strasse runs into the Maria Theresien Strasse, and where stood a tiny lady, holding a much smaller child by the hand, and looking about her in a perplexed, terrified way that at once roused the sympathy of the two girls.

'Of course we'll help,' said Jo impulsively. 'Come along, Frieda! We must see about this!'

The small, wistful face at her elbow brightened. 'I *thought* you'd help. Besides, you're both wearing the Guide Badge. Guides always help, don't they?'

'Rather!' said Jo. 'But what do you know about Guides?'

'Oh, I know about them. I was going to be a Brownie when I was seven, only we left Brisbane where we lived before then, and went up-country, and there weren't any. So I couldn't, you see. Here's Mummy!' And she suddenly released her hand from Jo's hold, and darted forward. 'Mummy! it's all right! They're Guides, and they speak English, and they'll tell us what to do.'

The little lady turned round sharply. 'Daisy! Oh, my darling, you shouldn't have run away like that! You might have been lost or run over.'

Daisy nodded her head contentedly, 'It's all right,

Mummy. I wouldn't have done it if I hadn't heard them speaking English.'

'May we help you?' asked Frieda in her pretty, gentle way, seeing that Jo was too much taken up with staring at the younger child in a puzzled fashion to remember her manners. 'Your little one says that you are in difficulties.'

'Oh, you do understand English?' cried the little lady. 'Oh, you don't know how thankful I am for that! We only reached here yesterday, and we don't know German, and it's all so—so frightening! And Daisy and Primula Mary are so small, and they have no one but me to look after them.'

Jo removed her eyes from Primula Mary and saw that the speaker was in deep mourning. Her splendid, black eyes softened at once, and when she spoke her beautiful voice was rich and sweet with sympathy.

'Can we help you? Where do you want to be? Are you staying at an hotel?'

'We are at the Anich, in the Anich Strasse,' explained the little lady, with a wistful upward glance at the tall girl who seemed to tower above her. 'We went to the station to make some inquiries about trains for to-morrow, and I thought I knew the way back. But I seem to be confused; and Baby is getting tired; and I couldn't find anyone who understood.'

'The Anich Strasse? That's a little way from here,' said Jo. 'It's right up the Maria Theresien Strasse, on the other side. Shall we take you back? I can carry Primula Mary if she'll let me.' She stooped down to the child; but the tired baby drew back behind her mother, with a whimper.

' I'm afraid she's shy,' said her mother apologeti-
cally. ' But I can carry her myself.' And she lifted
the child, with a smile. ' There, Babykins ! We'll
soon be back, and then Mummy will tuck you up in
the nice, big bed for your morning nap.'

She fell into step with Jo, while Frieda came behind,
Daisy clinging trustfully to her hand, sure that everything would go right now.

' It's not so fearfully far, really,' said Jo, as they
waited till the traffic cleared. ' Once we get across—
and we'll make a long crossing of it—it won't be too
far away. But I wish the baby would let me carry
her. You look tired out yourself.'

' Oh, I'm not so much tired as worried,' owned the
little lady somewhat breathlessly. ' And I'm quite
accustomed to carrying her.'

By this time the motors and lorries and bicycles
had gone past, and there was a clear crossing for the
moment. Jo seized the opportunity, and with a hand
on her new acquaintance's arm, steered her across,
leaving Frieda to follow with Daisy.

' There ! Now it isn't far to your hotel,' said the
Head Girl, as they reached the pavement in safety.
' Here comes Frieda with your other kiddy.'

' Is your friend's name " Frieda " ? ' asked the little
lady. ' What a pretty girl she is, and what a sweet
low voice she has ! You are English, I know, but
surely she isn't. She doesn't look like it.'

' Yes ; I'm English all right. But Frieda is an
Innsbrucker. She's Tyrolean born and bred, and
very proud of it. But we go to the same school—up
at the Tiern See. Why, what on earth's the matter ? '
asked Jo, ending on a note of consternation, for the
little lady had almost dropped Primula Mary as she

suddenly stopped dead, and turned on the big girl a face gone deadly white.

'The school at Tiern See?' she gasped. 'Do you—oh, do you mean the Chalet School?'

'Yes,' said Jo briefly. 'What about it?'

'The school that Madge Bettany started?'

'Certainly!' Jo's tones became slightly haughty. Who on earth was this stranger who spoke so familiarly of her sister?

'Then—then—oh, what is your name?'

'I am Josephine Bettany,' returned Jo, producing her six syllables with a flourish. 'But I must say I fail to see——'

'Oh! Don't you know? Can't you see? I'm Margot Venables—I *was* Margot Russell!'

Jo whistled—a long, low whistle, and Frieda promptly came up to them with Daisy.

'Jo, what is wrong?' she asked anxiously.

'This lady says that she is Margot Venables—Jem's sister in Australia,' said Jo. 'But I don't know what on earth she's doing in Innsbruck!'

But little Mrs Venables was already pouring out breathless explanations. 'Oh, you couldn't know, of course. But you *must* have heard that when I married Stephen I quarrelled with my people. They didn't want me to have him. But we loved each other, and I ran away with him. I did write when Daisy was born to say that I had a little daughter—our first baby was a boy—and I was giving her Mother's name, only she would have to be "Daisy." But no one ever took any notice of the letter. And then Stephen—my husband, you know—said that that was to be the end of it. I had him and the children, and I must be content with them. But he died a year ago from

snake-bite. Our three boys had died before that—we
had left Brisbane, and gone right up-country, to try
sugar-cane planting. Stephen thought he would be
sure to make it pay. But he never did. Primula
Mary came two years ago while we were there. Then,
when he died and things had been settled up, there
was very little left—only just enough to enable us to
get back to Brisbane. Primula Mary was poorly ;
and Daisy was growing very weedy, too. I knew
French and Italian, and I'd always managed to keep
them up by reading. I got some teaching to do, and
an old friend of ours, a nurse, gave us a home with her.
She was very good to us, and I was able to save.
Then she died too, of septic pneumonia, just four
months ago. She left me the little she had, as she had
no relations, and I sold up the house, and we came to
Brindisi. From there I came on by train to seek Jem,
for I knew he was somewhere near Innsbruck. Oh,
what a journey it was ! A kind lady on the train
recommended the Anich Hotel, and we came there,
and I have just been to the station to find out how we
are to get up to the Tiern See. I knew that Jem had
married Madge Bettany of the Chalet School—I saw
the announcement in *The Times* which someone left
us one day. I thought I could get the address here,
and I did find out about the school. I thought I
could learn from the people there just where Jem was,
and we should get on to him somehow. I mean to ask
him if he can find me a job as housekeeper or something—anything, so that the children and I can keep
together. He wasn't in all the trouble, though I
know he never liked Stephen. Only my husband
wouldn't let me write to any of them, and so I'm out
of touch with everyone. But if you are a Bettany,

then you must know all about them. Oh, do come to the hotel, and tell me everything ! '

Jo looked at Frieda. ' What about it, Frieda ? ' she asked.

' I think you should go, Joey,' said Frieda promptly. ' I can go on to the Mariahilf and tell them where you are, and someone will come for you to the Anich.'

' You'll do no such thing,' retorted Jo. ' You've been in all this, and you'll just go through to the bitter end.' She glanced at Primula Mary. ' Of course, I know now why the babe struck me as being so weirdly familiar. She's the image of Jem. I simply couldn't place it at all.—We'll come with you, Mrs Venables. And of course Jem and Madge will give you a hand. To begin with, Daisy can quite well come to the school. Let's see ; she's nine, isn't she ? '

' Nine last March,' replied her mother, the tears brimming her eyes. ' Oh, do come, both of you ! I simply can't believe that all my troubles are at an end ! '

CHAPTER V

MARGOT'S STORY

WHEN Jem heard of it, he gave Joey a sound lecture for going anywhere with a stranger in the impulsive manner she had done, and for dragging Frieda along with her. As he said, it was a thoroughly stupid and dangerous thing to do.

'You couldn't be sure that it was Margot,' he said severely. 'She might just have been pitching you a yarn. You might have got into Heaven knows whose hands, and we might never have seen either of you again! Really, Jo, at your age I do think you ought to show a little more common sense than that!'

'But it was just because Frieda *was* with me,' argued Jo. 'Besides, nothing could be more like you than Primula Mary. She might be your own baby. She's far more like you than either David or Sybil.'

'It doesn't matter. Please understand that you are never to do such a mad thing again. That is a promise, Jo. Otherwise, Madge and I shall never be at peace about you.'

'Oh, all right,' said Jo resignedly. 'But you are an old fuss!'

However, that all came much later—to be accurate, the next day. At present, Jo and Frieda are left standing in the Maria Theresien Strasse with Mrs Venables and her little girls, and much has to come before Jem's lecture.

It took them some little time to reach the Anich, for Mrs Venables was shaking with sudden relief, and Daisy was tired. However, they got there at last, and then Primula Mary suddenly found her voice and uttered her woes in no uncertain tone. It was a good twenty minutes before she was hushed and got off to sleep; but at last her long lashes fell, and she was 'over.' Daisy was left with a story-book to sit by her little sister, and the two girls with Mrs Venables retired to the privacy of the sitting-room (which Joey had insisted on engaging while the tired baby was being put to sleep), and heard her story.

Mrs Venables was very loyal to her dead husband; but it was pitifully obvious, even to the inexperienced girls, that he had killed her love for him years before. He had been a weak man, one of those wasters who can be the delight of company but are tyrants at home. He had never accomplished anything, though he was always going to do wonders. His poor little wife had had to bear the brunt of all the financial worries, for he seemed to have no idea of the value of money, and would order largely without considering how he was going to pay. Later, he had taken to drinking, though she only spoke of it vaguely, and he had been as great a care to her as her children. There had been three little boys, as well as Daisy and Primula Mary; but they had all pined and died in the cruel climate of North Queensland. Margot Venables said very little about them. At the time, Primula Mary had been a fragile baby of six weeks old, and the necessity for continual care of her had deadened the first pangs of loss to the poor little mother.

'Jimmy went first,' she said, telling her story.

' Then Frankie and Steve followed him. I—I didn't
seem to feel it at the time. I was numb, I think.
And then Baby needed all my time and care. And
Daisy was beginning to fail. I began to think they
would follow the boys. And then one day, Ah Sing,
our house-boy, came to tell me that the master was
sick.

' I thought at first that he meant—meant—well,
Stephen didn't often take too much. I think he tried
to forget about the boys—he was so proud of them ;
and Jimmy and Frankie used to follow him about so.
But—' She stopped, flushed and ashamed.

' All right,' said Jo swiftly. ' We understand. Go
on with the rest of the story.'

' It wasn't that at all. Ah Sing hadn't wanted to
frighten me ; he was trying to break the news to me
gently. Stephen had been careless—he often was—
and he trod on a sleeping snake. It swung up and
bit his hand. He had no chance ; there were only
Ah Sing and one or two other Chinese there. And he
had gone out without his permanganate crystals. He
died quickly, they told me. And Ah Sing said he had
no pain. I have often wondered since how true it was.
They—they wouldn't let me see him. Ah Sing said
it was no good ; and the babies needed me. He told
me to stay with the little girls, and he would see to all.
He was so good to me, Ah Sing. The children adored
him ; and he nearly worshipped them.

' Stephen was buried beside our little boys that
evening—burial has to follow quickly on death in
that climate—and the Burdens, two brothers who had
the plantation next to ours, came over to see to the
funeral. Tom Burden was very good to me. He and
his brother offered to take the land off my hands at

once, and I know they gave me more than it was really worth. But they knew that there were debts; and I had to have something to help me to get the little girls away. Ah Sing packed for us—faithful Ah Sing!—and the Burdens put us aboard the next steamer that called in at the station—oh yes; we had to go by boat. There is no railway there—and we left. How thankful I was to see the last of it—that awful, awful country that had taken my boys, and might have taken my little girls! During the voyage down the coast, I didn't try to think—I couldn't. I was still dazed and numb. It wasn't till we got to Brisbane that I realised that all I had in the world for the little girls and myself was the clothes we had with us, and about fifty pounds in money. When that was spent, we must starve or go to the workhouse if I couldn't get work.'

'Oh, poor you!' cried Jo; while Frieda's blue eyes brimmed over at the thought of all this little, frail-looking woman had undergone.

'I remembered Nurse Rickards, who was Daisy's nurse,' went on Mrs Venables, taking no notice of the interruption. 'I had always liked her, and we had been real friends. I knew her address, and I took the children and tramped all the way from the docks to her house—she lived in one of the suburbs. She was at home, fortunately for us, for I fainted across the doorstep when she opened the door. She took us in, and brought me round, and got me to bed; and she had the children washed and fed and in bed, too, before I could even realise that we had found a haven for that day, at least. She wouldn't let me talk. She simply brought me some tea, and then she left me to sleep. For three days she treated me like that, giving me food, and keeping the children happy and quiet. Then, when she knew that I was stronger, she let me tell her everything. She had just finished work on a case ; but she had another to go to in about a week. She suggested that we should live in her house " to keep it aired," she said. That would save us rent. And when I felt able to work, she found me pupils in French and drawing. It wasn't a great deal, but it meant something coming in. She made me put my fifty pounds into the bank, and said we must live on my earnings, and she would help. She was doing well, and I could pay her a trifle for board if I liked. I know now that she banked every penny I ever gave her. She almost clothed the little girls. She was always sewing and knitting for them, and she could make the daintiest things out of practically nothing. Daisy went to the school near by, and Primula Mary could always be left safely with the woman who used to come in to do the work.

' It was a hard life ; but after the plantation, it was Paradise ! Daisy began to pick up again, and Primula Mary seemed stronger, too. Then, Nellie Rickards, the best friend that any woman ever had, caught 'flu.

' She never had a chance. It turned to pneumonia almost at once. She had been working hard on a difficult case and she was worn out. The lungs turned septic, and she died almost before I knew she was ill.

' Even after her death I felt her care for us. She had left me everything she had, including her house and its contents. She left me a letter she had written the night before she gave in, in which she said that if anything happened to her, I was to sell off everything and go to my brother. She was sure he would help me. She had even left instructions about how to find out about boats and trains ; and reminded me that I ought to get warm clothing for the children and myself in case we needed it on the voyage.

'She enclosed another letter to a solicitor whose wife she had saved when she was dying from gas-poisoning, asking him to see to us, and to help me with the sale and booking the passages. She left him a small sum in payment, and begged him to try and do the work for that. He refused even that. He said he could never repay what he owed her, and he was thankful to do anything she asked.

'And so we came. The voyage did Daisy good. She is a different child from the white-faced, fine-drawn little thing who left Australia. But Primula was ill at first, and she is still frail. Jem is a doctor, and I thought he would advise me what to do for her. Only, I didn't know where he was exactly. I came here to Innsbruck because I knew it was the principal city of the Tyrol, and I thought I might possibly hear something of him here. When I went to the station this morning I tried to find out, but I am still stupid and dazed, I think. They said something about the Sonnalpe—I know that. And they told me I must go to Wiesing, and then get to the Sonnalpe from there. But it seems such an undertaking with two little children ! '

'You needn't worry about that,' said Jo gently. 'Naturally, Jem will come here for you—or send someone if he can't leave. Look here, Mrs Venables, the best plan will be to get Die Rosen on the 'phone. If he isn't in, my sister will be. We'll let them know where you are, and ask for instructions. That will be best.—Don't you think so, Frieda ? '

Frieda agreed. ' I will see to the telephoning,' she said, ' while Frau Venables makes arrangements with you.'

So it was decided; and while Jo, energetic and impulsive as usual, suggested various plans to Mrs Venables, Frieda rang up Die Rosen, the Russell's home at the Sonnalpe, and broke the news to Dr Jem, who happened to answer the 'phone himself. He was incredulous, at first. But as Frieda retailed in brief the story to which she had just listened, he became more and more serious. Finally, he bade her ring up her parents, telling them where she and Joey were and asking that someone should come and fetch them to the Mariahilf at once. In the meantime, he himself would come to Innsbruck by the first train he could catch, and interview this lady who called herself his sister.

Then he rang off, and Frieda, beginning to realise what a hazardous thing she and Jo had done, rang up her home, and presently returned to the sitting-room to inform Jo and Mrs Venables that Dr Jem was coming down, and that her brother-in-law, Kurt von Eschenau, was coming to take Jo and herself home in a few minutes.

' What about Bernie and the boy ? ' asked Jo.

' *Much* better. We may be allowed to see Bernie for a few minutes,' said Frieda, with sparkling eyes.

' It's Frieda's sister,' explained Jo, turning to Mrs Venables. ' Her first son is just three weeks old, and he got a chill, and gave them all a nasty shock. But he's evidently getting over it.—Who spoke, Frieda ? '

' Mamma,' said Frieda. ' But Kurt was there, too. He will be here soon, Jo, for Mamma said he would bring the auto.'

'And when is Jem coming?'

'By the earliest train,' replied Frieda. 'I gave him the address, Mrs Venables, and he said he would be here as soon as possible.'

'I wonder he doesn't think I'm a fraud,' murmured Mrs Venables. 'After all these years, he must have thought I was dead.'

'I don't think he thought that,' said Jo. 'I know he mentioned you when we were choosing Sybil's name, and he said we couldn't call her "Margot," because you were that already, and Daisy was another Margaret. My sister is "Madge," and we all hate "Maggie." And her small cousin, my brother Dick's eldest girl, is "Peggy" already, so she simply *had* to have another name. She's "Sybil Margaret."'

'Has Jem a daughter?' exclaimed his sister. 'How old is she?'

'Nearly two months now,' said Jo. 'Oh yes; Jem certainly has a daughter. And there's David as well. He will be two this month. And besides them, Madge and Jem take care of Dick's twin children, Rix and Peggy, as aforementioned. They are the eldest pair of that family. Oh, there are heaps of babies at the Sonnalpe!'

'I can't realise it, somehow,' murmured Mrs Venables, with a catch in her breath. 'I knew Jem was married, of course. But I didn't know that there were cousins for Daisy and Primula Mary. Somehow, I can't see Jem as anyone's father! He was such a scamp of a boy!'

'Oh, you'll get used to it before many days are over,' said Jo cheerfully. 'And my brother and his wife are coming home this summer, and bringing their other two with them—Bride and Noel.'

' I thought the baby was to be " Jack " ? ' put in Frieda.

' So he was. But somehow, no one ever calls him anything but Noel; so Noel he will have to be. Hello! That sounds like Kurt below!' She ran to the window and craned out. 'Yes; it's his car all right. We must go.—Good-bye, Mrs Venables. Jem will be here soon, and he'll see that you are all right. I expect the next time we see you will be up at the Sonnalpe.—Come on, Frieda! Kurt will raise the whole street with that horn of his if we keep him waiting. "Impatient" doesn't *begin* to describe him!'

Mrs Venables smiled wistfully as she shook hands with the girls. ' Oh, how thankful I am to have met you! I feel as if all my troubles had been completely smoothed away.'

' Oh, you would have managed quite nicely if you'd been put to it,' said Jo hastily.

Margot Venables shook her head. She knew, better than Jo, that she was very nearly at the end of things.

' You will love our dear Madame,' said Frieda, speaking of Mrs Russell, who was always known by this title among the girls of the Chalet School. ' She is so good and kind, and she will help you.'

Then she and Jo went off to join Kurt, who, despairing of making them hear the violent fantasia he had been performing on his Klaxon, and also becoming rather anxious at their non-appearance, was just coming into the hotel in search of them.

' How long you have been!' he greeted them. ' Did you not hear me?'

' You weren't bad to hear,' Jo told him, as she followed him to the car.

'How are Bernhilda and Stefan ? ' asked Frieda anxiously.

'Better,' he replied, speaking in German. 'We had a fright about the boy. But he is doing well, now. Bernhilda was very troubled about his illness, and it has set her back. But both your mother and Doctor Erckhardt think she will be well, now that she is no longer anxious about him. She is longing to see you both—Mind the wheel and your frock, Jo !—and to show him to you. What brought you two to Innsbruck, by the by ? '

'The dentist,' said Jo, with a grimace. 'I had toothache badly all yesterday, and Matey caught me out at once—our own Matron, I mean : not Matron Besly.'

'Who is she ? ' he asked, as he touched the self-starter. 'Ought I to know her ? '

'No ; you have never met her. She is the Matron at our new house,' explained Frieda.

'Ah ! I see. And how is Marie ? Did she not need the dentist's aid ? ' he asked, as he turned the car out of the Anich Strasse and into the Innrain.

'No ; Marie's teeth were passed. I believe Wanda took her to their dentist in Salzburg last week,' said his sister-in-law.

'And why did you go to the Anich ? ' he asked.

'Oh, that was Daisy's fault in the beginning,' said Jo. 'Daisy ? Oh, she is my—well, I think niece-in-law is as near as I can come to it. Her mother is Jem's sister from Australia. Her husband died, and left her with Daisy and Primula Mary—the boys died first. So she decided to come back to Jem, as she has next to no money, and Australia doesn't seem to have been suiting the children.'

'Primula Mary is so like Dr Jem,' said Frieda, as Jo wound up her somewhat involved explanation. 'She is much fairer, of course ; but she has his blue eyes, and the same nose and mouth. She is pretty, but so very shy.'

'She'll get over that in the nursery at Die Rosen,' said Jo decidedly. 'I defy anyone to be shy there !'

'Is Frau Venables older or younger than Dr Jem ?' asked Frieda.

'Three years older, I believe. She must be about thirty-eight, I should think. I'm not sure, though.'

'Well,' said Kurt, as with a masterly sweep he drew up the car before the door of the tall house where he and his wife had a flat on the fifth floor, while her parents lived in the one on the fourth. 'I shall be interested to hear how it goes when the Herr Doktor comes down. Here we are, so jump out. Go to das Mammachen first, and ask her if you may see Bernhilda. And if you do, then do not excite her. Say nothing about Frau Venables and your adventure with her. Do you understand, Mädchen ?'

'Oh, bother !' said Jo. 'I was just looking forward to telling Bernie the whole story—which you don't know yet, Kurt. We'll have to tell you if we can't tell Bernhilda. I simply *must* discuss it with someone. It's the most exciting thing that ever happened to me, I think.'

'I shall like to hear. But I will not have Bernhilda disturbed and agitated,' he said decidedly. 'So you must give me your word of honour that neither of you will say anything about it to her. Do you hear ?'

Jo frowned. Then she laughed. 'Oh, very well. Time enough for Bernie to hear when you're all at the Sonnalpe, I suppose. You are going to Gisela as soon as she's fit again, aren't you? Then you'll see Margot, and Daisy, and Primula Mary.—Come on, Frieda! Race you up to the fourth étage!'

CHAPTER VI

JEM ARRIVES

AFTER a most refreshing time with the elder Mensches—a time which included a ten minutes' visit to Bernhilda and her son—the two prefects, accompanied by Kurt von Eschenau, made their way to the station where they were to meet Matron and the rest of her party. Matron was not there when they arrived, for they had set off early, owing to the Mensches' clock being fast. The three of them were standing in a group, chatting about little Stefan, when Jo was suddenly grasped by the shoulder, and swung round to face a tall, fair man, whose clear-cut face wore a grim look that startled her.

'Jem!' she exclaimed. 'Haven't you got here before this? I thought you'd have been down by the noon train!'

'Talk sense, Joey! How could I possibly catch it? I had to wait for this, of course,' he said irritably. Then he turned to the others. 'Good-afternoon, Frieda.—Hello, von Eschenau! Look here; I'm going to take Jo with me. Frieda must stay and help Matron with the other children, but I need Jo. Will you explain, old man? Sorry I can't stop; but if we're to see into this fairy-tale the girls seem to have unearthed and catch the last train back, we must go at once.'

Kurt nodded. 'Of course. I hope all goes well, Russell, and that your sister will find happiness here among us all. Jo has told us some of her story. To judge by it, she has had a very bad time.'

'Margot—if it *is* Margot, and not an impostor—made her own bed when she ran away with Venables,' said Jem Russell curtly, not too pleased to find that Joey had broadcast the tale already. 'If she has found it uncomfortable, that was her own lookout. But you're all coming up to stay with the Mensches as soon as Bernhilda can be moved, I hear ; so you'll get all the news then. Meanwhile, I've got to investigate this, and as it is Jo who seems to have landed us with the whole affair, Jo must come along with me and help to disentangle it.'

'You needn't worry about its being an impostor,' said Jo calmly, though inwardly she was quaking. She had never seen Jem so angry before. 'Anything more funnily like you than Primula Mary I have yet to behold. David is Madge's own boy ; and Sybil is like no one but herself at present. But Primula Mary might be your own child, and not just a niece.'

Jem looked at her with compressed lips. 'We'll see,' he said after a pause. 'Come along now.—Tell Mademoiselle, Frieda, that if I can't get Jo back to school to-night, I'll bring her up first thing to-morrow morning.'

'Yes,' said Frieda. 'Good-bye, Joey dear. I shall be longing to know the rest of the story.'

'Good-bye,' said Jo. 'See you to-night, if poss.—Good-bye, Kurt. We've had a lovely time, and I think little Stefan is a pet !'

'Good-bye, von Eschenau,' said Jem. 'Frieda, you might try to hold your tongue about all this—if you *can* ! I'm not anxious to have my private affairs cried from the housetops, you know.'

With this somewhat bitter remark, he marched Jo off, leaving Frieda suddenly scarlet and Kurt not very sure what to say. Then the sister and brother-in-law were out of the station, and crossing the great Bahn-Hof Platz towards the Rudolf Strasse which leads directly to the Anich Strasse.

Jo cast doubtful glances at her brother-in-law as she hurried along by his side. She knew he was angry; and racked her brains to think what else she could have done in the circumstances in which Daisy's hail had plunged them. At length she spoke, just as they reached the Margaret Platz.

'You sound pretty mad, Jem.'

'So I am "pretty mad," as you call it,' he told her. 'Really, Jo, I wonder what insane thing you will do next! To go off like that with a perfect stranger! You must be crazy! Not to mention the fact that Matron trusted you and Frieda to go straight to the Mariahilf, and not to wander about Innsbruck as you seem to have been doing!'

Jo went scarlet. This side of her conduct had not struck her so far.

'We *were* going straight there,' she said in injured tones. 'Only we found we were early, and decided to go and get something to take to Baby Stefan. And then Daisy came rushing after us because she heard us talking English, and we went to see if we could help—after all, we *are* Guides!—and it was when we were taking them back to the Anich, as they had got confused about the way, that we found out who they were. She asked about Frieda's name, and I told her we were up at the Tiern See at school, and she asked if it was the Chalet School. She did give me a fright! She went so white I thought she was going to faint;

and she nearly dropped Primula Mary. Then she told me who she was, and all about it, and Frieda came to ring you up, and—well, there you are!' And Jo suddenly ran down.

The doctor was frowning. He had been very fond of his sister, and her elopement had been a great shock to him at the time. But his parents' indignation and her action had meant the breaking-off of all communication, and though he himself had written later on, the letter had been returned with 'not known' scribbled across it, and he had given it up. He had known from the one letter that did arrive from her that her little daughter was called Daisy, and that was all. With all this in his mind, he strode on at his best pace, till Jo was panting with the effort to keep up with him.

'Jem!' she gasped at length. 'This isn't a Marathon! And Margot won't run away before we get there. She's simply longing to see you again. And anyway, she has the two children to think about. Daisy is only nine, and Primula Mary is about two. How could she move about easily with two babies like that?'

He slackened his pace a little. 'Sorry, Joey! I didn't mean to race you breathless.'

'Well, there's one thing,' said Jo, 'we'll get a rest at the Anich.'

He nodded; but he was thinking too busily to say much, and they went on in silence. When they reached the hotel, he marched in, and up to the bureau, where the girl, recognising Joey, smiled a welcome.

'Grüss Gott, mein Herr! You desire rooms? Yes?'

'No,' he replied in the German she had used. 'I wish only to speak with Frau Venables. Is she here?'

'The sad little English lady with the two children like spring flowers? But yes, mein Herr. They are in their salon that das Fräulein here engaged this morning. Shall I send a message to them?'

The doctor turned a look of amazement on Joey, who stood at his side. Her sensitive face flushed with embarrassment. 'It seemed so horrid for them to have to feed in the Speisesaal,' she murmured. 'Primula Mary is only a baby. And I have heaps of money, anyhow.'

'Well, we'd better go up, I suppose,' he said. 'You seem to know the way, Joey, so we won't bother Fräulein to send up. Lead on, and let's get this thing settled.'

Joey skipped upstairs, and he followed. At the door of the sitting-room she had engaged, she stopped and tapped. A startled 'Come in!' answered her, and she opened it and went in.

'Mrs Venables—Margot!' she cried, impulsive as usual; 'here's Jem!' And then she stood back to let her brother-in-law pass her.

Mrs Venables had risen in surprise. She looked up at the tall fair man who had followed the girl into the room. 'Jem!' she cried. 'Oh, Jimsie!'

The next minute she was in his arms, sobbing in her relief. The two little girls stared round-eyed at the sight of their mother being picked up and hugged by the tall stranger. But Daisy knew Jo, so she decided that it must be all right.

'Have you come to tea?' she asked. 'Oh, do sit 'side me! I'll get chairs!' And she jumped up and began to drag a heavy chair to the table.

'Tea isn't a bad notion,' said Jo, going to her help. 'Not that it's *tea* you seem to be having,' she added.

'No; but it's tea-*time*,' replied Daisy sagely. 'Where will the gentleman sit, please?'

'Wants my mink!' observed Primula Mary suddenly. 'Wants my mink an' b'e'n-butter!'

'She means milk and bread-and-butter,' said Daisy confidentially. 'Could you butter it for her? I do make it so messy when I try.'

Jo went to the table and began to spread a slice of the delicious, holey bread with the sweet butter. She gave it to the baby. 'There you are, pet. Eat that.—Is this the milk, Daisy? Suppose I give you some, too? You don't seem to have begun your meal yet, and Mummy and Uncle Jem have such a lot to say to each other.'

'Uncle Jem is cuddling Mummy like's if she was Primula,' observed Daisy, glancing across to where the doctor, with his sister in his arms, was sitting on the sofa, talking in quick, low tones, while she wiped away the fast-falling tears.

'Yes; but then he's so big, and she's so tiny,' said Jo wisely. 'You *have* got a wee Mummy, Daisy!'

'Mummy kying,' said Primula Mary, waving her bread-and-butter towards them. 'Mummy mustn't kye! Baby kye, too!' And up went her lip.

'No, you don't!' said Jo promptly. 'Look, Primula! See the lovely jam I'm going to put on your bread!—I suppose she *may* have jam, Daisy?'

'Oh yes,' said Daisy. 'Jam me some, too, please—oh, what is your name?'

'You'd better call me Auntie Jo,' returned the young lady thoughtfully. 'That's about as near to the relationship as I can come, anyway.'

'Auntie Jo ? That's nice ! It's so short ! And I never had an auntie before,' decided Daisy. 'Oh, thank you, Auntie ! ' as Jo bestowed a lavishly-spread slice of bread-and-jam on her. Primula was already at work, and gradually becoming joyously sticky.

Jo poured herself out some coffee, helped herself to bread-and-butter and jam, and settled down contentedly to her meal until such time as Jem and the children's mother should awaken to the fact that they were not alone. This was not long in happening. The doctor, with a final kiss, set his sister on her feet. Mrs Venables gave her eyes a last scrub with her damp handkerchief, and he got up and stretched himself.

'I simply couldn't believe Frieda's yarn, you know, Margie ! But thank Heaven it's all right, and we've got you safe now. And don't you want to show me your two little maids ? '

Margot nodded, and advanced to the table where the little ones and Jo were enjoying a good meal, regardless—so far as the children were concerned—of what was going on round them.

'This is Daisy,' she said, a hand on the fair head, with its straight shock of silky hair. 'You knew about her, of course. And this is Primula Mary, my baby. I called her Primula because my friend, Nurse Rickards, had sent me a water-colour sketch of a cluster of primulas the day she was born. We were right up-country then ; and oh ! you don't know how that picture made me long for England and the spring flowers ! '

The doctor gave the children a keen look as he kissed first one and then the other. 'Daisy looks well,' he said, with a smile at the little maiden who was looking up at him with fearless blue eyes. 'How old is the baby?'

'She was two last November,' said her mother. 'The voyage did a great deal for Daisy; but Baby isn't—isn't quite as strong as she might be.' She finished up with a little quiver in her voice. Only too well she knew that the child was very fragile.

'Won't they finish off our nursery nicely, Jem?' asked Jo, who had caught the quiver. 'Davie is so dark, and so is Rix. And though Peggy is fair, it's a kind of *silvern* fairness, and these two are golden. Sybil is ginger, of course,' she added, with a provocative glance at him.

'I'll thank you, Jo Bettany, to remember that your youngest niece is chestnut—not ginger!' retorted Sybil's father, rising, as she had expected, to her bait.

'Oh well, it all comes to the same thing; and that's plain red,' said Jo.

'Is your little girl really red?' asked Margot, who had recovered her self-possession again.

'Her hair is,' said the doctor. 'She has chestnut curls—such a thick mop, too. The curls come from my wife, though you mightn't think it to look at Jo,' he added, with a teasing look at his young sister-in-law, whose black locks were as straight and lank as a Red Indian's.

'Ah, we never had any curls in our family,' said Mrs Venables, with a caressing touch to the thick, primrose-coloured thatch on her baby's head.

'Curly hair doesn't run in the Russell family,' he agreed. Then he laughed. 'Jo told me that Primula Mary was my image, and for once she hasn't drawn the long bow.'

' Well, I like that ! ' gasped Jo. ' Are you accusing me of being a liar ? '

' No, my child ; so keep calm ! But you do see such impossible likenesses in people sometimes, that I simply couldn't take your word for it.'

' More b'e'n-dam,' interrupted Primula Mary at this point.

' Yes, darling. But let Mummy wipe your mouth first. Such a sticky girl as you are ! Uncle Jem will never like such a messy little girl.'

She wiped the sticky mouth, while Joey spread another slice, and Daisy shyly pulled her uncle to the chair she had carried to the table. Jo rang for the chamber-maid, and when she came, bade her bring more china, and cakes, as well as fresh coffee. Then they settled down to enjoy the meal and talk. It was quite late by the time they finished, for there was so much for the brother and sister to hear about each other. Jo attended to the wants of the children, to leave their mother free, and when they had finished she bore them off to the bedroom to play, while Mrs Venables told her brother as much as she *could* tell anyone about her life in Australia. It was little more than she had told the two girls. Loyalty to her dead husband kept her as silent as possible about the life she had led with him. But the doctor was skilled to read between the lines, and he soon knew that Margot had bitterly repented her own wilfulness.

' I had the children,' she ended, ' or I could never have lived through it. And Stephen didn't mean to be bad, Jem ; only he was so weak, and he could never say " no " if it was easier to say " yes." '

' And that is a bad thing for a man, especially when he has a wife and children depending on him,' said the doctor sternly. 'Well, Margot, it seems to me that there is only one thing to do. You must all come back with us to-morrow. It is too late now for us to get up to the Tiern See, so I will see about rooms here presently. Can you pack and be ready to catch the nine o'clock train to Spärtz in the morning?'

His sister smiled wistfully. 'I could set off to-night if need be.'

'Oh, I don't think there's any need of that,' he returned. 'Fortunately, we have no very bad cases at the Sanatorium just now; and the other fellows are there in a case of emergency. Besides, your little people should be getting to bed. You send them off early, I expect.'

'Baby goes at six,' she replied. 'But I've let Daisy sit up much later these past few months. Was it selfish of me, Jem? But sometimes I felt that I couldn't bear to be alone, and Daisy is very companionable, though she is only nine.'

'When will she be ten?' he asked.

'Not till next March. She is just nine now. Jimmy was the eldest. He would have been nearly twelve. But the climate was too much for the boys. They just faded away in that awful heat.'

The doctor kissed her. 'Yes, dear. But now you have come to our wonderful mountain air, and even Primula Mary will be a different child before long.'

'I shall be so thankful! I have been in terror lest I should lose her too. You can't know, Jem, how I hated coming away and leaving those little graves behind me.'

'Try not to dwell on it, Margot. After all, the little lads have been spared the heat and battle of the day. You have these little girls left to care for; and you will have to be father as well as mother to them now. You will need all your strength for that.' But he looked very grave as he said it.

' Oh, I know. But at least I shall not have to stand quite alone now. I shall have you behind me—and your wife, too ? '

' Yes, honey. Madge is longing to get you all up there. She made me promise that if it was really you, and not one of Jo's wild-goose chases, I would bring you all up as soon as possible.'

' And there will be Jo, too. What a dear girl she is, Jem ! Do you know, just before she and her friend came up to me, I was beginning to think that I must give it all up. I felt as if I would gladly have died if I could only have taken my little girls with me.'

' Don't talk like that, Margot. That was just the result of the heavy strain under which you have been living so long. Please God, we shall be able to lift that from you. You have a home, and a brother to provide for you.'

' You are such a dear brother, Jem.' Then she asked suddenly, ' Mother and Father ? '

' Father was killed in a motoring accident seven years ago,' he said reluctantly. ' Mother only survived him three months. She spoke of you towards the end,' he added. ' You were a great deal on her mind, I fancy, and she often wished she could hear from you.'

' Stephen would not let me write,' said his sister, tears in her eyes. ' And I dared not go against him. He was jealous of me, Jem. He hated to think I had anyone but him. I think he was even jealous of our children. But I am glad Mother forgave me before she died. I—I would have liked to see them again.'

'They would have liked to see you, once the first bitterness was over,' he said, getting up. 'But, Margot, I must see about those rooms. And you ought to get your babies to bed. No need to keep Daisy up to-night.'

'No ; but she has been such a comfort to me,' said his sister, as she got up to go and seek the children.

'Daisy is getting a big girl,' he said, with a smile. 'Next term we must send her down to the Chalet School. She would love it there.'

Then he went off to arrange about the rooms for himself and Jo, while Margot put her little girls to bed, helped by the Head Girl of the Chalet School, who proved remarkably efficient.

'But that's the result of plenty of practice, as the White Knight said,' she explained, when Margot exclaimed at the briskly business-like way with which she undressed Daisy and tubbed her. 'I'll stay a while and read to Daisy, shall I ? It's not so very late yet.'

Daisy, who had been inclined to pout over the early bed, cleared up at that. She had taken a great fancy to Jo, perhaps because she had had so little to do with any girls of her kind before. Margot was glad to agree, so Jo curled up at the foot of the bed and told fairy-stories to an audience of one, till she discovered that Daisy was sound asleep. Primula, of course, had been 'over' nearly an hour before.

'Good girl, Joey !' said Jem, as late that night he escorted her to her bedroom door. 'You shall have your reward in due course.'

'So I was right after all, you see,' said Jo triumphantly. 'It *was* Margot ! Aren't you glad Frieda and I came with her after all ? If we'd behaved properly and refused to come, you mightn't have found her so easily, and anyway, not so soon.'

' Go to bed, you impertinent baggage ! ' he retorted. ' Remember you must be up early in the morning. I daren't face Mademoiselle if I let you miss more than half your morning's work.'

' Oh, work ! ' repeated Jo scornfully. Then she hugged him. ' All the same, Jem, you aren't half a bad sort. And I like Margot already. I'm jolly glad I found her ! ' And with this, she retired to bed and to sleep untroubled by either dreams or toothache.

CHAPTER VII

A BRUSH WITH THE NEW MATRON

AFTER quite a successful journey up to the Tiern See next day, Jo said good-bye to the new relations with the promise that she might come up to the Sonnalpe for the week-end of the following week, and hurried round the lake to school, where she decided that her best plan was to go straight to class, and run over to the middle house at the end of the morning. So she reported to Mademoiselle Lepâttre, who bade her come back at break, which would take place in about half-an-hour's time, and tell her all the news.

'You had better go to your history at once, my dear Jo,' said the Head Mistress. 'I know, of course, that our Dr Jem has found his sister, for Frieda told me so last night. But I shall be glad to hear what you can tell me later. Go now, dear child.'

Jo retired with the usual curtsey, and went off to apologise to Miss Stewart, the history mistress. After that she sat down and gave her whole attention to the doings in Europe during the Commonwealth in England. In fact, her morning was so full that she had no time for extraneous matters. She did occasionally wonder how Margot and the children were getting on, and if they had reached Die Rosen yet. But work at the Chalet School was strenuous during working-hours—or rather, it was intended to be. Some people managed to take things easily !—and by the time she had left the laboratory, where morning school for the Sixth ended that day with a two-hours science lesson, she had been working at full pitch and felt somewhat tired.

It happened to be her day on duty, so she marched to the side-door where the middles were waiting for her, since Miss Wilson had kept her class later than usual, and marshalled them across to their own house. On the way she noticed that two or three people seemed thoroughly disgruntled. She had had no time to speak to the other prefects, for talking was *not* encouraged during science, and she had spent the whole of break in the study. She wondered what had been happening during her absence, and being Jo, she set to work to find out.

' What's the matter, Corney ? ' she demanded of Cornelia Flower, one of the gloomiest-looking of the party. ' Got into trouble at school ? '

' No,' growled Cornelia.

' Then what's the trouble ? You look like a thunderstorm ! '

Cornelia growled again and hunched her shoulders.

' What is it, Evvy ? ' asked Jo, turning to fair-curled Evadne Lannis, Cornelia's compatriot and frequent ally in crime. ' What's wrong with you folk ? '

Evadne thought a moment. ' It's just Matron Besly,' she said at length.

' What about her ? ' demanded Jo sharply. ' What have you all been doing ? No more " midnights," I hope ? '

Whereat Joyce Linton, who was with them, went dark red. She had been the moving spirit of a ' midnight ' the previous term, and Nemesis had overtaken her in the most unpleasant form of all. She didn't like Jo's reference to her past sins.

'That's so likely, isn't it?' retorted Evadne with spirit. 'Once of that is quite enough, thank you!'

'Then what is it?'

'Oh, I guess she doesn't quite understand,' began Evadne confusedly.

'*Who* doesn't understand *what*? Oh, do get on, some of you, before I shake someone!—Lonny, can *you* tell me? What have you all been doing?'

Lonny—otherwise Ilonka Barkocz, a Hungarian girl—paused. 'It's so difficult, Jo. Only Matron went all round the dormies last night, and confiscated our books for early-morning reading.'

'Oho!' quoth Jo. 'So *that* business is coming up again, is it?'

'I wondered if you'd remember,' said Evadne.

'Remember what?' asked Cornelia, rousing out of her gloom at this cryptic allusion.

'We had a Matron here years ago—before you came—when Madame was Head,' explained Evadne. '*She* tried to put a stop to our early morning reading. She was a—a——'

'Now you just be careful what you say,' warned Jo. 'See how much pocket-money you can manage to keep *out* of the fines-box this term, for a change.'

'Well, anyhow, she was a bit of a trial,' emended Evadne. 'She left in a hurry, after several things had—er—*happened*!'

Ilonka began to gurgle. 'Do you remember when we all began to yell at the tops of our voices when we talked?' she asked. 'And Madame was *so* angry about it ! I think we—all of us who were middles then—had to write out a hundred times :

> " Her voice was ever sweet, gentle, and low ;
> An excellent thing in woman."

You see, Corney, *Matron* shouted when she spoke.'

A grin of pure delight illuminated Cornelia's face at this. ' What a great scheme ! ' she said. ' Whose idea was it—yours, Jo ? '

' I have no idea who suggested it,' said Ilonka. ' But we all did it.'

' It was Elisaveta's idea, if you must know,' said Jo, referring to the young Crown Princess of Belsornia, who had had two happy terms at the school, until the death of her grandfather, and the rescinding of the Salic Law in Belsornia, had brought her too near the throne to be permitted to continue her education out of the country. ' Yes ; it was a good idea. *How* furious my sister was about it ! '

' I wish I had been here then,' mourned Cornelia.

' But did she really stop the early-morning reading ? ' demanded Joyce Linton.

' Tried to, anyway,' said Jo. ' We only read on Sundays then. It wasn't till later that we were allowed to have our books upstairs in summer so long as we don't touch them till half-past six. Then my sister and Mademoiselle decided that as so many of us woke early in the light mornings, we had better be allowed to read if we liked. Of course, a good many people don't wake up ; and others prefer to go out and play tennis. But it's quite jolly to be able to get through a chapter or so if you want to.'

' Well, you can't do it now,' said Cornelia, assuming

her look of gloom again. 'Matron has taken every book in the place but our Bibles and Prayer-Books, and she says there's to be no more of it.'

'But—' Jo suddenly stopped short and bit her lips.

'What were you going to say?' asked Evadne with interest.

'Never mind. Here we are, and as we're late, it'll mean a rush. Hurry up, and don't be late for Mittagessen.'

With this, she ran off to the splashery reserved for the prefects, leaving the middles staring after her before they turned and looked at each other.

'It's all very well,' began Joyce, as they took Jo's advice and hastened to prepare for their midday meal, 'but I love reading in bed in the mornings, now that it's light; and I don't see why Matron should shove her oar in like this. And she's just come, too!' she added with a virtuous air.

'Don't worry! Jo will see to it somehow,' said Evadne.

'Don't see how she can. She can't very well tell Matron that she's an ass, and we're always allowed to read,' grumbled Cornelia.

'I know that! But she'll do something about it, all the same. You wait and you'll see!' And with this final remark, Evadne hung up her towel and retired to the common-room, leaving her friends to finish their ablutions somewhat hastily as the gong for Mittagessen sounded a minute or two later.

She was quite right in her supposition. Jo was thinking the matter over, even as she served the stewed steak which the Lower Fifth, whose day for

Domestic Economy it was, had cooked for the school dinner. It was a difficult question, for, as Cornelia had truly remarked, even the Head Girl could scarcely tackle Matron in quite that way. Jo had come to no decision by the time the meal was ended, and she went upstairs to change into her gym. tunic for games, still uncertain what to do.

She was quick in her movements, and she was soon ready. Then she glanced round for her book, as she had a few minutes to spare. It was gone, and she realised that Matron must have been to her room, as well as the dormitories. Jo went dark red at this. As a prefect, and Head Girl at that, she was supposed to be exempt from all bedroom supervision, and this was a deliberate violation of her rights. She got to her feet, meaning to go and tackle Matron at once, when there was a knock at the door, and then it opened, and Frieda burst in, startlingly indignant for gentle Frieda.

' What has gone wrong ? ' demanded Jo, in German, which was the language for the day.

' My book has been taken,' cried Frieda, her blue eyes sparkling with anger. ' I heard that the middles say that Matron has confiscated all books, and says that there is to be no more reading in bed in the mornings. But she has no right—*no right at all*—to go into our rooms. We are on honour, always, and no one supervises us in that way. We are prefects ! '

' She's taken mine, too,' said Jo. ' I wonder if she's done the same with Marie and Simone ? Let's go and see. We can't have this sort of thing going on. It will undermine our prestige as prefects if it is permitted.'

However, they were not to be troubled to seek the other two, for they came in at that moment, fully as indignant as their confrères, and demanding to know what they should do about it.

' Come in and sit down,' said Jo. ' Shut the door, Simone ; and don't yell, any of you. Matron may be in her room.'

' It is a shame ! ' stormed Marie. ' What right has she to do this kind of thing ? We have always been allowed to read, so long as we kept the rules about it. I know Bill and Charlie never suggested this, or they would have spoken to us first.'

' Keep cool,' said Jo sharply. ' Losing your temper won't make any better of matters. Of course we can't allow it to go on. The difficulty is to decide what we can do about it.'

' Report to Bill—I think we ought,' said Simone, with a wag of her small head which loosened part of the still precariously pinned-up roll of black hair which caused her so much trouble, since, ten months ago, it had been neatly bobbed.

' How can I possibly do that ? ' asked Jo irritably. ' Can't you see the picture ! " Please, Miss Wilson, I wish to report that Matron has been going into our rooms and confiscating our books." I should only get ticked off for impertinence. Bill would never listen to tales about another member of the Staff from just a schoolgirl—unless it was anything frightfully serious, that is. No mistress worth her salt would.'

There was silence. The girls all realised the truth of this dictum. But they were not disposed to take what had happened lying down, and they felt that they must do something about it. Frieda turned to Jo's mirror to make sure that the heavy plaits she wore in a coronal round her head were perfectly tidy, and her action reminded Simone to feel her own locks. She gave an exclamation of horror when she found part of them straggling over her shoulder.

'Oh, my hair! I shall never keep it up— never!'

'It will be better when it has grown a little longer,' said Marie soothingly. 'It comes down now because it is so short still.'

'And so fine,' added Jo. 'But it does take a long time to grow, doesn't it?'

'Well, *you* cannot say anything!' cried Simone, as she tucked in the last pin. 'Surely you should have had your hair trimmed when you were in Innsbruck yesterday, Jo? I am sure Herr Alphen would have been delighted to do it for you—especially if you had asked him to put on it Holy Water.'

The girls laughed at this, though Jo replied, 'That was Grizel, and not me. He's never forgotten it, either,' she added reminiscently. 'And *I* shall never forget his face! I thought he was going to have a fit!'

'But why did you not have your hair cut?' persisted Simone. 'It is quite long, and it looks more untidy than ever.'

Jo flushed, and for once in her life looked shy. 'Well, if you must know, I'm growing it,' she said. 'My sister said that she thought that as I am growing up—worse luck!—and as long hair was coming back into fashion, I'd better let mine begin, and see how we liked it. I can always have it cut again if we *don't* like it.'

'But you still keep your fringe,' said Marie.

'Yes; I shall keep that. Madge thought I could

wear my hair in ear-phones when it is long enough,
and keep my fringe with that style. She says,' added
Jo with a grin, ' that no one would know me if I gave
up my fringe.'

' I am glad of that,' said Frieda, leaving the mirror.
' It is so much better, Jo ; and it makes us all alike.'

' Impossible ! None of you look like a Skye
terrier ! ' retorted Jo.

' But that will soon pass. Your hair grows so
quickly. And I can show you how to keep it tidy
once it is long enough to turn up just a little. And in
the meantime, could you not wear a snood as girls
are doing now.'

' No, thank you ! I never have any money as it
is !—Yes ; come in ! ' For a tap had come to the
door.

It was Evadne who stood there, and she had brought
a message from Matron. ' Please, Jo, Matron says
will you go to her in her room at once.'

' Very well,' said Jo resignedly. ' Frieda, will you
take the middles over for me, if Matron keeps me ?—
How are you all managing, Evvy ? Everyone downstairs good and quiet ? '

' Quite,' said Evadne. ' Corney is in charge just
now, though it's my day. But we thought it better
not to leave some of those junior middles entirely
alone. You know what some of them are ! '

Jo stifled a laugh at the gravity with which this was
said. A new arrangement had come into force with
the establishment of the new house. This was the
rule that all girls must lie down for their midday rest.
Hitherto they had been allowed to sit about and talk,
so long as they were quiet. But now they were all
provided with cushions and mattresses or rugs, and

no speaking was permitted. In the Chalet itself, the prefects had overseen the rest; but now they were to be freed from this duty, which must fall on the four seniors among the middles—this term, on Evadne Lannis, Cornelia Flower, Ilonka Barkocz, and Giovanna Donati, and there was not a doubt but that they would keep order most efficiently. But it was not yet three weeks since all four had been mere middles under authority, and the sudden attack of responsibility which had seized on them since their appointment made the older girls chuckle in secret.

Jo nodded to Evadne, who went back to her duties, and strolled along to Matron's room, grinning to herself as she went. But all desire to laugh, or even smile, went from her at that lady's first words.

'Come in, Jo. And now I want to know why you have not troubled to report yourself to me, although you must have been in the school at least four hours now.'

'I reported to Mademoiselle,' said Jo stiffly. 'She is Head Mistress, and I went straight to her.'

'That is all very well. But you had break and before luncheon to see me. I am Matron here, and you should have come to me at once as soon as she had finished with you.'

Jo had recovered herself a little. 'Mademoiselle sent me to class as soon as she had seen me, but told me to go to her for break,' she said quietly. 'I was with her the whole of break, and as we were late in finishing our science lesson, it was practically time for Mittagessen by the time I had brought the middles over.'

'That makes no difference. You should have left

the middles to someone else and come to me
direct.'

' Is it a new rule ? ' asked naughty Jo, composing
her features into a look of deep perplexity. ' We
never had to report to Matron before.'

' It's *my* rule ! ' snapped Matron. ' For the future,
when you go out anywhere, you must report to me
on your return.'

Jo's eyes flashed, but she kept herself in hand,
though there was something peculiarly galling to her
in Matron s tone. ' If it is a rule,' she said, ' I must
enter it on the rules list. Mademoiselle asked me to
let her have all lists to-night for signature. I will
enter it up, Matron.'

' That refers to school rules. This is house rules,
and has nothing to do with them.' Matron had not
yet spoken to Mademoiselle about her idea, and she
was not anxious to have it brought to the Head's
notice before she did so.

' *All* rules lists, whether for school or house, have to
go to Mademoiselle to be countersigned,' returned Jo,
still quietly, though she was beginning to boil.

Matron was nonplussed for the moment, so she said
nothing. Jo, meantime, had one of her usual impulses,
and changed the subject. ' Oh, Matron, there is something I want to ask you about. The girls tell me that
it is you who have confiscated all our books for early-
morning reading. But the rule says that girls who
wish to read after half-past six may do so provided
they sit up, and don't try to read lying down ; and,
of course, wear a bed-jacket. Has Mademoiselle
revoked this rule ? Because there is no need for me
to copy it out if she has, and she has said nothing to
me about it.'

Matron was in a quandary. The stopping reading in bed was her own idea. She had had no notion that it was so hedged round, and had imagined that the girls might read lying flat. She honestly thought this very bad for their eyes—so it is—hence her arbitrary behaviour.

'Surely you don't mean to say that that is in the rules?' she asked slowly, trying to gain time to think.

'I'll bring you the copy,' said Jo, moving to the door to do so. But she was pulled up at once.

'There is no need to do so, thank you. I can read my own copy. In the meantime, you owe me an apology, and I sent for you to make it.'

Jo's eyes flashed dangerously. 'I'm sorry, Matron, but as I knew nothing about this rule of yours, I don't think I do owe you one. And in any case,' she added, 'before any rule can become a rule, it must be passed by Mademoiselle. And my sister, Mrs Russell, must pass it too.'

'How dare you speak to me like that?' cried Matron. 'Understand at once, Josephine, that I will put up with no impudence from you, Head Girl or no Head Girl!'

'I was only telling you what is always done here,' said Jo, still in that deadly quiet tone. 'There was no impudence in that.'

The next moment she was thankful that she had not given way to the fury that was boiling within her, for there was a rap at the door, and then Miss Wilson came into the room.

'Well, Joey,' she said, as she saw the Head Girl, 'I hear that you have brought Dr Jem's sister and her small girls safely to the Tiern See. Have you heard

if they have arrived safely at Die Rosen yet ?   And
do we get any new pupils ? '

' I hope Daisy will come down, Miss Wilson,' said
Jo.   ' Primula Mary is rather too small yet, though.
She's only two.'

' Primula Mary ?   What a pretty name !   However,
I haven't time to stay talking here.   I was looking for
you to ask you for the rules lists, as I want to
sign them, and Mademoiselle has, I know, asked for
them for to-night.   Let me have them, Joey, for I'm
going to Spärtz, and shan't be back till late to-night.
Matron will let me sign them here, I know.   Run
along, dear.'

Jo went off, and the Head of the new house sat
down and smiled at her Matron.   ' Jo is a dear girl !
You'll soon find that out for yourself, Matron, if you
haven't found it out already.   We shall all miss her
horribly when she leaves.   She's a real strength in
the school, and sets an admirable tone.   And when I
think what a scaramouche she used to be ! '   And Miss
Wilson began to laugh.

' Indeed ? ' said Matron stiffly.

Miss Wilson opened her eyes.   ' Yes ; indeed she
is !   She is so firm with the younger girls, and yet she
contrives to be friendly with them too.   And then she
is so capable, and so courteous.   In many ways I
consider her one of the best Head Girls we have ever
had—and we have had some excellent ones, I can
assure you.'

' Oh ? '   Matron did not seem interested in the
subject.   Miss Wilson said no more ; but she put it
aside in her mind, intending to think it over later,
and go into it with Matron if necessary.   Meanwhile,
Jo having come back with the lists, she glanced over

them, and then signed them with her firm, clear signature, ' H. M. Wilson.'

Now, Jo was not, as a rule, vindictive. But Matron had contrived to rouse all her worst feelings that afternoon, and there was a certain malice in her voice as she pointed to the rule about early-morning reading and said, ' I suppose that rule remains as it is, Miss Wilson ? '

' Remains as it is ?   What do you mean ? ' demanded Miss Wilson.

' Only that Matron says it has been rescinded,' said Jo innocently.   ' I haven't had time to hear about it to-day until just now.   But I knew, of course, that you had a Staff meeting last night.   So I thought I'd better ask to make sure.'

Miss Wilson glanced quickly at her.   Jo's voice and manner were abnormally innocent ; but ' Bill ' had not known her for nearly six years without learning a good deal about her.   ' I imagine Matron was referring to the story-books some people try to smuggle into preparation,' she said shortly.   ' We certainly spoke of that last night.   Mademoiselle said that it was to be put down at once, and with a firm hand.   So please be on the alert, Jo.   As for the early-morning reading, nothing was said about that, of course.   Why should there be anything ?   I wish you would try to listen properly when people discuss things with you, Jo ! '

Jo said nothing.   She stood there, the very picture of a proper Head Girl, her cheeks tinged with pink, her lashes down.   But Miss Wilson knew perfectly well that beneath those long lashes her eyes were gleaming.   And Jo was quite aware that the mistress understood, as if she had been told point-blank, what

had happened. She was also aware of the fact that
'Bill' was merely saving Matron's face in scolding
herself thus. So she took the tartness of the rebuke
with becoming meekness ; apologised for her stupidity
and then fell silent. Miss Wilson finished signing the
lists, and then told Jo curtly to be sure to take them
to Mademoiselle in good time.

'And you'd better go off to games at once,' she
added. 'Miss Nalder won't be pleased at your lateness.'

'No, Miss Wilson,' cooed Jo in tones of dulcet
sweetness. She took up the lists and departed,
chuckling inwardly to think that she had got the
better of Matron. Miss Wilson waited until she
had gone. Then she turned to the angry woman
beside her.

'Matron,' she said in a firm but gentle tone, 'it is
the rule here that *no* new rule may be put into force
until it has been discussed with Mademoiselle, the
Staff, and Mrs Russell. We have found this answer
very well, as it gives us time to consider any suggestion
from all points of view. Nothing is so annoying as
having to rescind any rule that may be found to have
been framed too hastily. Either of your colleagues,
who have both been here some time, will tell you this.
Now I must go, or I shall be late. Guten Tag !' And
she followed Jo out of the room, and hurried off to
her own to get ready.

But when she was going down the mountain-path
that leads to Spärtz by the banks of the little stream
which frolics gaily down to the Inn, and supplies
power for the saw-mills half-way down the mountain-
side, she suddenly stamped her foot. 'That wicked
child ! How dared she do such a thing ? And what,

I wonder, has Matron Besly done to rouse such villainy in Jo ? I do hope to goodness that things will simmer down between them. I'd like a peaceful term for a change ! '

Poor Miss Wilson ! From that afternoon onwards it was war to the knife between Matron and Jo !

CHAPTER VIII

THE PREFECTS IN COUNCIL

'WELL, how do you like it over there now that you've had a little while of it?' asked Vanna di Ricci, one of the prefects, as Jo, accompanied by Simone Lecoutier, entered the prefects' room at the Chalet.

Jo looked round the little room which had been used by the grandees of the school ever since its first days, and heaved a sigh partly of satisfaction, partly of regret, as she sank into her chair at the head of the table. 'Oh, bliss! You don't know how I've missed all this! Over there? Oh, it's quite jolly, of course. We have a gorgeous room, and a bedroom to oneself has its advantages, though I miss the fun we used to have in the dormies. But this is *ours*. The first prefects helped to make it, and no other prefects' room will ever seem quite the same to me.—And I know all the others think the same—n'est-ce pas, Simone?' she added to her friend.

Simone nodded her head cautiously. 'It is very pleasant, as Jo says; and our room is pretty. But I agree that I prefer this because the first prefects gave it to us. Gisela gave those pictures, and the bookshelves in that corner were Gertrud's, and Bernhilda gave us the inkstand. Yes; and Bette's gift was the clock. And the others have added to it. There is Grizel's bust of Beethoven, and the one of Bach that Mary gave; and——'

'Oh, don't go through the whole list, for goodness' sake!' implored Jo. 'What a memory you've got! I doubt if I could manage all that at a moment's notice.'

Simone laughed. 'Well, at least this is all given by ourselves; and the other room is just part of the school furniture. It is not the same thing at all, Vanna.'

'I can understand that,' said quiet Carla von Flügen. 'And we miss you four so much.'

'Nice of you,' said Jo. 'How is Luigia getting on, Bianca?'

'She is very happy,' said Bianca di Ferrara, a slight, Italian girl, whose elder sister, an old pupil of the school, had been clothed as a novice in the Poor Clares early in the previous autumn. 'She is looking forward to taking her final vows, and then she will be indeed happy.'

Joey nodded, her mind going back to the days when slim, dark-eyed Luigia had been a happy, care-free girl like themselves. It seemed to her that if some of the elder ones had husbands and children, Luigia had taken an even greater step forward than they.

'How late Frieda and Marie are!' exclaimed Eva von Heiling, another of the prefects. 'And where is Paula?'

'Paula is having her lesson with Herr Anserl,' said Marie herself, as she appeared at this moment. 'I cannot think why Onkel Siegmund should have insisted on her taking lessons with him for the rest of her school-life! She is not naturally musical, and she must make him so furious.'

'She does!' said Vanna di Ricci with feeling. 'She has the lesson before mine on Mondays, and I can never do anything right for him on those days. It is well that Paula's lesson on the Thursday is the last of the day.'

'And it's better still that no one has ever suggested that *I* should have lessons from him,' put in Jo, who was the pupil of patient Miss Denny, the assistant music-mistress. The piano was not her strong point, but she possessed a lovely voice, which was already being carefully trained by Mr Denny, the school's eccentric singing-master, and Miss Denny's brother.

The assembled prefects laughed at the idea.

'If you had lessons from him, Jo,' said Anne Seymour, one of the sub-prefects, 'there'd be no roof left on the school.'

'Well, I couldn't be much worse than you!' retorted Jo.

Anne chuckled. 'Music never was my strong point. Drawing's *my* subject.'

'Well, it certainly isn't mine,' sighed Jo, who had had such a violent battle with short-tempered Herr Laubach, the drawing-master, two terms ago, that it had been decided that her lessons in art had better end.

'Here comes Paula,' said Carla in her quiet voice. 'Poor Paula! You look as if it had not been a placid lesson.'

Paula, a dark, somewhat ordinary-looking girl of sixteen, heaved a deep sigh as she came in and sat down. 'It has been terrible! Oh, why did Papa think that he wanted me to be a musician? Irma is far more musical than I, and when she is strong enough to leave the Annexe and come back here, she could go to him, and she would never enrage him as I do.'

'She's much better, isn't she?' asked Anne.

'Oh, much better. She has had only one bad cold

all the winter, and Dr Jem thinks she may come back in another year.'

'Just as well,' said Jo. 'The Annexe is getting on the full side now. Laurenz Maïco will be down after next winter; and Amy Stevens is coming in September. Jem says that she is perfectly fit now; and, of course, the Annexe is only intended for very delicate people. As soon as they get strong enough, they have to be drafted here. Juliet won't be sorry, I know. She said during the holiday that she had as many as they could manage, and they have four applications for next term already.'

'Will the Robin come back?' asked Simone, referring to Jo's little adopted sister, whose father, Captain Humphries, was secretary to the Sonnalpe Sanatorium.

Jo shook her head, a shadow falling across her face. 'No; Jem says that her school-days must all be spent up there. She is better, but she is still very frail. And you know how her mother died.

Simone was sorry she had spoken. The Robin's pretty, Polish mother had died of tuberculosis, brought on by the privations she had undergone during the war, and her little daughter was very fragile indeed. Luckily the door opened once more, and Frieda came in, full of apologies for her lateness.

'But indeed I couldn't help it, for Matron detained me,' she explained.

'But why didn't you tell her that we had a meeting?' demanded Jo. 'Matey's never unreasonable, and she'd have let you come at once.'

'It was not Matey, Jo. And our new Matron does not quite see things as Matey does,' said Frieda carefully.

' Isn't she decent ? ' asked Anne curiously.

' She is still new, and she does not yet understand,' said Frieda, true to her name's meaning of ' peace.'

' That means that she is *not* nice,' translated Bianca, who was a shrewd young person. ' I am sorry for that. I hope she will not be so bad as that Matron Webb we had here when we were middles. Do you remember ? '

Jo nodded. ' I should think I do ! Oh, she isn't like that ! But, as Frieda says, she's new, and she certainly doesn't understand.'

' And she will not try to understand, either,' put in Simone viciously.

Jo, deciding that this had gone far enough—there was never any knowing what Simone might say next when she was in the mood—rapped on the table, and brought the meeting to order.

' Now then, you people, we haven't too much time. Let's start business, Frieda, if you have last term's minutes, perhaps someone will move that you read them to us.'

It was duly proposed and seconded, and Frieda stood up and read the account of the doings of last term. They were passed unanimously, and Jo signed them with the script that was decidedly neater than it had been when she first was called on to perform such an act.

' Well, that's that,' she said. ' Now about duties. They come next, I think. As we four have to see to prep over at Middle House, as well as escorting the middles back and forth, perhaps the rest of the prefects will divide junior prep and break duty among them. Arrange it to suit yourselves, and let me know what you decide to-morrow. Library, I will keep on as usual. Stacie Benson will remain editor of the magazine. She has done very well, and I don't think we could improve on her.'

'I agree,' said Frieda. 'Stacie has done very well.'

'And the other special duties ? ' said Marie.

'Well, I want Eva to keep on the pets ; and Louise might help her there.—Hobbies will fall to you, Vanna, and Paula will help—nicht wahr ? ' And she turned to Paula.

'Yes, Joey. But I know very little about some of them,' said Paula.

'That's not to be wondered at. Some of the babes do go in for such weird hobbies. However, this is the summer term, so they won't have much time for such things.—Anne,' she turned to pretty Anne Seymour, 'you will be the sub-prefect of the games, we hope. I rather think Marie wants you to captain the tennis, too.—Wasn't that what you said, Marie ? '

Marie nodded her head. 'Yes, Anne. I hope you will take the tennis, for I must see to the cricket and boating again.'

Anne, looking rather serious over the responsibility, agreed to this, and Jo went on to the next item. 'Carla, you'll be music monitress as usual, and Margia Stevens will help you. She'll have to take it on next term, anyway, because you'll have left—like most of us, worse luck. You may as well get her trained to his ways while you can. It isn't everyone who could manage Vater Bär as you do ! ' By which rude epithet she referred to Herr Anserl, who was a terror to his music pupils, though out of lessons he was very popular with the girls.

'Does Margia know ? ' asked Carla.

'No, my love. I'm leaving it to you to break the

glad news. Won't she be pleased, though ! ' And Jo chuckled whole-heartedly.

' I think I would rather you told her,' said Carla decidedly. ' And ought she not to be here now ? I thought that Mademoiselle had appointed her as sub-prefect ? '

' Yes ; but she was rather headachy, so Matey sent her to bed,' explained Jo. ' That's one reason why I'm leaving you to do the telling. You'll see her before I shall.'

' And do I take stationery again ? ' asked Frieda, more to stop Carla from arguing the point than for any other reason.

' If you don't mind.—Luigia Meracini, wake up ! You look half-asleep, and you may as well know that I've put you with Frieda for stationery this term. You're a neat and tidy creature, and ought to be able to manage it very well.'

Luigia, a dreamy girl of sixteen, started guiltily at the sound of her name. ' I beg your pardon, Joey. What am I to do ? ' she asked.

' Oh ! ' groaned Jo. ' Aren't you the limit ?— Sorry, everyone ; I know it's slang, but it really is the only word that expresses Luigia !—I said I was giving you to Frieda to help with the stationery, my child. Don't go to sleep when you're on duty, that's all. If you do, some of those middles will get books out of you that they've no right to have.'

Luigia blushed. ' I am sorry, Jo. I will do my best,' she said earnestly.

' And what do I do ? ' demanded Arda van der Windt, a pleasant-faced Dutch girl of Luigia's age.

' You help me and Sophie with library and magazines. It won't mean a great deal of work, and

I hope you'll take it over next term, though that, of course, must lie with whoever is Head Girl then.'

The girls looked at each other in silence. None of them liked to remember the fact that this was Jo's last term. But they knew that they must face up to it. After all, as Marie remarked later, many of them were also leaving, and they could not hope to remain schoolgirls for ever.

' And what is my duty, Jo ? ' asked Thora Helgersen, a big Norwegian, whose mother had died up at the Sonnalpe recently. ' You know that I leave at Christmas ? My father wishes me to go home then to keep house for him and look after Astrid and the boys—though Astrid will come here when she is old enough.'

' I know. Don't you think you could see to Staff break ? It only means seeing that they get their lemonade and biscuits at break, and bring the tray away afterwards.'

Thora nodded. ' Yes ; I could do that.'

' Then the duties are pretty well settled, I think,' said Jo, glancing round. ' Does everyone agree to these arrangements ? If not, speak now or for ever hold your peace ! No one ? Good !—Then here's the list, Frieda. You can enter it in the notes later on. And give it to Cyrilla Maurús, and tell her to make the usual three copies to put up. I'll see to the one for Mademoiselle.'

' Ought there not to be five copies this term ? ' asked Frieda. ' We shall need one for middle house, you know, and I think there ought to be one for the Staff as well.'

' Oh, bother ! That's true. Then Elsie Carr can see to the other. She and Cyrilla are getting off very lightly this term for subs.—Tell her to make two copies,

Carla, will you. She's by way of being artistic, isn't she? Will you see to that?'

Carla amiably agreed, and then Jo sat up very straight. 'The next piece of business is that Mademoiselle thinks that now we have three houses, they should have better names than those they have at present. The school, as a whole, is always "The Chalet School." But our three houses, she thinks, should each be dedicated to a Saint. We have always considered the Madonna as our special Patron. But I rather like the idea of a special Saint for each house. Mademoiselle wishes us to choose to-night for the Chalet itself, and middle house. Le Petit Chalet is to be dedicated to St Agnes, because she is one of the best known of the child-saints. The special virtue to be learned from her is gentleness, and steadfastness too. Now what about our houses? By the way, we must choose women, of course, because the idea is that we take our saints as a kind of pattern. Will you all get paper and pencil, and write down the saint you choose for each house?'

The girls found paper and pencil, and presently scribbled down the saint they chose for each house. Joey acted as scrutator, with Frieda and Carla to help her. They examined the papers carefully, and then the Head Girl sat back in her chair. 'There are six votes for Ste Thérèse de Lisieux; and six for St Clare,' she announced. 'There are also three for St Scholastika; but she's ruled out. Have you *quite* forgotten the Saints? We don't want them to think that we're copying them; and they probably wouldn't like it, either.'

'I forgot the Saints,' admitted Thora, speaking of the girls' school which was situated at the other side

of the lake. ' So it lies between little Ste Thérèse and
St Clare. We must vote again, as they are level.'

' Not at all,' said Marie. ' We will take St Clare
for middle house, for she teaches us complete sub-
mission to orders, as well as charity for all, and I
think that is what most of us over there need to learn.
And the Chalet shall have Ste Thérèse, whose life
teaches us love toward God.—Will that do, Jo ? '

' Will anyone second that ? ' asked Jo, with a nod
at Marie.

' I will,' said Bianca, ' though I wish that *we* might
have had Santa Chiara.'

However, when it was put to the vote, it was found
that once more the girls were unanimous.

' Is that all, Joey ? ' asked Carla.

But Jo had still something more for them. ' This
is the term we celebrate my sister's birthday,' she
said. ' As there will be no half-term this term——'

' No half-term ? ' exclaimed half-a-dozen voices,
full of consternation.

' Did you really expect it ? ' asked Jo blandly. ' I
suppose you know that this is only a nine-weeks term ? '

' I had forgotten it was so short,' admitted Marie,
the first to speak.

' But, Jo, we had hoped that you and Marie and
Simone would come to stay with us for the week-end,'
said Frieda in dismayed tones. ' We shall hope to see
much of you and Marie still after this term ; but
Simone returns to Paris, and it will be three years at
the least before she can return here.'

' I know,' said Jo slowly. ' However, it can't be
helped. Mademoiselle says that if we three can be
spared, and you, too, we may have a week-end with
you at the Mariahilf. She quite understands how we

feel about it.   And Simone *is* coming here every summer for a holiday.—Aren't you, Simone ? '

' Cousine Thérèse says that she will arrange it,' said Simone, who was looking depressed. ' I hope she may, for so much may happen in three years.'

' I should think so,' agreed Jo. ' Why, within three years of leaving school Bernhilda and Gisela and Wanda were all married. And Marie, at any rate, will be settled before we know where we are. Frieda, too, I expect.'

Marie von Eschenau blushed at this, though Frieda did not change colour. But then, Marie at eighteen had already met the man she was to wed, and had some inkling as to her future destiny. Frieda knew nothing about hers as yet.

' You may be married yourself,' said Simone pessimistically, answering Jo's last remark.

' You never know,' Jo informed her calmly. ' However, that's not the question at present. What I was going to tell you all is about the arrangements for my sister's birthday. But if you don't want to hear, I can leave it till Mademoiselle tells the School.'

' Joey, don't be mean ! ' said Anne Seymour. ' Never mind those three ! If Simone chooses to make herself miserable about what may happen, that's no reason why the rest of us should be kept waiting. Tell us what they propose to do.'

She was backed up by the rest, even Simone forgetting her present grievance to clamour loudly for the news. Jo looked round them all, and then relented.

' Oh, all right ! Well, my sister thought we would like to go up the Zillerthal this time. We've done a good many other things, and it's years since we were there. It will be quite new to most of the School ;

and those of us who were there three years ago won't mind seeing it again.'

'No, indeed,' said Frieda. 'Joey, what a good idea! Though we shall miss many who were with us then,' she added, with a sigh.

'When do we go?' asked Louise Redfield, who had not known most of the girls of whom they spoke, and, consequently, could not enter into their regret.

'The fifth Saturday of the term, if it's a fine day,' said Jo. 'If not, then we'll go the next Saturday. We shall set out very early in the morning, and not come back till late at night. The juniors, by the way, will not come with us. They are all going up to the Sonnalpe with Miss Norman and Miss Edwards, who will take charge of them and the Annexe people, so that Juliet and Grizel may come with us.'

'Oh, that is very good!' cried Marie. 'It will be more like old times to have them with us. But if we could only have Wanda, and Gisela and Bernhilda, and Luigia and the others, how much pleasanter it would be!'

'We're going to have Rosalie Dene, anyhow,' said Jo, naming another old girl who had just come to the Sonnalpe to be Dr Russell's private secretary. 'Mary, of course, can't get away. And Bette and Gertrud are both too busy just now. *But*'—here she paused impressively until even Frieda the peaceful felt inclined to shake her—'but Elisaveta is coming for a fortnight just then, and will be with us whichever day we go.'

A chorus of joy broke out at this. Everyone present knew the young Crown Princess of Belsornia, for they had been in camp with her the previous summer, when the Chalet School Guides had had a glorious camp on the shores of the Baumersee, a beautiful little lake very near the German border.

'I say! What fun!' cried Louise. 'I reckon the Quintette will be thrilled to the limit when they hear that! They were very chummy with Elisaveta at camp.'

'Let's hope they won't be moved to investigate any hornets' nests we may come across,' said Jo, with a chuckle, as she remembered what had happened when Elisaveta, Maria Marani, Hilda Bhaer, and Evadne Lannis had found one, and not knowing what it was, had thrown sticks at it until a straight shot from Evadne had brought down the great paper-bag-like thing, and set the hornets buzzing furiously after them, out for revenge.

'*I* hope you and Juliet will refrain from trying to catch fish,' laughed Frieda, with reference to one of Jo's own exploits.

'Don't worry! I doubt if there's anything bigger in the Ziller than tiddlers,' retorted Jo.

'Perhaps Simone will wish to wash for gold again,' suggested Marie, with a teasing glance at Simone.

'Indeed, that was Margia's idea,' returned Simone seriously. 'Besides, I was only a child then. One does not do such things when one is grown-up.'

'Your hair is coming down,' said Jo detachedly.

Simone sighed heavily, and she twisted up the tiresome locks, her sudden accession of elderliness gone at this reminder.

'Well, anyway, it will be a great expedition,' declared Louise. 'Is that all, Jo? Or have you any more news for us?'

Jo shook her head. 'No; I think that's everything. And there goes your bell for Abendessen. We four must fly, or Matron will be on our track.'

'Don't you like her?' asked Paula von Rothenfels curiously. 'I think she is quite pretty to look at.'

'Oh, she's a fluffy little idiot,' said Jo, who had had another passage-of-arms with Matron Besly just before coming over to the Chalet, and who had not yet recovered her temper over it, or she would certainly never have spoken like that. 'She'll never do for us—that's certain! The middles will play her up to their hearts' content, if I know anything about middles!'

'Well, you ought to!' said Vanna. 'You used to be the leader in all the pranks that went on when we were middles, Jo.'

Jo laughed. 'I managed to get a good deal of fun out of life,' she admitted. 'Well, there's only this term left to me now, and I'm going to enjoy it all I can. Oh dear! How I wish I were a middle still! It seems to me that once you get past fifteen, you lose half your fun.'

'Such as flouring the hair of other girls?' asked Frieda, with a twinkle at her.

'I like that! You were in that as much as I was!'

'Do you remember the mess Corney made when you suggested that perhaps corn-flour and water might make blanc-mange of her hair?' asked Marie, with a peal of laughter.

'I remember how hard I had to work with Yvette's hair,' sighed Frieda. 'She has so much, and it is so long, and the corn-flour would *not* wash out, though I rubbed so hard.'

'I believe Anita was worse,' Simone joined in eagerly. '*Never* have I worked harder!'

'That was the term we had the feud with the Saints,' Carla von Flügen reminded them. 'Who could have foreseen that we should come to be real

friends with them as we are now ? And Miss Browne
is quite nice when you get to know her.'

A tap at the door brought these reminiscences of
their gay and varied past to a close, for when Vanna,
who was nearest, opened it, Matron stood there.

'Have you forgotten that there is such a meal as
Abendessen ? ' she demanded.

Everyone jumped up. 'Oh, Matey, we'd no idea
it was so late ! ' cried Jo. 'We've been discussing
old times, and quite forgot about Abendessen. Matron
Besly *won't* be pleased ! '

'That's all right,' said Matron. 'I rang up middle
house and asked Miss Wilson if you four might stay
over here, and she says you may. You are very late,
of course ; and you'll have to run as soon as the
meal is over. But it will save trouble for the middle
house Staff. Go and make yourselves fit to be seen
now, and then hurry down to the Speisesaal.'

They streamed past her out of the room. Jo came
last. As she passed the little lady in the fresh uniform
who had been domestic autocrat at the Chalet School
for more than three years now, she slipped an arm
round her shoulders, and gave her a hug.

'Matey, you're a sport ! ' she declared.

Matron freed herself vigorously. 'My uniform is
clean on to-day, and I'd like it to last the week out,'
she said tersely. 'It certainly won't do that if you
treat me in this unseemly way. Don't blarney, Jo ! '

But Jo merely chuckled. She knew herself to be
privileged. Though wild horses wouldn't have dragged
it out of Matron, Jo Bettany occupied the warmest
corner of her heart ; and however much she might
protest at the crumpling of her clean uniform, she
glowed to the cause of the crumples inwardly.

CHAPTER IX

MATRON BESLY SCORES

THINGS went on quietly in the school for the next week or so. Dr Russell, having got his sister and her little girls safely at Die Rosen, quickly decided that Daisy had better go to the Annexe for that term. When the Christmas term came, she was to go down to Briesau to the Chalet School proper as a pupil. But just for the few weeks that remained, he thought it best to have her near her mother.

Once she had safely reached haven, Margot Venables broke down. She had contrived to keep up as long as she was the only prop of her children; but once she had her brother and his sweet wife behind her, collapse followed inevitably from the reaction. News came down to Joey and Frieda that she had been removed to a distant wing of Die Rosen, where the noise of the children and the ordinary comings and goings of the household could not disturb her. Daisy went happily to school with Miss Carrick, better known to the Chalet girls as Juliet; and Primula Mary settled down in the big nursery, where she became the sworn ally of her cousin David, who was a few months younger than she. The doctor did not say much to the girls, but it was obvious that he felt very anxious about his sister. The long strain under which she had been, added to the effects of the killing climate of North Queensland, had told heavily on her, and he was terribly worried when he saw how her strength had been drained.

Joey spent the week-end following the prefects' meeting up at the Sonnalpe, where she was rapturously welcomed by her nieces and nephews, the Robin, her little adopted sister, and Dr Jem and his wife, her own adored sister, once Madge Bettany of the Chalet School.

'Margot looks awfully changed, Jem,' she said anxiously to him, as they walked down the corridor that joined this wing to the main portion of the house. 'What's wrong with her?'

'Worn out,' he said curtly.

'She looks—she looks—so tiny,' went on Jo, thinking aloud. 'I thought she was the tiniest woman I had ever seen when I first met her. But even in these few days she seems to have dwindled.'

'Herr von der Witt is coming along next week,' said her brother-in-law. 'I shall ask him to look at Margot then.'

Joey said no more; but she guessed what he was feeling. As she told her sister later on, there was nothing to be gained by rubbing things in.

Madge Russell, slight, dark-haired, brown-eyed, with a world of sweetness in her delicate face, shook her head. 'Jem hasn't said much to me,' she said, running her fingers through the shaggy black locks pressed against her knee. 'But I know he *is* very anxious.'

Joey looked up lovingly into the deep brown eyes that were the dearest eyes in the world to her. 'But you have your own ideas?'

Madge shook her head again. 'I am not going to say anything, Joey. We shall know better when Herr

von der Witt has seen her. I know that Jack May-
nard and Gottfried Mensch have both insisted on a
consultation.'

Jo's eyes darkened. 'Surely they don't think—'
she began, half-fearfully.

'No ; not that, Joey. Margot's lungs are perfectly
sound. But I think they are afraid that all she has
undergone may have undermined her nerves and her
constitution, and they are afraid that she may become
permanently invalided. It will be a terrible thing for
Daisy and Primula Mary if that is so.'

'Not as long as they have you,' said Jo.

When she went down on the Monday, she answered
Frieda's eager queries very sombrely, however.
'Margot is ill. She is very ill. They have taken her
into the new wing Jem had built on last spring, and
the children are only allowed to see her twice a day.
Gottfried and Jack have insisted on a consultation
with Herr von der Witt when he gets there next week.
They will know better what to think when that's over.
Yes ; I saw Gisela—had Kaffee und Kuchen with
them yesterday, as a matter of fact. Natalie is growing such a big girl now, Frieda. She toddles all over,
and she calls Gisela " Mam-mam," and is getting quite
chatty.'

'Well, she is thirteen months now,' said Frieda,
smiling happily. 'I had a letter from Mamma this
morning, Jo, and Bernhilda and Kurt are taking little
Stefan up to Das Pferd next week, and Bernhilda
expects to stay there till the summer is over. Kurt
must be in Innsbruck, of course ; but he will be able
to spend Sundays with them, and he will have his
holidays there, too.'

'Good ! That means all our babies together, then,'

said Jo. 'And Gertrud is to be married to that new doctor they have there in the X-ray room in June. Fancy Gertrud being Frau von Ronschlar! There's one thing, Frieda, we do manage to stick pretty near to each other. Don't you dare to marry anyone who wants to take you away!'

'That is not likely,' said Frieda. 'And how is Rosalie?'

'Oh, very well. And she likes her work so much. She's just the same as she always was—very quiet and mousy. But Jem says that she's an excellent private secretary, and Uncle Ted swears that his work is twice as easy since she came. How have things gone while I've been away?'

Frieda frowned. 'Not very well. I'm sorry, Jo, but Matron is so very trying. You remember how angry she was because we stayed to supper at the Chalet—I mean, Ste Thérèse's—after our meeting? Even though Matey told her that she had rung Bill up about it.'

Jo nodded. She was not likely to forget in a hurry the trouble there had been over that. Matron Besly chose to consider that the girls had put a slight on her by not asking her permission. 'You don't need to remind me of that, my dear! But surely she hasn't raked it up again? I should have thought she'd said enough already.'

'Well, Mademoiselle sent over for me for something last night. I met Matron in the corridor, with my blazer on, and she asked me where I was going. I told her that Mademoiselle had sent for me. She asked if I were going to stay for Abendessen, as she wished to know.'

'What a nerve!' said Jo indignantly. 'I hope

you informed her that Mademoiselle, as Head of the school, has every right to keep any of us as long as she likes without any warning to *her*!'

'Jo! How could I be so rude?' cried Frieda.

Jo looked somewhat ashamed of herself. When she lost her temper she frequently said more than she meant, and she knew quite well that the remark she had suggested to Frieda would have been impertinent, to say the least of it. Luckily, Frieda was possessed of a much more even temper and she had said nothing so discourteous.

'I only told her that I had no idea; but if Mademoiselle wished me to stay, I would ask her to ring up.'

'You've the temper of a saint,' declared Jo. 'Well; did Mademoiselle keep you?'

'Yes; and she said there was no need to ring up, as Miss Stewart was going across and she would tell Miss Wilson. Only Charlie never said a word to Matron, and when I got back, there was trouble.'

Jo flared up at once. 'What—after that? The woman must be mad!'

'No,' said Frieda thoughtfully. 'I think it is that she knows she is very young compared with our own Matey and Matron Gould, and she fears that we shall set her on one side.'

'Then she *is* mad! Whoever heard such rubbish?'

Frieda paid no heed to this. Instead, she began to laugh.

'What's the joke?' demanded Jo, still with a frown.

'It is only that Corney, and Evvy, and Giovanna, and Lonny are being so dignified, now that they are seniors at St Clare's,' said Frieda. 'And yesterday, when Corney heard Mary Shaw using slang, she

scolded her and—' Here, Frieda was again overcome
with laughter.

'What on earth happened?' asked Jo, forgetting
Matron in her curiosity. 'I see that the bare idea of
Corney ticking off anyone for slang is humorous, to
say the least of it. It's a case of Satan rebuking
Satan, with a vengeance! But what is so awfully
funny about it?'

'Why,' said Frieda, still gurgling, 'Mary was rude.
She answered Corney back. And Corney said, "When
I tell you not to talk slang, you little ham-handed,
left-footed bonehead, you, I guess you'll not talk it
unless you want to get in wrong!" Bill was coming
along, and she heard that. She had no idea, of
course, what it was all about; but she came to rebuke
Corney for her language. What she must have felt
when Corney explained that she was scolding Mary
for saying "Sez you!" I can only guess!'

Jo rocked with laughter. 'Oh—*oh*—OH! I *knew*
Corney would be funny, but I never thought she'd be
as funny as all that! I wonder what Bill made of it
all?'

'I have not heard that part,' said Frieda.

'But what has all this to do with Matron Besly?'
asked Jo, sobering a little. 'What did she say to
you about being away, by the way?'

'She said that she was Matron, and it was my duty
to inform her. I could scarcely say that it was
Charlie's fault, could I? So I could say nothing, and
had to be quiet.'

Jo frowned. 'That woman is well on the way to
making a complete idiot of herself! No other Matron
we've ever had has behaved like this. Even Matron
Webb has stopped short of that.'

' Yes ; but she did much worse,' remarked Frieda.
' Do you remember the day she locked up the Robin
in her own room ? '

' I should think I do ! Why, she even refused to
give my sister the key at first. Robin was badly
upset by it all. Jem was afraid that it might make
her ill.' Jo's face grew very dark as she recalled the
episode.

' I cannot imagine Matron Besly doing such a thing
as that,' said Frieda.

' Oh, I don't think she would myself. But she's
got an absurd idea of her own dignity, and she's taken
it into her head to stand on it—don't be silly, Frieda !
I mean her dignity, of course !—and the result is that
she's in danger of becoming thoroughly *un*-dignified,'
said Jo, who was quite sharp enough to see this,
though Frieda had not gone quite so far.

' Well, I suppose we must just put up with it,'
sighed her friend.

' She'll get a lesson some day that she'll never
forget,' said Jo with conviction. ' The only thing is
that I don't want it to come from the middles.
They're quite bad enough without any encouragement
of that kind.'

Then the bell rang for the end of break, and
they had to part, for Jo was due at chemistry, and
Frieda, who had dropped science, having no aptitude
for it, had extra Italian in this period.

The next step of the affair occurred at midnight
that night. As I have explained, above the dormitories and rooms at the front of the new house was the
roof-garden, with two great skylights which were intended to give light to the cubicles at the back of the
dormitories. When the girls first went to St Clare's,

as the new house was now definitely christened, they had all been escorted over the whole building, and shown the roof-garden among other things. Cornelia and her crew had later been heard to bemoan the fact that now they were in positions of responsibility they must behave themselves. They felt that it would have been possible to have such a good time with those skylights !

But if they were well on the way to a certain amount of reform, there were other people among the middles who had had no such restrictions placed on them, and these folk put their heads together to discuss various ideas of their own.

They were seven in number, with Mary Shaw of the slang affair and Kitty Burnett, whose claim to fame was that her elder sister had been a very popular Head Girl at the school, as leaders. The others were Biddy O'Ryan, a wild Irish scamp ; Emmie Linders, Enid Sothern, Irma Ancokzky, and Alixe von Elsen, a quiet-looking child of twelve, who now and then recalled to her elders and betters that still waters have a habit of running deep. This crowd had seen the advantages of the skylights even before Joey Bettany most unwisely demonstrated how they could be opened from the outside.

' I do think we ought to be able to do something with them,' said Mary, as she and her tribe sat at the top of a bank and watched a tennis doubles between Jo Bettany and Frieda Mensch, Louise Redfield and Marie von Eschenau. ' It seems such a waste if we don't.'

' What can we do, though ? ' asked Kitty.—' Oh, good shot, Louise !

' I only wish one of them was on top of Corney

Flower's room,' sighed Mary. ' I owe her one for dog-fighting me about slang. And if you'd only *heard* the lingo she used ! ' she added virtuously. ' It would have made you want to curl up and die ! There's one consolation, Bill gave it to her as hot as *she* did to me ! '

' But as Corney's room is not near the skylights, that is impossible,' said Emmie Linders, handing round a box of sweets. ' Try one of these, Mary. Papa sent them yesterday.'

' Then how did you keep 'em ? It's a wonder that cat Matron didn't grab them.'

' He sent them to Mademoiselle to give to me,' said Emmie serenely. ' She made me promise not to eat them all at once, and said I might have them, as it is a small box.'

' Good for Mademoiselle ! And I know Corney's room isn't near the skylights,' went on Mary, reverting to the former topic. ' But it seems to me that we ought to be able to manage to settle her somehow, if we could only get up to the garden after everyone's gone to bed.'

' We couldn't get out without being caught,' objected Kitty. ' Frieda's door opens almost bang on to the staircase, and she sleeps with one ear open, I'm positive.'

' But we shouldn't have to pass Jo's door, and she's *much* worse,' said Mary with conviction.

' No ; that is true,' observed Emmie.

' Could we not possibly get up there without being caught ? ' asked Alixe, a sparkle in her greeny-blue eyes which usually looked so dreamy and far-away.

' We *might*, if we were very careful, perhaps,' said Mary thoughtfully. ' Have you got an idea, Alixe ?

You've been sitting mighty tight about it, if you have.'

'I have an idea, yes. If you think we could get out of our dormitories and go up the stairs without being heard, we might do it,' said Alixe.

'Well, how are we fixed ?' demanded Mary. 'Let's see; you and Biddy and me in the Leafy dorm, Kitty in the Wheatfield.—Who's head of it, Kit ? I forget.'

'Maria Marani. But once she gets off to sleep, she's pretty safe, as a rule,' said Kitty. 'The only bother is that I'm right at the far end, and it would mean either going through the dorm, or else risking Jo hearing me, and going out by my own door and past the splasheries and her room.'

'You don't really go past her room,' said Mary soothingly. 'The door's just beyond the end of the corridor. Still, perhaps it would be as well not to risk it. You'll just have to go through like a mouse.'

'And then Stacie Benson's more likely than not to be awake,' said Kitty. 'She never seems to sleep, that girl.—Oh, who's won the game—Joey and Frieda ? How do the games stand, somebody ?'

'Five—three,' said Irma Ancokzky. 'Jo's playing very well to-night, nicht wahr ?'

'She is; but she's so chancy,' said Enid. 'Last time I saw her play, she sent half her balls into the net.—About our idea. Couldn't you risk Jo, Kitty ? Doesn't the near door creak rather badly ?'

'Yes,' said Kitty. 'I suppose I'd better risk it. Stacie would be certain to hear me. She's got ears like a lynx !'

'You always have a down on that girl,' said Mary. 'Why ?'

' I told you what she did to me her first term here.'

' Yes—smacked your face. But, gracious, Kit, that's years ago ! You've surely forgiven her by this time ? '

' I don't like her, anyhow,' said Kitty, who possessed a most unpraiseworthy tenacity for a grudge.

' But Stacie has nothing to do with this,' objected Alixe. ' We can speak of her later. Now, let us see what we can do to pay Cornelia back for scolding Mary.'

Finally, after much talk, it was decided that that night they should all try to creep out of their dormitories and up the stairs to the roof-garden at midnight. Arrived there, they were to put into execution a plan which Alixe and Enid outlined for the benefit of the others, and which, if it worked according to plan, would certainly go a long way towards repaying Cornelia for the lecture to which she had treated Mary the previous day.

This settled, they scattered at once in search of the materials they needed, and finally marched in late for Abendessen, to find that Matron was, to quote Enid, ' in the vilest temper going,' and ready to snap them up for the least thing.

Abendessen for the seniors came later, for they had an extra hour for work when it became too dark for them to see to play tennis. The arrangement was Mademoiselle's own, but Matron chose to feel injured over it because it meant two meals instead of one. That the people to object should have been the kitchen staff, who never troubled their heads about it, did not strike her. All she knew was that on certain evenings of the week it fell to her lot to be present at both meals, and so cut into her evening. She considered that if prefects and senior girls had to have their meal later, they could quite well have looked after themselves. Or one of the Staff might have taken it for the whole week. In her opinion, the Staff at St Clare's got off very lightly with regard to duty.

For once, the eight girls concerned thoroughly agreed with her, though they never said so. They were not anxious to be supervised by the new Matron, who was no favourite and never likely to become one.

' I can't think why Mademoiselle should want us to be looked after at meals as if we were Mary Shaw and Co.,' said Jo grumblingly, as she led the way to the splasheries to make herself tidy. ' Goodness knows, we get enough and to spare of Matron as it is ! '

She had no idea of letting Matron hear her senti-ments ; but her clear carrying voice reached the head of the stairs where Matron was standing, and she flushed indignantly as she listened.

The eight girls standing behind their chairs, wait-ing for Grace to be said, sent startled glances at each other when she rustled in, with her mouth set in a straight line and her head carried at an angle that told them that something had gone wrong. She looked them over before she began. But when she spoke, it was to the point.

' Jo Bettany, your hair is disgracefully untidy ! Go and make it tidy at once. And please remind me to see that it is cut the next time Herr Alphen is here.'

Jo said nothing. With Cornelia and her clan present, the Head Girl could scarcely set the example of answering back. So she left her place and went back to the splasheries to contend with her shaggy locks in complete silence. But Cornelia was tied by no such considerations.

'Jo can't have her hair cut, Matron,' she said calmly. 'Madame says she is to let it grow.'

'Will you kindly cease being so officious, and mind your own business,' snapped Matron. 'An order-mark!'

Cornelia subsided, duly squashed for the moment; and presently Jo returned with her offending shagginess brushed and combed into a temporary neatness and her mouth set as straight as Matron's own. The rest were sitting, eating their salad and rolls in dead silence. The four senior middles might be 'agin the Government' as exemplified by Jo and her compeers, but that did not make them feel any more pleasant towards Matron for speaking to the Head Girl as she had done. Indeed, in their eyes, she had contravened a highly important unwritten law of the school; which was that no prefect might be found fault with in public unless for a glaring misdemeanour.

The three prefects tried to put *their* feelings of outrage into the way in which they pressed salad and rolls and milk on Jo, while almost ignoring the presence of her enemy. The atmosphere was heavy with disapproval, and Matron felt it—as she was meant to do.

When the meal was ended and the girls stood up to go, she rapped sharply on the table. 'Before you go,' she said icily, 'I wish you all to understand for the future that if you do not come into meals properly tidy, I shall send you away from the table. I don't care *who* it is! I will not have this rushing in, looking anyhow!'

So far she was within her right, and if she had

been wise she would have left matters there. But Matron was anything but wise ; and she was letting the dislike she had conceived for Jo Bettany rule her to such an extent that she forgot all discretion. Now, catching sight of the black look on Jo's face, she added overbearingly, ' And please don't look so sulky because you are found fault with, Jo. You are too old to be so childish ! '

Now, Joey had borne a good deal, and she had been angry enough before, though she had managed to control herself, but to be spoken to like this— and before Cornelia and her confrères—was more than she could stand. In a thorough passion, she replied in her coldest tones, ' You forget that I am Head Girl, Matron. If you wish to speak to me in that way, the rule of this school is that you do it in private.'

So far she got before Matron recovered her breath. Then, even as seven separate gasps told of the shock Jo's outburst had been to the others, the angry head of the domestic side of St Clare's recovered herself, saw her chance, and took it.

' And I presume that, as Head Girl, you also consider it to be the rule for you to be impudent to your betters ? '

Thanks to a kick from Frieda, Jo remained silent ; but her face showed quite plainly what her thoughts were. Matron rubbed it well in.

' I am afraid that whatever your previous rules may have been, you must abide by this of mine— that such behaviour to myself from any girl in the school will be punished. You will report yourself to Mademoiselle for impudence to me. Now you may all go.'

They turned and left the room, Joey leading with her head well in the air, though her cheeks were scarlet. Never, since she had been a wicked middle and responsible for more than half the mischief that went on in the school, had she been spoken to like this. She paid no heed to any of the others, but turning down the corridor, went swiftly along it, and out by the side-door that led to Ste Thérèse's.

What happened in Mademoiselle's study, she never told even the faithful trio. Even her beloved sister never heard of it. But one thing is certain: as far as possible, Jo Bettany gave Matron Besly a very wide berth after this. And however Matron may have infuriated her, she never spoke her mind again.

CHAPTER X

IN the pretty room at the south end of St Clare's, Cornelia Flower and Ilonka Barkocz lay sound asleep, the moonlight pouring through the open casement across the floor. It was a very warm night for the middle of May, and the two senior middles, tired out with a hard set of tennis at the end of a strenuous day, slept the sleep of the justly weary.

Presently, the moonlight was slightly obscured as something drifted down before the window—a fairly ghastly-looking something—and dangled there. At the same moment, there came from somewhere above a string to which a small object had been attached, and this object was swung gently against the casement.

Tap—tap—tap !

Cornelia moved in her sleep and muttered something. But she did not rouse up, and after a moment or two the tapping began again. Still Cornelia slept, though her rest was becoming more broken. Those above on the roof-garden could not know this, and they groaned softly as no apparent notice was taken of the tapping, for Ilonka was a notoriously heavy sleeper, though they had thought better things of Cornelia.

' I believe she's too dead asleep to bother,' muttered Enid Sothern at length. ' We can't go on with this much longer, you know. We might break a pane or something.'

' P'r'aps she's seen It, and doesn't bother about It,' suggested Mary Shaw, with a smothered giggle. ' If so, I reckon Corney Flower's the coolest hand on this earth. I'd raise the roof if I saw Baby Voodoo peeping in at me. I know that ! '

' Let me try,' whispered Alixe von Elsen, pressing forward.

' Here you are, but be careful not to break the glass or Bill will hear of it, and she would be so angry,' replied Emmie Linders, giving her the string to which they had tied a light fishing-rod sinker.

Alixe tried. But no more than Emmie could she rouse that rival to the Seven Sleepers, Cornelia Flower.

From where they stood, they were not able to see the lattices very clearly, and though they felt that they had guessed right with the position of Baby Voodoo, they could only guess at the whereabouts of the open leaf of the window. What is more, though none of them had realised it, when Alixe had taken Emmie's place she had moved a little to the right, and the sinker was swinging and tapping against the casement of the Head Girl's room.

Joey Bettany, too furious over all that had happened that evening to sleep early, had been lying watching the stars through the open window. It was so warm that she had flung both halves open to get all the air she could, and Alixe's unwary movement had put her into the right position to touch the extreme outer-pane of the diamond-shaped glass in the frames.

The brilliant moonlight fell on the sinker, and for an instant Jo could scarcely believe her eyes as she saw it gleam. She had thought that it must be a thrush with a shelled snail, though her own common sense should have told her that the only birds likely to be about at that time of night would be either owls or nightingales. She got quietly out of bed, and stole to the window, and looked up. She could hear low murmurs, but could see nothing except the sinker attached to the string. The middles had drawn up Baby Voodoo for a minute or so just before she arrived.

' It's those imps of middles ! ' thought the Head Girl, as she turned away to seek her dressing-gown and bedroom-slippers. ' Wonder who it is ? Not Corney and Co., surely ! Well, I'll just slip up—they are on the roof, of course—and catch them red-handed ! '

With this idea in her mind, she opened her door noiselessly, and slipped out into the corridor. The whole house seemed hushed in sleep, and the silent corridors were lit up only by the moonlight that came in through the long windows at each end of the cross passages. Jo went softly along, and then mounted the stairs. A little breeze met her as she went up, and told her that the girls were certainly on the roof. She was about to go to the open door when a sudden idea struck her. They had used the door ; but even if she shut that, there was nothing to prevent them from using one of the windows of the various rooms that looked out on to the roof-garden, and then they might escape her. She turned down the passage, and proceeded to shut and lock such doors as stood open, moving with caution, for though she guessed that the servants would not be easily disturbed, she was not anxious to bring any of them on the scene. That done, she came back ; shut and bolted the door ; and then, drawing her dressing-gown comfortably round

her, settled down on the top step of the two that led
up to the door, and waited.

Meanwhile, the seven on the roof were still trying
to rouse Cornelia with a perseverance worthy of a
better cause. One by one they each tried swinging
the sinker. But as they all took up Alixe's place
most carefully, and as Joey was not in her room,
nothing resulted. Baby Voodoo was no light weight,
either, dangled from the end of a cord, and dropped
some fifteen or sixteen feet down. Finally, they gave
it up as a bad job ; drew up the sinker and their pet ;
and, since they felt that to be up on the roof-garden
at that hour was a thing not likely to happen to them
again in a hurry, they strolled round it, admiring the
view, and commenting on the tubs of flowering bushes
and boxes of hardy annuals which had been set here
and there. Deck-chairs and chaises-longues stood
about, too, for the Staff were in the habit of coming
up here to chat or do corrections in the evening, now
that the weather was warmer. The seven tried them
all, and even found a half-finished packet of milk
chocolate left by someone.

'Do you think we might eat it ? ' asked Mary
wistfully. ' I'm beginning to feel real hungry.'

'It isn't ours. We can't take it,' said Enid, with
a longing glance at it. ' It's horrid luck, 'cos I feel
as empty as anything. But we can't exactly steal
someone else's chocolate.'

They put it back where they had found it, and
went on. Perhaps this little episode had lessened
their first joy ; at any rate, Kitty Burnett turned
to the door into the house.

'It must be getting awfully late,' she said. ' We'd
better get back. I have to go past Jo's room—oh,

very well, then, if you *must* fuss !—*near* it ! It was bad enough before. But at *this* time of night it'll be heaps worse.'

'Quite so !' thought the unseen listener to herself, as she pressed up against the door to keep out of sight. The upper half was glassed in, with stout shutters for bad weather ; but the lower half was of wood. Jo ducked her head, chuckling softly to herself, and waited.

'I suppose we must,' sighed Emmie Linders. 'It is very beautiful up here, Kitty — sehr schöne Bilder !'

'Oh, do talk English !' snapped Kitty, who was beginning to dread her solitary walk back to her cubicle more and more. The moon was gradually drawing towards the back of the house, and there were long shadows falling across the roof-garden that made her feel nervous.

Emmie subsided, duly snubbed, and Alixe took up the tale. 'Yes ; we had better go, I think. Biddy sleeps next to Luise von Starken, you know, and if she should wake and hear Biddy going to her cubicle, she may very likely think it is a ghost and scream, and then Bill will come, and there will be bad trouble, nicht wahr ? '

Biddy O'Ryan gurgled at this. 'I'll be a banshee, shall I ?' she suggested; 'an' flap me arms, an' wail like the banshees of old Ireland do.'

'Oh, dry up !' said Enid, with a shiver. 'It's quite spooky enough up here without your talk ! '

'Sure, an' 'twas your own suggestion—Baby Voodoo an' all !' retorted Biddy defiantly.

But the little group were rapidly becoming infected, and just then an eerie screech from the playing-field made them all jump. It was only an owl hunting for his supper ; but the septet were too scary to think coherently now. It had wanted only that last thing to finish most of them, and as the screech died away into silence, they scuttled across the roof towards the door, terrified.

Mary led the way, and Kitty was not far behind her. She flung herself on the door-handle, and twisted it sharply. To her horror, the door refused to budge. She twisted again, the others pressing round her. Enid, indeed, kept her hands over her eyes, for she was thoroughly frightened by this time. The twisting had no more effect than before. Mary shook the door, and thereby nearly upset Jo Bettany, who was leaning against it, nearly choking with laughter. But it was all in vain. That door held fast.

' Oh, Mary, do open it quickly ! ' implored Kitty in shaking tones.

' I—I *can't* ! ' gasped Mary. ' It's stuck or—or something ! '

' Oh,' cried Alixe in her own tongue, ' do you think that one of the servants came out and saw it open, and—and locked it ? '

The bare idea of anything so awful nearly panicked the lot on the spot. And then Biddy, who had been carrying Baby Voodoo, suddenly swung the creature over her shoulder as she pressed forward to see what she could do. Emmie, who was standing near, caught sight of it unexpectedly and promptly shrieked, whereupon Jo, realising that the small girls were now thoroughly frightened, rose to her feet and confronted them through the glass.

The sight of her was the finishing stroke. With one accord they all burst into tears and sobs, even

Biddy forgetting her usual bravery, and gulping as loudly as the rest.

Jo promptly unlocked the door and came out, shutting it behind her. Then she caught sight of Baby Voodoo, and jumped. Nor was it to be wondered at. The thing was made of an old navy-blue jumper of Kitty's, and attired in someone's outgrown white petticoat. The face had been painted on the blue wool with luminous paint, which Biddy had got from somewhere—where, they never knew · though Jo always suspected Hansi, the boy-of-all-work at the school—and the effect of the thing grinning up at her in the moonlight from the roof where Biddy had flung it when she had joined the chorus of wailers, was enough to upset stronger nerves than Jo Bettany's. She recovered herself before the middles had had time to see the effect of their bogy on her, however, and dealt with the weeping throng firmly and efficiently.

'Do you people *want* Miss Wilson to come and catch you out here at this time of night ? ' she queried. ' What do you think she would say ? '

This had the effect of hushing their sobs. Most emphatically no one desired either Miss Wilson or any other member of the Staff to come on the scene.

' I think,' said Jo in her severest tones, ' that we had better go in. I suppose you realise that it is nearly one o'clock in the morning ? '

Meekly they all followed her in. Meekly they accompanied her down the corridor, after she had picked up Baby Voodoo from the roof and locked the door behind them. Then she ushered them into the chief practising-room, and shut the door after them. She glared round at them with a chilly glare, and they all shook in their shoes. 'Well, what does *this* mean?' she asked, waving Baby Voodoo at them.

Emmie nearly screamed again as the ghastly thing leered at her from Jo's hand. Only the thought of the appalling retribution that would follow if Miss Wilson heard and came up checked her. Besides, she had been in one awful row at the end of the previous term, and she had not yet forgotten all her father had had to say when he had read her report. She did not want a repetition of that.

Jo tossed the thing contemptuously down on the lid of the grand piano in the corner. 'All things considered, I think you'd best get back to bed now,' she said. 'I'll see you all before Frühstück in my room in the morning. Come along; and tread softly if you don't want it to get to Miss Wilson's ears that you're promenading about the house at this unholy hour.'

Shepherded by her, they all crept downstairs. She waited to see them into their cubicles, and even tucked them up before she left them. Contrary to Kitty's uncharitable remarks, Stacie Benson was fast asleep when Jo was seeing to the small girl, and knew nothing about what had occurred until later on.

When Kitty—the last of them—was safely between the sheets, Jo returned to her own room, where she curled up in bed, with a low chuckle as she remembered the consternation on their faces when they saw her at the door.

'I must try to think up something neat in the way of punishment,' she thought drowsily, as she snuggled down. 'O—ooh! How comfy bed is! It was chilly up there, with not very much on. Let's hope those monkeys haven't taken cold, or the fat *will* be in the fire ! '

With this pious wish, she turned on her side again and fell asleep. She was thoroughly tired out, and this latest exploit of the middles had driven all recollection of Matron's trying ways out of her head. That Baby Voodoo was left lying on the piano where she had flung it was another thing she had forgotten. Jo was peacefully and contentedly slumbering.

But if Jo had forgotten the bogy, someone else had remembered it before long. Alixe von Elsen, drowsing on her pillow, was suddenly startled into complete wakefulness as she remembered that Joey had flung the thing down on the grand piano, and that, so far as the middle knew, no one had bothered about it again.

' Oh ! ' thought the small girl, as she sat up in bed. ' Whatever shall we do ? If Bill or Matron find Baby, there will be such terrible trouble. Jo can be hateful, but I prefer her to Bill any day ! '

Alixe had soon recovered from her panic—sooner, in fact, than anyone else. She was naturally a plucky child. and the very sight of the Head Girl had helped her to pull herself together. Now she set her teeth, and made up her mind to go back to the practising-room and rescue their creation before anyone else could see it. She got out of bed again, put on her dressing-gown and bedroom-slippers, and stole softly to the door. She was just about to open it when the sudden sound of voices brought her up with a shock.

' I certainly heard someone moving about,' said one voice, which she at once recognised as Miss Wilson's. ' No, Con ! Don't you bother ! I 'll just go the rounds and see that everyone is safe.'

' It's no bother. And if I do half the place, and you do the other half, we shall get through just twice as quickly,' said a second voice, which Alixe knew to be Miss Stewart's. ' You take this half of the house and I'll take that. We'll meet here, and report when we've finished—unless we bring any captives with us ! ' she wound up laughingly.

Alixe nearly dropped where she stood. Could mistresses really think of such things as unlawful expeditions in the small hours of the morning a joke, when their pupils were not there to see them ? But she dared wait no longer. Baby Voodoo must take its chance. Already she could hear the light footsteps coming towards their room. She slipped back, and into bed as quickly as she could. As it was, she was only just under the clothes when the door opened, and Miss Stewart's soft Highland voice asked, ' Are you all right in here ? '

Naturally, there was no answer. Alixe was the only one awake, and she had no intention of apprising the mistress of that fact. She curled up tightly with her head half under the clothes, and prayed fervently that Miss Stewart would not take it into her head to visit each cubicle.

Vain hope ! Miss Stewart was a conscientious girl, and she gently opened the curtains of every cubicle and flashed round her tiny torchlight, being careful not to catch the faces of the sleepers. This saved Alixe, who was, to all appearances, sound asleep. The mistress made no effort to uncover her, thinking that she might wake the child. But she decided to speak to Matron about Alixe's burying of herself like that. It was not healthy, and she must have bad dreams if she generally slept in a heap like that !

Then she switched off her light, and withdrew as quietly as she had come.

It seemed ages to the worried Alixe before she heard the voices of the mistresses again, and this time she could not make out the words. Still, so far as she could judge, they had found no one awake, and certainly could not have seen Baby Voodoo. Alixe heaved a sigh, made up her mind to wake early next morning and remove the thing before any unauthorised person should get hold of it, and then stretched herself out and really fell asleep.

Naturally, after the very sensational night she had spent, Alixe never stirred until Violet Allison, the head of the dormitory, came in and shook her awake next morning.

' Oh, do wake up, Alixe ! The rising-bell rang ages ago, and you'll be horribly late if you don't hurry ! '

Alixe sat up with a groan. ' It *can't* be time to get up yet ! I haven't been in bed five minutes ! ' And she showed every sign of dropping down on her pillow again and resuming her slumbers.

' It's nearly twenty past seven,' said Violet, pull-off the bed-clothes. ' Get up, Alixe, do. You'll be fearfully late as it is. Nearly everyone else is just about ready. There's only Emmie much behind ; and I've just wakened Irma. Whatever were you three doing last night that you're so sleepy this morning ? '

Her words brought back to the suddenly awakened Alixe just what they *had* been doing, and her own resolve. She tumbled out of bed in a hurry, and snatched up her towels to fly to the bathroom. She had just reached the door when an ear-splitting yell sounded from upstairs, and the next moment there came the sound of someone racing along the overhead corridor, and then practically *falling* down the stairs.

At once half-a-dozen people tore to the door, Irma among them. Emmie, who had just come from the bathroom, and was in the middle of dressing, had to stay where she was until she had some more clothes on. But the rest were in time to see Anna, one of the maids, come rolling down the stairs, pick herself up, and make a dive for the next flight, with a face as white as milk.

Needless to state, every girl in the building was on the spot the next minute, even Emmie having got into some clothes and rushed to the door. Anna went hurtling down the stairs, yell after yell bursting from her, till she was met at the foot by Miss Wilson, who shook her with great promptitude, making her bite her tongue involuntarily. However, though the girl screamed again, it was with pain this time, and she recovered herself a little after that. Perhaps Miss Wilson's stern expression helped her.

' What is the matter, Anna ? ' asked the mistress severely. ' Have you taken leave of your senses ? '

' Ich habe den Teufel im Musikzimmer gesehen ! ' sobbed Anna.

' What ? ' Miss Wilson looked completely flummoxed for once.

' Oh, mein Fräulein,' gasped Anna, the tears streaming down her cheeks, ' ich habe den Teufel im Musikzimmer gesehen ! '

' Nonsense ! ' Bill's tones took on a certain sharpness which all her pupils recognised at once. ' The music-room is the last place in which the devil is likely to appear, and he isn't likely to appear in person, in any case. Stop that silly crying at once, and tell me where you were and what you were doing when you *thought* you saw him.'

Seven pairs of eyes met unbidden. Every one of their owners knew what it was that Anna *had* seen, and every one of the seven was frenziedly turning over in her mind wild schemes for rescuing Baby Voodoo before ' Bill ' could get there. Jo also guessed what had happened. For a moment she debated within herself whether she could possibly rush off and hide the awful thing before the science mistress should have seen it. But the next moment, ' Bill ' put a stop to all such ideas.

' Go back to your rooms at once, girls ! ' she said severely. ' Miss Stewart, will you please see that they all go back ?—Matron, if you will come with me, we will search the top-floor, and see what it is that has frightened Anna.' She turned to Karin, the cook, who had come from the kitchen, and was now busily scolding the still-sobbing Anna. ' Karin, please take Anna to the kitchen, and give her some strong coffee. I can see that she has had a fright, though that need not make her lose her head in this way.'

' But it is ridiculous, mein Fräulein ! ' scolded Karin. ' If Anna were a good girl, she would not need to be afraid if the devil and all his company from hell were to appear to her ! There, silly girl ! Cease thy howling like a dog that is turned out of the house for stealing, and come with me ! Cease, I bid thee ! '

Having seen Anna bustled off to the kitchen regions, Miss Wilson marched up the stairs, followed by Matron, who looked rather startled.

' I will take this side and you take that,' she said to her colleague, when they had reached the head of the stairs and were standing opposite the door that led to the roof-garden. 'We'll soon see what has startled that stupid girl like this!'

Matron meekly turned to the left, while 'Bill' turned to the right, and walked into the storeroom where some of the girls practised. She sent a sweeping glance round, but could see nothing out of the way there.

Neither did the box-room next door reveal anything. The maid's room next to it also revealed a blank. Then she heard a startled exclamation from Matron, and sped back along the corridor to her. In the practising-room, which looked up the valley to the mouth of the Tiern Pass, she found her compeer, standing by the piano, looking still startled, while in her hands she held Baby Voodoo. Even in the semi-twilight of the room—Anna had gone to dust and open the jalousies when she saw the creature—the middles' creation had a fearsome aspect, and if this were what Anna had seen, Miss Wilson was no longer surprised that she had lost her head so thoroughly.

'What an awful thing!' she ejaculated, as she surveyed it. 'Where on earth did you find it?'

'It was lying across the far end of the piano,' said Matron, with a little shudder. 'I saw it the moment I entered the room, for it was lying on its side. As you see, the jalousies are still closed, and that end is in the shadow, in any case. I nearly screamed myself.'

'I don't wonder!' said Miss Wilson. 'Now I wonder who is responsible for this—er—work of art?'

'We can easily find that out,' returned Matron, beginning to pull the thing to pieces. 'This jumper and petticoat are sure to be marked.'

But 'Bill' stopped her. 'Wait a moment, Matron,

I think we had better take it as it is to Anna, and let
her see it. Otherwise, I am afraid she may refuse to
come up here again to dust, and that will be awkward.
Give it to me, and I'll see her. Then I'll take it to
the Staff room, and you can come along after Frühstück, and we'll go over it together, unless someone
has owned up in the meantime.'

'They'll never do that,' said Matron gloomily.

'Oh yes, they will if we ask them,' returned
Miss Wilson with decision. 'Our girls are imps—
the middles, at any rate—but I have never found
one of them cowardly or dishonourable.' With this
she left the room, and went downstairs, carrying
Baby Voodoo in her arms. She made straight for
the kitchen, where she exhibited her find with a cheery,
'Come here, Anna. Come and see what scared you
so much.'

At sight of that awful thing, Anna began to weep
and protest again, and one or two others of the maids
shrieked. But Karin ruled her kitchen with a rod
of iron, and she soon settled them by promising to
put the head of anyone who was foolish under the
pump outside. As she was both strong and determined, and would not have thought twice about
doing it, the threat took effect. Anna was persuaded
to dry her tears, and come and look closely at the
thing; and the other maids thronged round, too.

'Some of the young ladies must have been playing
a silly joke on each other,' said Miss Wilson. 'That
is all, you see. There is never any need to be afraid
of the devil, unless you do wrong. Now you will
all have Frühstück, and then Anna will go and finish
her dusting, nicht wahr?'

Knowing that two of the others would be busy

with their bedrooms at that time, Anna reluctantly agreed to this, and 'Bill' left the kitchen, and went to the Staff room to deposit her find on the table, where Miss Nalder and Miss Stewart saw it unexpectedly ten minutes later, and both yelled at the first shock. Baby Voodoo's career of crime had been short, but it had certainly been eventful, though it had gone much further than his creators had ever intended.

After Frühstück, Miss Wilson blandly invited the perpetrators of the 'joke' to give themselves up, and, in much fear and trembling, the seven rose. To everyone's amazement, Joey Bettany got up with them.

'*Joey!*' gasped the thunderstruck Miss Wilson.

'Oh, I didn't make the thing, *nor* dandle it about,' said Jo, with scarlet cheeks, though her black eyes were dancing with amusement. 'I'm afraid I'm responsible for Anna's shock, though. I found him last night and dropped him somewhere in the practising-room at the back. I meant to bring him away and—er—reduce him to his component parts; but I'm afraid, in all the excitement, I forgot. I'm very sorry, Miss Wilson.'

'I see,' said 'Bill' drily. She knew perfectly well how much Jo was enjoying the sensation she had created. 'Very well, Jo. That will do.—Everyone may go now but the seven middles standing up. They will stay behind.'

The girls filed out, all of them dying to know what had been happening. Matron, Miss Nalder, and Miss Stewart followed them, the last-named leaning over her friend to murmur as she passed, 'Nell, as you are strong, be merciful! Those unfortunate children look all in as it is. It strikes me that this has been another midnight affair.'

'Trust me!' said Miss Wilson. 'I can see they are done up just as well as you can. I'll be gentle with them.'

And she was; though the seven, who were soon weeping like water-spouts, didn't think so at the time. She catechised them until she had got to the bottom of the affair. Then she treated them to a sharp lecture, finally condemning them all to spend the afternoon in bed.

Considering the fright Joey had given them the night before, they all thought she might have omitted that last. They were too young to realise that it was more in the nature of a rest-cure than a punishment. However, when they had had time to think it over, they realised that they had really escaped very lightly. But after that, Miss Wilson took possession of that key, and commanded the prefects to see that the door was securely fastened every night when they locked up.

'If we had had you, Matey,' said Miss Wilson affectionately to Matron Lloyd, as they were discussing the affair over their coffee-cups on the roof-garden that afternoon, 'it could never have happened. You'd have heard those imps, and hauled them back to bed, with a dose of something unpleasant, long before it got that far. But Matron Besly seems to sleep like the dead. As for Jo's part in the business, wasn't it exactly like her?'

Matron Lloyd chuckled. 'Jo's a scatterbrain. And I'd like to remind you of *one* midnight affair last term, of which I knew nothing until the sword of Damocles fell on those unfortunate children, Joyce,

Mary, and Thekla. It *had* to come out then. But so far as Matron Besly is concerned, unless she pulls up and shows herself more capable than she is at present, I'm going to recommend Mademoiselle to get rid of her. She's next to no use; and she's putting the backs of the girls up very badly. She has neither tact nor judgment. I'm going to have a talk with her some time this week; but I'm afraid it won't be much good. She's very little use to us—that's certain!'

CHAPTER XI

SUNDAY'S EVENTS

MATRON Lloyd duly had her talk with her young confrère, but, as she had shrewdly surmised, it did little good. Matron Besly was up in arms as soon as Jo Bettany's name was mentioned, and refused to listen to anything.

'I don't like Josephine Bettany,' she said coldly. 'She is thoroughly conceited, and thinks she can be as impudent as she likes to me.'

'Matey' eyed her thoughtfully. 'I wonder just why you should think Jo, of all girls, conceited?' she said. 'That's just what she isn't.'

'I consider her the most conceited specimen of schoolgirl I have ever met,' retorted Matron Besly, her head well in the air.

'Well, I advise you to keep your opinion to yourself,' said Matron calmly. 'You won't find any sympathisers on that subject here. After all, we people have known her for some years. You have only been here two or three weeks.'

'That's probably just why,' returned Matron Besly. 'I have come fresh to the school, and see clear-eyed. You, who have been here so long, are naturally prejudiced.'

'Well, at any rate, don't pull up any of the prefects before the rest of the School,' advised 'Matey,' giving it up as a bad job. 'That sort of thing never does—more especially in a school of mixed nations like this.'

143

Matron Besly stared at her. 'Do you mean that I am expected to pass over faults?' she exclaimed.

'Nonsense, Matron!' Matron Lloyd was beginning to lose patience with this wrong-headed girl. 'Of course, I mean nothing of the kind. But if it is necessary to speak to any of the prefects, kindly do so in private. That has always been the rule here, and I don't advise you to try to upset existing conditions.'

Matron Besly sniffed, and flounced off. She was very young—too young to realise that if she persisted in her chosen course, she would be undermining the discipline of the school. And she was too inexperienced to grasp that she was doing herself no good by her attitude towards the Head of the domestic side of the school. Matron Gould, her other colleague, would never have behaved like this. But then, Matron Gould, in her earliest days, would never have treated any of the prefects as the new-comer had done.

Meanwhile, with Matron and Jo and Frieda at daggers drawn, the middles thoroughly subdued as the result of the affair with Baby Voodoo, and Evadne, Cornelia, and Co. standing on their dignity, the School was more upset than it had been for some time. It was a relief when Sunday came, bringing with it its usual sense of peace and happy rest.

As a little girl, Margia Stevens had once told her mother that they had 'such gentle Sundays,' and the quaint phrase exactly describes the atmosphere which generally informed the whole School on that day.

Mr Eastly, the Protestant chaplain who served the church at the Sonnalpe, had set up a curate lately, as his regular work made it difficult for him to come down to the Tiern See to take service for the girls. Mr Bernard was a young fellow, who had been sent out to the life-giving air of the mountain district, because, though he was not ill, it seemed likely that if he stayed in England he would be. He had come down the previous night, so as to be able to hold a communion service at eight in the morning, and it was attended, not only by all the girls who had been confirmed, but also by several visitors, who were now beginning to flock to the shores of the beautiful lake. There was also Mass in the little whitewashed Catholic church not far from the school, so there was quite an exodus early that day.

Frühstück was at nine, and after that the girls attended to their bedroom duties, and then took chairs out into the gardens, where they sat quietly reading, talking, or writing letters until it was time to put on hats and gloves and go to the mid-morning services. To-day was a special day, for in the evening they were to hear the story of the three Saints who had been chosen as patrons of the three houses.

' I know nothing about any of them,' declared Jo Bettany, as she sprawled in a deck-chair in front of Ste Thérèse's.

' Joey ! ' cried Marie with horror. ' But, of course, you know the story of little St Agnes and her lamb ? '

' And you know about Santa Chiara, who was the friend of San Francesco d'Assisi ? ' added Bianca di Ferrara. ' It was she who founded the Poor Clares.'

' Oh well, I do know that much,' conceded Joey, nibbling the top of her fountain-pen. ' And I happen to know that Ste Thérèse of Lisieux was a little Carmelite nun, and she wouldn't be much over sixty if she were living now. But that's all.'

'Have you not read *La Vie d'une Ame*?' asked Simone Lecoutier.

Joey shook her head. 'I have not. Have you got it?'

'But yes. It is in my room. I will give it to you later.'

'Good! I like fresh things to read,' declared Jo, who was an omnivorous reader—so much so, that it came as rather a shock to many of the girls to find that she had not read this book, which has been translated into many languages and finds readers among all sects.

'Are we to be together to hear them—all the houses, I mean?' inquired Anne Seymour.

'You know as much as I do,' yawned Jo—the sun was hot, and she felt sleepy. 'Bianca, you're more or less head of the Chalet nowadays. What have you heard?'

'I? Nothing,' said Bianca, looking up for a moment from her home-letter.

'Oh well; we'll hear all about it presently, I suppose,' said Jo, with another yawn. 'Who's this coming along?'

'It's your Matron,' said Anne, sitting up to see. 'I say! She seems in rather a bait!'

'Oh, *bother*!' Jo also sat up. 'What's gone wrong *now*?'

Matron Besly stalked up to the group, and fixed the Head Girl with a baleful eye. 'Josephine, where are the rest of St Clare's?'

Jo got to her feet and cast a swift glance round. 'Evadne and the rest of the seniors are with Margia Stevens and Elsie Carr over there, Matron,' she said politely. 'I believe some of the younger girls went across to St Agnes's with Miss Norman and Miss Edwards, to listen to the junior reading. I don't know where the others are.'

' And may I ask what your business is, then ? ' demanded Matron. ' If you are Head Girl here, it is your duty to know where the younger ones are out of school-hours. I told Joyce Linton, Maria Marani, Kitty Burnett, and Aimée Béranger to come to me for medicine, and not one of them has come.'

Jo went red, and the sympathetic members of her party promptly became violently interested in something—unspecified—that was going on at the far side of the garden, and moved off in a body.

' Well ? ' demanded Matron. ' I am waiting for an answer to my question. What do you imagine your business as Head Girl to be ? '

' I am not on duty to-day,' said Jo stiffly. ' No prefect ever is on a Sunday. I believe Miss Leslie is in charge, but I couldn't say without looking at the list on the notice-board.'

Matron snorted unbelievingly. ' Indeed ? Well, whether you are on duty or not, I must insist that you keep an eye on the girls during all free periods——'

' Matron Besly ! ' It was Matron Lloyd, who had seen the pair and had come unheard across the grass to them. She guessed that there was trouble in the offing, and had hastened to smooth matters over if she could.

Matron Besly whirled round, the colour deepening in her face. ' Did you want me ? ' she asked.

But Jo broke in. She was too furious to heed the fact that she was breaking all rules of etiquette. Matron Besly's manner and tone got her on the raw, and, for once, she was in a thorough-paced rage. 'Matron, will you please explain to Matron Besly exactly what my duties are ? I'm afraid she won't take it from me ; and I'm sick of being hauled over the coals by a complete new-comer for things that aren't my fault or my business ! '

Matron Lloyd held up a hand at this point. ' That will do, Jo ! You forget yourself, I think ! Kindly go and join the other prefects. You can come to me in my room presently. I have a message for you from Mademoiselle.'

Still seething, Jo turned on her heel and fled. Matron Lloyd looked at her subordinate contemplatively. ' I see you don't intend to take my advice,' she said.

' You heard that last piece of impudence ? ' exclaimed Matron Besly, nearly as furious as Jo herself. ' *That* is the sort of thing I have to endure from Jo Bettany ; and the rest are almost as bad ! They follow her example, of course.'

' What had you been saying to Jo ? ' demanded ' Matey.'

' I merely asked her where the rest of the middles were.'

' Was that really all you said ? '

' Are you accusing me of being a liar ? '

' Don't talk nonsense, Matron ! ' The elder woman's voice was coldly contemptuous. ' I want to know what words you used when you asked Jo that question. And what else you added, too.'

Matron Besly repeated her speech as well as she could. She faltered and mumbled over it, for she knew that she had exceeded her authority by saying what she had. But no girl in the school had ever

been able to outface 'Matey'; and the younger
Matron was no exception to that rule.

Finally, when she had a fair account of the scene,
Matron Lloyd sighed. 'I wish you had seen fit to
do as I asked. As it is, I think the best thing will
be for you to see Mademoiselle. In any case, Jo, as
she seems to have told you herself, is responsible for
no one but herself to-day. I can quite understand
why she was so discourteous just now, and I can't
say I am surprised at her.'

'Oh, I might have expected you would stick up for
her!' sneered Matron Besly, flinging all caution to
the winds. 'But I never yet toadied to anyone—
even if she *is* sister to one of the proprietors of the
school!'

Matron Lloyd opened her mouth; then she shut
it again firmly. But any girl who had merited her
expression would have shaken in her shoes. At last
she spoke. 'This must go to Mademoiselle, Matron.
In the meanwhile pray consider yourself freed from
all duty for the rest of the day. Give me the names of
the girls you were seeking, and I will attend to them.'

'I shall do no such thing! The middles are my
concern!'

Matron Lloyd looked at her in silence. Then she
turned and left her, following Jo down to the lake,
where that young lady was trying to walk off some
of her fury.

'Jo!' she called.

Jo turned. 'Matron? Yes; what is it?'

'Do you know the names of the girls who were to
have had medicine?'

'Joyce Linton, Maria Marani, Kitty Burnett, and
Aimée Béranger,' said Jo curtly.

' Thank you. By the way, Jo, Mademoiselle asked me to tell you that there is to be a Tzigane band at the Kron Prinz Karl this afternoon. If you prefects and the seniors like to go and have Kaffee there, you may. Go and tell the others, will you ? And let me know how many are going, so that I can ring up Herr Braun and ask him to reserve tables for you.'

Jo nodded sombrely, and went off, while Matron, having done what she could to smooth down the young lady's ruffled feathers, called to Elsie Carr, who happened to come in sight just then, and bade her send the wanted quartette to her room at once.

Elsie sped off on her errand, and ran the four to earth at the far side of the playing-field, grouped round Stacie Benson, who was entertaining them with tales from the Greek myths. On hearing the elder girl's message, they all started guiltily, and Joyce and Maria went red.

' What crime have you committed *now* ? ' asked Elsie, quite as if she had never been anything but a model throughout her career.

' It's that wretched Matron of ours ! ' declared Kitty. ' She saw us after Frühstück, and said that we were looking yellow, and looked at our tongues. Then she said we were to go to her for medicine before Mittagessen ; but I forgot every word about it till this moment.'

' And so she's reported you to Matey ? ' laughed pretty Elsie. ' Well, you'd better go and get it over, whatever it is—castor-oil, eh, Joyce ? '

Joyce could go no redder, but her blue eyes flashed at this reminder of one of her worst exploits during the previous term. However, she had made up her mind to reform, so Elsie's teasing drew no more from her than a curt, ' Perhaps ! '

' Oh, Elsie, I hope not ! ' cried Maria Marani, with a reminiscent shudder. 'Besides, we feel quite well ! '

' Oh, I don't suppose it 'll be anything worse than magnesia,' said Elsie magnanimously. ' Matey never gives castor except for something really bad ; and none of you *look* like it.'

Slightly consoled, they wended their way to 'Matey's ' room, where she requested them to show their tongues, felt their hands, and finally gave them a small dose of some innocuous mixture of her own. So far as she could see they needed nothing ; but she must uphold her colleague.

The next episode of that stirring Sunday occurred when the prefects were setting forth in full force, attired in their white frocks, with shady white hats, and carrying their blazers. They were all chattering excitedly, for though the Tzigane bands frequently come up to the lake on summer Sundays, this was the first of the season. None of the younger girls were going ; but Mademoiselle had agreed that the members of the Sixth and Upper Fifth might attend. Some of the resident Staff would be there ; and Mr Denny, the school's eccentric singing-master, and his sister had told her they would be going, so the girls would be well chaperoned, even though they were to sit by themselves.

Matron Besly, slightly uneasy about her forth-coming interview with Mademoiselle on the morrow, and knowing nothing of the School's interest in the picturesque orchestras, met them as they were parading across the plank bridge that connected the school with the public footpath, and promptly demanded to know where they were going.

Big Sophie Hamel answered her. ' We go to hear the Tzigane band at the Kron Prinz Karl.'

' *What?* ' gasped Matron.

' But yes,' said Simone demurely. ' Mademoiselle has given us permission, and so we go.'

' Impossible ! Girls like you to go and sit outside a rowdy hotel and listen to a gipsy band ! Perhaps get into talk with goodness-knows-who ! Don't tell me such lies, Simone ! '

Simone straightway lost her temper, and, being Simone, her self-control as well. Her face flushed, and she flared out in her own tongue, ' I do not tell lies ! How dare you say such things to me ! '

Mercifully, Matron's French was not her strong point, and Simone's wrath made her less coherent than usual. But it was impossible to mistake her tone, and it was to that Matron replied. ' I have told you girls before that I will put up with no rudeness from you. Go back to your own house, Simone, and remain in your room till I give you permission to come out of it.'

What would have happened it is hard to say, but just then Mademoiselle herself appeared to see them off. She surveyed them critically ; told Simone that her hair was coming down at one side ; asked Jo to see about some method of keeping hers in better order ; and then told them they might go. ' I may walk along later and join you,' she added. ' Adieu, mes enfants. Amusez-vous ! '

Gripping Simone's arm so that she could not get away, Jo led them off, and Matron was left standing there, absolutely dumbfounded. What sort of a school was this that not only permitted such things, but encouraged them?

But Mademoiselle had now turned her attention to the young woman near her. 'I think, Matron,' she said in her careful English, 'that until we have had our interview to-morrow, I should prefer you to have nothing to do with the prefects or the seniors.'

Matron bowed, unable to trust herself to speak. She hurried off, and went to her own room, where she shut herself in. She was rather afraid of what was coming, after that last speech. But how could any sane Englishwoman know that girls of that age were allowed such outrageous freedom.

Meanwhile, the prefects, knowing that *they* had scored this time, went on, chuckling quietly to themselves. They were no more unkind than most girls, but it must be admitted that they fully appreciated the situation. Matron had asked for a snub, and she had got it, with a vengeance.

They promenaded round the lake, and came to the big hotel, standing on the right bank of the little stream that bisects the valley just here. Here, tables with gay umbrellas were set outside, and visitors from all over, as well as trippers, up from the Innthal towns for the day, were seated, drinking coffee and the light beers and wines of the district, and enjoying the warm sunlight, the lovely lake, and the enthralling music of the band. Near the hotel itself were the two tables set aside for them, with cakes of every kind piled high in baskets, and good old Herr Braun, proprietor of the hotel, and the School's firm friend, waiting for them to take possession. They sat down, and proceeded to enjoy themselves thoroughly.

The band had come up from the plain during the

morning, and had already played for nearly two hours. But when gipsies of the Hungarian breed give themselves to their music, they feel little fatigue until they have played themselves completely out— and that is not for some hours, as a rule.

This was a gay band, clad in the national dress, with long unkempt hair falling to their shoulders, and big gold earrings swinging from their ears. Their instruments were mainly strings and woodwind, though one of them beat time on a tabor. Now and then, to give the performers rest, some of them stood up and sang together their wild songs, such as those which inspired Liszt when he wrote his Hungarian Rhapsodies.

All the girls were accustomed to such airs with the exception of Gillian Linton, Joyce's elder sister, who, like Joyce, was only in her second term. She was not specially musical, but she was thrilled by this music.

' Isn't it glorious ? ' she cried. ' I never heard anything like it before.'

' Oh, the Tzigane always play like this,' said her friend, Elsie Carr. ' They are wonderful, aren't they ? Sometimes they have women with them, who dance and tell your fortune.'

' Have you ever had your fortune told ? ' asked Gillian.

' No fear ! It's a waste of money. And besides that, I don't think it's right,' replied Elsie firmly. ' Mademoiselle wouldn't allow it, either.'

Gillian looked unconvinced. ' I'd love to have mine told,' she murmured.

' Love to have what told ? ' asked Jo from the other table.

'My fortune,' said Gillian, shaking back one of her long black tails of hair. 'Ever had yours done, Jo?'

Jo grinned. 'Rather! My brother did it.'

'Your brother? Can he tell fortunes? How does he do it?'

'With cards. If that's all you want, I'll tell yours when we get back,' said wicked Jo, a look in her eyes that her friends knew well, though Gillian was too deeply engrossed with the idea to notice it.

'Will you promise?' she asked eagerly.

'Of course I will. Come to our prefects' room with us, and I'll do it then,' promised Jo.

Gillian thanked her, and turned back to watch the band again, while Jo's friends overwhelmed her, sotto voce, with inquiries as to what she was going to do.

'Tell Gill's fortune, of course,' said Jo matter-of-factly.

'It is wrong to tell fortunes,' Marie reminded her. 'Only God can know the future. And it is much worse on a Sunday.'

'What I'm going to do isn't wrong,' said Jo.

'Jo, what are you up to?'

'Not up to anything,' protested Jo.

'But yes; you never look like that unless you are planning something.'

However, Jo refused to give away her secret, and they had to subside, for Miss Wilson came over to them to make sure that they all had money for the collection which one of the gipsies was beginning to make.

After that they strolled home, and Gillian, quivering with excitement, followed by a disapproving Marie, Frieda, and Simone, was led by Jo to the prefects' room at St Clare's.

' Is the coast clear ? ' demanded the latter young lady. ' Then where are the cards, Marie ? '

' Jo, I wish you would not,' began Marie in troubled tones.

' Marie von Eschenau, don't be an ass ! ' was the unsatisfactory reply, as Jo rummaged in a drawer. ' Here we are. Clear that rug out of the way, Gill, and sit down.'

Gillian did as she was asked, and squatted on the floor. Jo sat down beside her. The other three looked on in a worried way.

' First of all,' said Jo, ' you must give me your word to do exactly as I tell you. Otherwise, the 'fluence—whatever that may be—may be broken, and then it would come wrong.'

' Oh, rather,' said Gillian. ' Of course I will.'

' That's a promise, mind ! ' Jo warned her. ' Now take the cards and shuffle them three times, wishing hard all the time.'

Gillian did as she was told in solemn silence. When she had finished, she looked up at Jo.

' Now set them on the floor and cut them twice— into three packs, I mean. Done it ? Good ! Now take them one by one and lay them, face upwards, in a perfect ring all round you. Mind, it *must* be a ring ! '

By this time, the other three were beginning to get a faint glimmer of what was coming, and their looks of disapproval faded. Gillian knelt up, and gravely distributed the cards round her, being most particular to make as perfect a circle as she could. When the last card was in its place, Jo faced her.

' You're *sure* you want your fortune told ? ' she asked.

' Of course I am ! Oh, do get on with it, Joey ! '

Jo surveyed the cards solemnly. Then she sat back on her heels. ' All right ! Now listen carefully. The past is that you sat down there and spread those cards out. The present is that you are listening to me. And your future is that you're going to pick them all up and put them tidy,' she said blandly.

Shrieks of laughter from the other three greeted this. Gillian stared at her. ' Oh, Jo ! You perfect pig ! And I thought you were really going to tell my fortune ! But you're wrong about the future, anyway,' she added, jumping up. ' You can pick those cards up yourself. I'm not going to.'

' Oh yes, you are ! You promised you'd do whatever I told you ! ' Jo reminded her.

' Oh, bother you ! So I did ! ' But Gillian was a good sport. She bent down and picked up the cards, replacing them in their case. Jo took them from her and put them back in the drawer. ' You can't say I didn't tell your fortune truly,' she said, as they turned to leave the room. ' And as for you three,' and she faced round on her friends, ' I'd no idea you could be so thick ! As if I ever believed in such rubbish as *fortune*-telling ! '

They had to admit that she had trapped them all neatly, and went off quite amicably, arm in arm, to the garden to listen to the brief but telling accounts Mademoiselle gave the united School of their patron saints. When it was over, they had Abendessen and Prayers, and so to bed, as Sam'l Pepys remarks, with minds full of the little Carmelite nun, Ste Thérèse of Lisieux--the Little Flower, as so many love to call her—who led such a pure and holy life on earth, and who was inspiring men and women of the present day with such love and reverence for her.

CHAPTER XII

THE REVIVAL OF THE S.S.M.

FRIEDA always declared that it was Joey Bettany who was really responsible for what happened next. Joey repudiated this; but she laughed over it, for all that. However it may be, it is certain that one day Evadne Lannis called Cornelia Flower to her in a mysterious way, and said, 'Corney, will you come to a meeting behind the bathing-shed this evening after Kaffee und Kuchen ?'

Cornelia opened her enormous blue eyes. 'Say ! What's biting you ?' she demanded.

'If you come, you'll see soon enough,' returned Evadne. 'I may tell you that you won't be the only one,' she added. 'Not by a jugful !'

Cornelia stared. 'Is it a joke ?' she asked doubtfully.

'Let's hope so—but not on any of us,' replied her fellow-criminal feelingly.

'Who, then ?'

'Come; and then you'll be put wise,' retorted Evadne. Then, as she heard Elsie Carr plaintively wailing for her, she ran off, leaving her compatriot in a pleasing state of anticipation.

Cornelia was not the only girl to feel that way. Before sixteen o'clock—four, by English time—a goodly number of the senior middles were on tiptoe with expectation, and they could scarcely bear to

sit through Kaffee und Kuchen, which, as the weather
was now so warm, was served in the garden.   The
girls themselves carried out the food and the big
coffee-urns, and when the meal was over, they took
everything back.   These were the conditions on which
they might have the meal out of doors, and, as a
rule, nobody made any complaint.   But on this
occasion several people were heard grumbling about
the nuisance it was to have to clear away for themselves.

'Well !   What's gone wrong with you now ? '
snapped Jo, when she heard Cornelia on the subject.
' We've *always* waited on ourselves when we have
Kaffee outside, as you perfectly well know.   You
just trot along with those baskets, and stop growling ! '

Cornelia went, but the rebellious expression on her
face showed how little she was influenced by the
Head Girl's remarks.   Jo followed her, carrying a
bouquet of milk-jugs—mercifully empty, or she
would inevitably have made a mess with milk.

Once the garden was cleared, and the girls were
all strolling about or making up sets for tennis, or
reading under the trees, the young American set off
for the bathing-shed at her best speed.   As it was a
very hot evening, the girls might do as they chose.
Heat in the Tyrol can mean something that England
may experience once in a century, and these were
growing girls.   Moreover, the school had to be run
on the lines laid down by the doctors at the Sonnalpe,
and one important rule was that no girl might be
strained.   Too many of them had relations in the
great Sanatorium up the mountains for any of those
responsible for their well-being to dare to run any
risks.

Cornelia slowed down as she crossed the stout log bridge that had been thrown across the deep ditch which surrounded the whole estate, and saved it from flooding, especially during the early spring, when the thaws brought down tons of water from the mountains. She reached the public footpath and turned to her right, and walked demurely along till she reached the fenced-off enclosure in which stood the big shed used by the School when bathing. At the far side she found Evadne, Elsie, and the ringleader of their set, Margia Stevens, a slight fifteen-year-old, with a short bush of curly hair, who was also the School's musical genius. Margia meant to become a concert-performer, and this term had been allowed to drop some school subjects so that she might have more time to give to her piano. The intervals between school-work and music she contrived to fill in very pleasantly with sundry sins.

Three years before, this character had founded a society, and now it seemed good to her to resurrect it—or such parts of it as were quite fitting. The original organisation had included Jo Bettany, Frieda Mensch, Marie von Eschenau, and sundry others among the prefects. Margia knew better than to inform them of what was toward; but she reckoned that she would have plenty of numbers without them.

'Prithee seat thee, maiden,' she commanded the startled Cornelia.

'Say! Can't you talk English?' demanded Cornelia.

'Yea, verily, maiden. And in good sooth, I do; but—oh, I can't keep it up! Wait till the others come, Corney, and then you'll know all about it.

I'm the President, by the way,' she added bewilderingly.

'The President? Help! I guess you've gone batty for keeps!' gasped Cornelia, her mind going wildly to his Excellency the President of the United States. 'Look here, Margia, you come along with me, and——'

'Oh, be quiet—do!' cried Elsie, pushing back her long dark locks from her hot face. 'Margia's all right; you'll see in a moment, anyway, for here come some of the others! Hope the rest will be quick, or they will be calling to us to go and do something!'

Her hope was speedily fulfilled, for before long twelve girls besides themselves were seated on the ground in a ring; Margia, as President, being perched on the thwarts of one of the boats. Of the whole sixteen of them, Margia, Evadne, Ilonka Barkocz, and Suzanne Mercier had been among the original members. Elsie and Cornelia were foregone conclusions, because Elsie was Margia's chief friend, as Cornelia was Evadne's. The rest were kindred spirits, such as Cyrilla Maurús, Maria Marani, Joyce and Gillian Linton, big Sophie Hamel's younger sister, Berta, Anita and Giovanna Donati, Yvette Mercier, Suzanne's younger sister, Luise von Rotheim, and Hilda Bhaer, a quiet, rather colourless girl, who was an intense admirer of Joyce Linton's, and so got into a good many more scrapes than she might otherwise have done.

This select band squatted on the grass, and listened with all its ears while the President explained her purpose in calling them together.

'Years ago,' she began, 'when Jo Bettany and

that crowd were middles, we had a Matron here who was the very limit.'

'I know,' put in Cornelia. 'I've heard of her. She was the one who locked the Robin in. And Joey and 'Veta and Bianca stuck snails on her window in the middle of the night so that they'd *scrudge* up the glass and make horrible noises. She thought it was ghosts, and came flying out of her room with her hair in curling-pins and her face all covered with cold-cream.'

Margia cast a freezing glance at the interrupter. 'The meeting is not yet open for discussion,' she said. 'You can wait till it is.' Cornelia subsided, duly snubbed, and Margia went on. 'Well, some of us decided to do something about it, so we formed a society. It was the S.S.M., or the Society for the Suppression of Matron. We all took a vow to do everything we could to make things hot for her, and force her to leave——'

'*Why?*' asked Hilda in awestruck tones.

'Because she was doing the school harm, and we couldn't let *that* go on. That was when we found out who 'Veta really was, by the way,' added the President in parenthesis.

'Didn't you know all along?' asked Elsie Carr.

'Not till then; but she gave herself away then, all right. We'd never thought she was anything special until then. Well, we did all we could—the snail business Corney was yarning about just now was one thing—and we'd have got her shifted all right ourselves; only she locked the Robin up, and cheeked Madame like everything—wouldn't give her the key, an' all that.' Margia was rather vague about this, for very few of the girls really knew what had taken

place on that momentous occasion. 'Anyhow,
Madame told her to clear out that very day—and she
did.'

'But what has all this to do with us?' asked
Gillian Linton plaintively.

'Just this. St Clare's has got a Matron who is a
nuisance, and so I thought we'd revive the S.S.M.
—see?'

They saw—naturally! And the noise they made
discussing what they should do about Matron was
enough to bring the entire Staff down on them, as
Margia did not hesitate to point out, once she could
make herself heard.

'Be quiet!' she insisted, clapping her hands loudly
for attention. 'Do you want everyone to hear?'

They calmed down a little, and then settled to a
quieter discussion of what they should do first.

'For,' said Evadne wisely, 'we'd better get
started, I guess. Nobody loves Matron Besly too
well. It's up to us to—sort of—well—ram it home.'

'I *wish* we could give her a scare with snails, like
Jo and 'Veta and Bianca,' sighed Ilonka. 'But our
windows at St Clare's are casements.'

'Yes; those small diamond panes wouldn't be
much good for that sort of thing,' agreed Margia.
'Besides, don't you think we'd better try to be
original?'

'She has early tea brought up every morning,'
said Joyce Linton suddenly. 'I've met Gretchen
bringing it when I've been going to my bath. Couldn't
we doctor it somehow?'

'Well—how?' asked Margia.

'Say—oh, what about salt?' suggested Cornelia
breathlessly.

'Who did you say brings it up?' demanded the President of Joyce.

'Gretchen.'

'Don't know her. Is she one of the Pfeiffens? There seems to be a never-ending string of that family, I know.'

'No; her name is Angbach, I believe,' said Evadne. 'But she's a pal of Rösli Pfeiffen's, I know.'

'Well, is she the kind of girl who lays the tray round loose somewhere, so that you could get at it?'

No one knew this, as no one had been sufficiently interested to notice.

'And,' pointed out Ilonka, 'if we put in salt or pepper, she will guess that it is one of us, and then there will be trouble.'

As nothing was more likely, this seemed to finish Joyce's suggestion, greatly to the relief of her elder sister. But Margia was not their leader for nothing. So while Joyce herself was scowling furiously, and the others were wondering how they could manage, the President was ruminating quickly, and soon came to a decision.

'I've got it! You know that horrid tartar stuff Matey gave Lonny last summer when she ate some unknown berries, just in *case*?'

Ilonka made a face. 'And I was so terribly sick! I remember it well, Margia. But we have none.'

'No; but I know where it is. I have to go to Matey every night, because I've been sleeping badly again, and Dr Jem's given me a tonic or something for last thing at night. I go at twenty-one o'clock, and often Matey isn't there, and she doesn't always

lock the medicine cupboard. I'll see if I can sneak
some of it, and then Joyce and Corney or someone
can try and get it into Matron's tea.'

Gillian looked up abruptly. 'I don't think you
ought to do that, Margia. It's all very well messing
about with salt and pepper and things that won't
hurt. But I'm sure you oughtn't to give anyone
an emetic like that.'

'Oh, rubbish!' said Margia. 'Matey gave Lonny
one last summer; and then they found out that
there hadn't been any need for it, after all. Those
berries were quite safe. Besides, Lonny and Corney
say that their Matron is being a perfect pig to the
prees and especially Jo Bettany, and it's high time
someone put a stop to it. Jo hasn't been an angel
to us by any means; but no one's got any right to
behave as Matron is behaving to her.'

Gillian was silenced for the moment. She owed
Jo Bettany a heavy debt of gratitude, though she
didn't exactly see how upsetting Matron, in the way
the more irresponsible members of the party were
coolly suggesting, was going to do any good either
to Joey or anyone else. Meanwhile, Margia was
calmly enlarging on her idea, and the rest were
taking it in. More: they were receiving it with
acclamations.

'You find out if Gretchen what's-her-name leaves
that tray about anywhere—say, she puts it down
while she opens the door,' said Margia to Cornelia
and Ilonka, whose room was next to Matron's. 'If
so, just nip out and drop what I give you into the
cup or the pot or something. That ought to do the
trick! And if she's sick, as she jolly well ought to
be, it'll give you all a day's rest from her, anyhow.'

They all agreed to this. And before Gillian, who happened to own a conscience, could think of any arguments which would turn them from their evil purposes—perhaps!—shrieks of ' Margia—Corney— Evvy! Where are you all ? ' caused the meeting to break up somewhat hurriedly.

Once they had had Abendessen, and were safely in their own dormitory for the night, Gillian did her best to make Margia give up the idea. But Margia refused firmly.

' Give it up ? Rather not! Something 's got to be done about all this! Joyce told me that that woman actually hauled Jo over the coals before every-one—just as if she was a kid like Joyce herself! You can't have that sort of thing going on. It 's our *duty* to stop it,' declared Miss Margia virtuously.

Gillian felt that Margia might be right there. Where she was not right was in the methods she proposed adopting. However, unless she told some-one in authority about it, she didn't see how she could stop it, and telling was the last thing she would do. If it had been her own sister who was to per-form the deed, she might have stepped in. But Margia had foreseen that, and it was one reason why she had deputed Cornelia and Ilonka to do it.

Two days later, the President passed Evadne a small packet during their first lesson. Evadne pocketed it with a righteous smirk, and later handed it on to Cornelia and Ilonka. They had found out that Gretchen invariably set the tray on the floor while she knocked and opened the door. They had arranged that one of them must do something to attract her attention while the other slipped the contents of the packet into the teapot. It ought to be easy enough to manage, for Gretchen was a regular peasant—heavy, slow, awkward in her movements, and not too bright.

That night, as they were going to bed, they made their final arrangements with much glee. Matron had caught Ilonka in the act of safety-pinning a suspender, and had read her a severe lecture on such slatternly behaviour. Besides this, she had seen fit to pull up Frieda Mensch for coming across from gym with her wonderful banner of hair floating loose over her shoulders—it had come down during the lesson— and two or three juniors, as well as most of the middles, had overheard her. The two St Clare seniors were indignant that one of their own special prefects should have been treated like this before the little ones, and Matron's act had sealed her doom.

Events turned out pretty much as they had planned —so far as putting the mixture into the tea was concerned, anyhow. Cornelia, watching for Gretchen, suddenly appeared in the doorway, uttering squawks that made the girl turn in amazement.

'Was ist es, denn?' she asked in her slow, peasant accent.

'Ow—ow! A spider gone down my neck!' squealed Cornelia, dancing about like a dervish. 'Take it off—take it off!'

Joey Bettany, attracted by the noise, came out of her room, just as the maid set down the tray and advanced on the squirmer.

'What on earth is the matter?' demanded the Head Girl. 'Corney, what on earth are you doing? D'you think you're a contortionist, by any chance?'

' A spider—down my neck ! Running all over me !' gasped Cornelia.

' Hold still, then !—Gretchen, grab her while I fish ! ' And Jo caught at the young sinner, and between them, she and Gretchen managed to get her to stand still. Then Jo made a dive, and presently produced a long-legged specimen of the spider-tribe, which she dropped out of the nearest window with a contemptuous, ' There you are ! He's gone now ! Go and get dressed, and stop that awful squirming and squalling ! '

Meanwhile Ilonka, who had been on the watch, had hurriedly tipped the contents of the packet into Matron's tea, skipped back to join the group by the door, and was occupied in condoling with the shaken Cornelia, even as Gretchen picked up her tray and carried it to Matron, who was sitting up in bed, demanding to know the cause of all the disturbance.

For a wonder, she was sympathetic. She hated spiders herself—how the middles would have rejoiced if such a piece of information had come *their* way !— and she felt that in Cornelia's place she might not have ended without hysterics. What she would have said if she had known that Cornelia had made a martyr of herself and allowed Ilonka to drop the creature down her neck so that there should be no question that he was there, it is hard to state ! The chances are that she would never have believed the story ; so it is as well that she never knew the truth.

However that may be, she poured out her tea ; stirred it complacently, then, as she was thirsty, she took a long drink. The next moment, the peace of the morning was again rudely broken. Matron was out of bed in an instant. The tray was lying upturned on the bed, the contents of the cup meandering over the bedclothes; and Matron herself was at the window spluttering wildly. Margia had not been quite so clever as she had thought—and a good thing, too!—and what Ilonka had put into that tea had been a good, heaping dessert-spoonful of Epsom-salts!

CHAPTER XIII

THE MIDDLES' NEXT EXPLOIT

NATURALLY, there was a tremendous fuss when it all came out. Matron at first declared that it had been an attempt to poison her; and, as Jo said later on, no wonder! Epsom-salts, even when you know what it is you are taking, is the reverse of pleasant. When you get it unexpectedly—and such a dose of it!—in an innocent cup of tea, it comes as a horrid shock. Luckily, no one had attempted to empty the pot, and Matron Lloyd, with the severe common sense that characterised her in all she did, insisted on tasting its contents. She diagnosed them at once, and by the time she had succeeded in calming down her colleague, to whom she had come at once on receipt of Miss Wilson's hurried telephone-call, the gong sounded for Frühstück, and the girls had to go down, all agog with excitement.

After Frühstück, Miss Wilson rose from her seat and settled matters out of hand. ' Who was responsible for putting the salts into Matron's morning tea ? ' she asked firmly.

Her eyes wandered to Mary Shaw and her clan, for she fully expected to hear that they were at the bottom of it, even though it seemed a somewhat daring plan for such children. Still, Joyce Linton was among their number, and Joyce had already shown herself to be an enterprising young lady on occasion. But this time ' Bill ' found herself mistaken, for Ilonka, blushing furiously, got up; and Cornelia, at the other table, was standing also.

'Please, Miss Wilson,' said Cornelia, 'it was my idea.'

'Yours, Cornelia?'

'Yes; but it was I who put it in,' chimed in Ilonka.

Miss Wilson was silent for a moment. When she spoke, her comment was of the briefest, but it made the pair feel ready to sink through the floor. 'And you two are seniors here!'

It was all she did say, but it was more than enough.

'I—we—we didn't think,' stammered Cornelia.

'So it seems. I will see you both in the Staff room over here in twenty minutes' time.—Now you may all go and attend to your bedroom work.'

But Joyce had jumped up. 'The first idea was mine, Miss Wilson,' she declared, giving Cornelia a look of indignation.

'Indeed, Joyce? So there are three babies among you middles?'

Joyce's golden head drooped, and she was scarlet to the tips of her dainty ears.

'Go now,' said Miss Wilson. 'You three will come to me at the time I gave you.'

She said Grace, and the astounded girls went out. They had all been under the impression that Cornelia, Ilonka, and Joyce had really reformed. Corney had been a firebrand; and Joyce had excelled some of the middles' doings last term. But the present one had seen them settling down amazingly.

'I could have understood it if it had happened last term,' said Jo to her own friends, as they stood in the corridor discussing the latest event. 'But

I really thought those imps had turned over a new leaf.'

' I expect they wish to revenge themselves on Matron for her treatment of the prefects, and especially of you, Jo,' said Marie thoughtfully. ' Corney is very fond of you ; and Matron has been so unpleasant to you.'

Jo went red. ' Then I wish to goodness the little idiots would try to show their affection a little less strenuously ! Well, they will know all about it by the time Bill has finished with them. She was too flabbergasted to say anything at the moment ; but she'll make them wish they hadn't been born before she's finished with them—and that's one comfort !— What *are* you giggling about, Marie ? '

' I was just thinking of your snails and Matron Webb,' choked Marie. ' This was quite as bad ! '

Jo made a sudden movement. ' I *say* ! I hadn't thought of that ! '

' Hadn't thought of what ? ' asked Frieda.

' Why, our old society—the S.S.M. Don't you remember ? '

They all remembered.

' I wonder,' went on Jo pensively, ' if those imps are trying to revive it ? Corney and Joyce weren't here, of course. But Evvy was—and she was in it, what's more ! Do you think that's what they've done ? '

Before anyone could voice an opinion, Matron herself was with them. ' Now then,' she snapped, ' why are you all loitering about here ? Go and attend to your rooms at once ! And take an order-mark, all of you, for not doing them as soon as you came upstairs.'

Malice sparkled in Simone's eyes. 'The prefects cannot have order-marks,' she informed the angry woman.

'Then they can just begin to take them now!' retorted Matron. 'Give them in when you go over. And you can take two more, Simone, for being impudent.'

Simone opened her mouth to reply; but Jo was too quick for her. 'Go on!' she muttered. 'Hold your tongue!'

Simone shut up her mouth at that. Jo's remark had reminded her that all doors were open, and the girls could hear every word of the conversation. A prefect must not set the middles the example in rebellion. But she went to her room with fury in her heart. Marie and Frieda followed her example, and there were left only Jo and Matron.

The latter was furious, not only with the girls, but with herself for making the fuss she had over the salts. She felt that she had made a fool of herself, and the girls would not forget it. She hated everyone this morning in consequence. So now she turned on the Head Girl and rent her.

'Yes; it's all very well to pretend to be on the side of law and order when it suits your book!' she flung at the tall girl, who overtopped her by a good inch. 'But that won't save you when I report you all to Mademoiselle, let me tell you! If you were a proper Head Girl, with proper influence, this sort of thing would never happen! You want to be taken down a peg or two! You are so conceited and swollen-headed that you imagine that you can rule this whole place, and you never see that you are nothing but a very ordinary, empty-headed schoolgirl, who needs putting in her proper place, once and for all ! '

But Jo was not to be provoked into answering, this morning. She kept a tight grip on her rising temper, and with a quiet look at Matron, she went silently to her room, closing the door behind her. Matron felt as if she could fling it wide again, and continue giving the Head Girl her opinion of her. But she still retained a modicum of common sense, so she went on, little recking that the middles, who had overheard all this, were secretly raging that any prefect should be spoken to like that.

Nothing was said then. The girls knew that Miss Wilson was too angry for them to dare to trifle with her. They went to their cubicles, and performed their various chores. Then they got ready to go over to the school. But inwardly they were boiling at the injustice of it all. Joyce Linton, indeed, rushed off to find her sister, the moment she was inside Ste Thérèse's, and startled her by bidding her tell Margia that a meeting of the S.S.M. must be convened forthwith, for Matron must be settled, and that right speedily !

But this came later. Before they got to school the sinful trio went to Miss Wilson, where they had a none too pleasant interview. That lady sympathised with them in her heart ; but such pranks were subversive of discipline, so she scolded them sharply, informed them that they were awarded two order-marks each, which meant that they would get a report ; and wound up by sending for Matron, and commanding them to apologise to her. Matron had arrived, still bristling, and listened to the limping and decidedly insincere apologies they made her.

' Very well,' she said, when they had finished. ' If you say you are sorry, I suppose I must accept it.' Then she turned to the Head of the house. ' I wish to inform you, Miss Wilson, that I have given Josephine Bettany, Frieda Mensch, Marie von Eschenau, and Simone Lecoutier an order-mark each, and two extra to Simone. I have told them to give them in, but I thought it best to inform you.'

Miss Wilson waved the trio away. ' Go at once, girls,' she said in the chilly tones she had been using to them.

They went, thankful to get off so easily. When they had gone, she turned to Matron. ' I am sorry, Matron, but order-marks are not given to the prefects here. Did they not say so ? And what have they been doing ? '

' Loitering on the stairs, talking, instead of going to their rooms at once,' flared out Matron. ' And I must say, Miss Wilson, that I consider it a great mistake to make so much of " the prefects." What are they, after all, but a set of schoolgirls, no better than the rest, and in some ways worse than the middles ? '

' However, as prefects, they have certain privileges,' replied Miss Wilson drily. ' Exemption from order and conduct marks are among these privileges, and not even the Head of the school can give them to a prefect. They have others, such as speaking in the corridors on occasion, and going, within certain bounds, about Briesau as they choose, so long as they report to either Mademoiselle or myself. And another thing, Matron, I think you will be well advised to remember that they have also a great deal of responsibility which does not fall on the others. They merit their freedom ; and no one who has been here any length of time ever dreams of drawing the reins quite as tightly as you seem to wish to do. It is a great mistake on your part, and has resulted in this morning's foolish, practical joke. That is all I have to say. And now, if you do not wish to detain me further, I must ask you to excuse me, as I have work to attend to over at the school.'

Overawed by her manner, Matron went out, and ' Bill,' heartily wishing that Matron Besly had never come to the school, stalked off in a thoroughly bad temper, which did not sweeten as the morning went on. Her classes had an unpleasant time of it, and those who knew, set it down—not unjustly—to Matron Besly's account.

Punctually after the rest-period that afternoon, the S.S.M. met—this time among the pine-woods that clothe the slopes of the hill on the western side of the little peninsula of Briesau. They were quite free to go there so long as they did not wander out of sight of the school, and so long as they had no duties elsewhere. It was too hot for games this afternoon, though one or two of the seniors were at tennis. The rest were either studying, or else lying about in chairs. This always happened at intervals during the summer term, though, as a rule, the greatest heats do not set in till the end of June. But this year was to produce a record heat-wave, and the girls had been excused from regular work, once the hottest part of the day set in.

Cornelia and Ilonka gave a somewhat vivid and overdrawn account of the morning's occurrence, at which those who had not been present rocked with laughter. Then Cornelia went on to tell how ungraciously Matron had received their apology, but was brought up short by an exclamation from Joyce Linton as she mentioned the order-marks Matron had ' awarded ' to the prefects.

' Yes—the pig ! And she talked like everything before the lot of us ! And to the *prefects*, too ! '

Margia, who had been rolling about among the pine-needles, sat up at this. ' What d'you mean ? '

' Why, she said the *horridest* things to Jo—abused her like a pickpocket—told her that she was conceited and swollen-headed——'

A howl of wrath made her break off at this point. Jo was beloved by the whole School ; and though she had plenty of faults, no one, with any truth, could ever have accused her of conceit. She was heedless, untidy, and tactless. She was a most unpunctual person, as a rule, and could generally be relied on to blurt out exactly what was in her mind, regardless of whether it was the right time or place for it or not. But she had far too much to do with her work, both in and out of school, to give much thought to herself, and Matron's accusation promptly roused the S.S.M. to fullest fury.

' Conceited and swollen-headed herself ! ' cried Margia. ' Why, if she *wasn't* such a conceited ape, she wouldn't make such an utter ass of herself ! That's just what's causing all the trouble. She thinks no one has a thought for anyone but *her* ! We'll show her ! Won't we just ! '

Gillian Linton raised her sapphire-blue eyes. ' But, Joyce, are you *sure* that's what Matron said to Jo ? ' she asked her sister.

Joyce's perfect little face became convulsed with rage. She wagged her head till her golden curls

tossed madly round her. 'You bet I'm sure!
Wasn't I there? And didn't I hear every word?
I'd—I'd——'

'Well, keep cool, anyway. Going into a fit won't
help matters much,' said Margia soothingly.

'But it is so unfair, and so untrue!' said Cyrilla
Maurús. 'Margia, we *must* try and stop this! If
Joyce heard it, then many of the much younger ones
must have heard it, and think how bad it will be for
them! Besides,' she added, 'this is Jo's last term,
and that horrible woman is making it so unpleasant
for her.'

'We'll stop it all right,' said Margia, whose brain
had been working quickly. 'I've got a great idea!
And the beauty of it is that she simply can't say
anything about it! At least, if she does, she's a
bigger idiot than I took her for!'

'What is it?' demanded half-a-dozen voices.

'Why,' drawled Margia, 'she's always thinking
we watch her and spend all our spare time thinking
about her. Well, let's do it!'

There was silence for a moment. Two or three
people looked puzzled. They did not see how this
would help matters. But Gillian was quicker than
they, and she grasped the point at once.

'You mean we are to stare at her whenever we
meet her, and make her feel uncomfortable about it?
Well, but that means it will fall mostly on St Clare's.
We don't see very much of her.'

'Still, I dare say we could *make* a few opportunities
for seeing her,' said Margia suggestively.

There was no doubt that they both could and
would. That the idea was a cruel one, especially
with anyone so self-conscious as Matron Besly, never

struck them. And if it had, they probably wouldn't have cared. All they wanted was to serve Matron out for the way she was breaking their own unwritten law, and it struck them that this was a brain-wave, once they saw it clearly.

'Guess she'll ask a few questions!' chuckled Evadne Lannis. 'What'll we say if she asks us what we're looking at?'

'Don't say anything. Just go *on* looking, and slide off,' Margia told her.

'Then she will give us order-marks, and I have so many as it is!' sighed Yvette Mercier.

'Oh well, if you're going to set your wretched order-marks above the outrageous way she's going on, do it,' retorted Margia. 'Only, when she drops on you for anything, don't come to us for sympathy —that's all!'

'Oh, I will do it,' protested Yvette, who would never have dared to go against public opinion. 'It was only that if she insists on a reply, I shall not know what to say.'

'Say, "Nothing!"' suggested Joyce, who had recovered her normal appearance by this time. 'It'll be perfectly true. *We* think she's nothing, don't we?'

This piece of casuistry went down well with them, and they finally parted for swimming, with their plot all thought out.

That very night they got to work. Matron, meeting the two Merciers in the corridor at St. Clare's, was startled at the intentness of their gaze at her. She was in a highly sensitive mood, and though she said nothing, she could feel that when she had passed them they had turned round and were staring after her.

When she had disappeared, the wicked pair looked at each other and grinned.

'She did not like that at all,' murmured Suzanne in her own language, lest Matron should be lingering within earshot and hear.

Yvette said nothing, but she chuckled softly, and the two went to bed that night, happy in the thought that the campaign had been opened.

All next day it was the same. Matron felt herself pursued by the eyes of the girls. Whenever she met them, they gazed at her. Sometimes it was with a startled air; sometimes with a thoughtfulness that she couldn't understand. Joyce Linton, who had plenty of brains under her golden curls, though she didn't always put them to the right use, regarded her with such mournfulness that Matron became convinced that she must be coming out in spots, and rushed off to her own room to inspect.

'Well, why are you staring at me?' she demanded sharply of Maria Marani, whom she met on the stairs ten minutes later.

'Nothing, Matron,' said Maria politely, keeping her dark eyes fixed on Matron's face.

'Then keep your eyes to yourself!' snapped Matron. She would have gone to Miss Wilson about it, but after the experience of the previous morning, she felt it would be wiser to give that lady a wide berth.

The next person she encountered was Cornelia Flower, who had been sent upstairs by Miss Stewart to seek her embroidery. Cornelia hated sewing with all her heart. She had already spent two terms on this embroidery, and there was every sign that she was likely to spend two more; and then it was questionable if it would be finished. She never touched it if she could help it ; and she had protested as it was. But 'Charlie' felt that it would be as well if she had something to keep her out of mischief, so sent her off for it. Evadne was reading, and Ilonka was busy with her lace-pillow, being desirous of getting on with a collar she was making for Jo, whenever that young lady was absent. As for Maria, she was busy with a water-colour sketch intended for her sister Gisela's birthday. Miss Stewart decided that if Cornelia were also engaged with something, she could draw her breath freely for the next half-hour or so.

' Where are you going ? ' asked Matron sharply— even now she could not take ' Bill's ' advice and slacken the reins a little.

' To my room to get my work. Miss Stewart told me to,' said Cornelia, raising her enormous blue eyes to Matron's face.

' Oh ! Then go along and be quick about it ! ' snapped Matron. ' And *stop* staring at me like that ! Has nobody ever told you how rude it is to stare at people ? '

' Yes ; but I wasn't staring *at* you,' replied Cornelia gravely.

Then she went on, leaving Matron looking uneasily after her, wondering exactly what she had meant by her last remark.

She was still looking when Jo came along, bearing her knitting. Jo, no more than Cornelia, loved sewing ; but she was reconciled to knitting and was busy with a frock for her small niece Sybil. She glanced at Matron as she went past, wondering to herself why the woman was staring after Cornelia like that ; but she made no comment.

Matron had caught the glance, and became un-easier than ever. What did it all mean ? Why were they all staring at her like that ? Once more she went to her room ; but the closest scrutiny of her reflection made her no wiser than she had been before.

It went on all day, and when bedtime came, Matron was a thoroughly puzzled and worried person. It is scarcely to be wondered at that she began to feel ill and upset. Unfortunately, her relations with the rest of the Staff were not sufficiently cordial for her to speak to them about it. She knew that she had antagonised them all by her treatment of the prefects ; and she had to suffer in silence.

The next day, as it happened, two strings in one of the pianos at the school snapped, and Margia Stevens was, accordingly, sent over to St Clare's for two hours' practice. She was highly gifted, and her music was her chief consideration now, so the practice could not be missed. Herr Anserl, the irritable music-master, would have had a good deal to say if it had been !

She had been badly upset when the accident to the piano was discovered, so she was correspondingly delighted when Mademoiselle sent for her, and told her that as all the other pianos at Ste Thérèse's were in use at the moment, she must go to St Clare's to the chief music-room, and work there. She went off happily with her music, and was climbing the stairs at St Clare's when she ran into Matron Besly.

Now Matron really knew very little about the part of the school with which she had no contact, and she had no idea that Margia's love for music amounted to a mania. So when she met a girl who, in her eyes, had no right at all in the house, running upstairs, and then suddenly grinning at sight of her—Margia's grin was one of pure pleasure at the thought of getting on with her work—she promptly took steps to demand the reason for it.

'What are you doing over here?' she asked sharply. 'And what do you mean by grinning at me like that?'

In her joy over her music, Margia had forgotten all about the S.S.M., but this sudden bombshell recalled her to their plans.

'Mademoiselle sent me over here to practise, as the piano I generally use has gone—two strings snapped with the heat,' she explained, keeping her grey eyes fixed on Matron's face. 'And I beg your pardon, Matron, but I wasn't grinning—at least, I didn't know that I was. You see, I'm so longing to get at my new Brahms.'

'Rubbish!' said Matron curtly. 'Don't tell me such nonsense as that! If you expect me to believe that any girl isn't overjoyed at getting *out* of her practising, you've made a mistake. And what is this tale of you, a girl from Ste Thérèse's, being sent over here to practise at all. *I* have heard nothing about it.'

Hitherto, Margia had really come very little into contact with the new Matron. So she opened her eyes widely at the remarks, and flushed with annoyance. 'Mademoiselle arranged the matter with *Miss Wilson*, who is the head of the house—naturally,' she said, with a wicked emphasis on 'Bill's' name.

'Indeed? Well, you can just go down to the common-room and wait there until I have rung up Mademoiselle and learnt that you are speaking the truth,' said Matron insultingly.

Furious at being doubted, Margia opened her mouth to reply. Then she realised that ' answering back ' would most certainly be punished. So she shut it again, and casting a queer look at Matron, went quietly downstairs to wait till that lady had rung up Mademoiselle at the Chalet, and learned that she had again made a mistake, and Margia had every right to be where she was.

' You can go up,' she told that young lady ungraciously, when she went to summon her from the common-room. ' And mind you don't ruin that beautiful piano by banging on it. I know what you girls are like ! '

Margia got up with dignity, and marched off ; but not without another look which contained amazement, pity, and—could it be ?—disgust, all nicely blent together. She practised her proper length of time—incidentally giving a shock to Matron, who was listening, and who could scarcely believe that such music came from a mere schoolgirl—and then shut the piano, closed the jalousies, to keep the room cool for the sake of the strings, gathered up her music, and went downstairs. Meeting Matron on her way to the door, she again cast upon her that look.

How much longer it might have gone on, it is hard to state. The members of the S.S.M. were quite sharp enough to see that Matron was becoming miserably uneasy. What was worse was that many of the younger girls were beginning to take it up, at first from sheer imitativeness, later because they tumbled to the joke. But when it had been going on for three days, Miss Stewart happened to be following Matron along the upper corridor when they met Yvette Mercier. The look that naughty Yvette gave

Matron aroused the mistress's curiosity at once. There was such a curious inwardness to it.

'Yvette, I want to speak to you,' she said. 'Come to my room, please.'

Yvette followed her into the pretty room, and stood very properly at attention, the picture of a model schoolgirl, with her long plaits dangling over her shoulders to her waist, her face demure and serious, her toes turned out, and her hands clasped behind her back.

'What are you imps doing, Yvette?' asked Miss Stewart grimly, not at all taken in by her appearance.

'Je ne comprends pas,' said Yvette promptly.

'Oh yes, you do—perfectly well. Why were you staring at Matron in that way?' asked 'Charlie.' 'And speak in English, please—you know that this is English day.'

'I—I only looked at her as I went past,' faltered Yvette, her heart going with a bump into her shoes. Too well she knew that 'Charlie' would never rest until she had dragged the whole story out, and Yvette was never much use at keeping secrets.

This was exactly what happened. Yvette did manage to lie low about the S.S.M.; but in five minutes Miss Stewart knew exactly why Matron had been treated to that comprehensive stare, and what was hoped would come of it. She scolded the girl sharply for rudeness and ill-breeding, and then sent her off to call the entire house to the common-room, whither she presently descended, and proceeded to give them a dressing-down that she had never bettered, winding up by forbidding them to stare rudely at anyone for the future.

'All the same,' said Jo, when she and her compeers were over in the prefects' room at Ste Thérèse's, 'I can't imagine why *we* came in for all that pi-jaw. I never look at Matron if I can help it—I'd just as soon look at a slug!'

Marie chuckled. 'I suppose we really deserved it, because we didn't notice what was going on. I must say I never saw it at all. But you'll have to confess, Jo, that this all points to one thing. Someone has started the S.S.M. again, and Matron Besly is being suppressed as hard as ever they can manage it.'

'Then I wish,' said Jo, as she took the glass of lemonade Carla was offering her, 'that the little wretches would leave dead things buried. I never did think exhumation was decent!'

CHAPTER XIV

AN EVENTFUL NIGHT

MISS STEWART duly reported to Miss Wilson what had occurred, and 'Bill,' who had, as Jo remarked later, an indecently long memory, was moved to make sundry investigations of her own. Unfortunately for the S.S.M., she had her own ways of finding out things, and before they quite knew how it had been done, she was in full possession of the facts of that interesting Society. She did nothing for two whole days. Then she summoned the various people her own common sense and powers of observation had told her were at the bottom of everything, and settled the matter once and for all.

'This silly Society of yours must stop,' she informed them in her blandest voice. 'It was all very well when you were little girls. Babies *must* have secrets of some kind or perish, I suppose! But at your age, I should have imagined that you were rather beyond such things. In any case, Matron's doings are no business of yours. Officiousness is always the mark of ill-breeding, so please let me hear no more of this sort of thing. I thought that at least you were gentlewomen.'

Spoken with her intonation, this speech made the members of the Society writhe inwardly. There was only one person in the school who could beat 'Bill' at gentle irony, and that was Miss Annersley, the senior mistress, who was usually the gentlest soul alive. But now and then she roused up, and even 'Bill' the sarcastic could not better her on such occasions.

In the present instance, the S.S.M. died the death, and the middles gave their attention for the time being to their lawful occasions. For the next few days there was peace in the school, and the worried prefects heaved a sigh of relief, and seized the opportunity to get on with work, games, and boating. Then a fresh attack of trouble broke out.

In the original house—now Ste Thérèse's—the dormitories had all been on the small side, the largest holding no more than ten beds. Here, at St Clare's, with one dormitory holding eighteen cubicles, and another with sixteen, there was more scope for everyone. Moreover, the prefects' room had always been upstairs at the Chalet; for the past year, the library had been on the first floor; and the Staff sitting-room had been at the other end of the corridor. This had meant that no mischief could be easily perpetrated until the last of the Staff had gone to bed. As that was generally between eleven and twelve, most people among the middles had been sound asleep by that time, though there had been notable exceptions here and there. But in St Clare's, the prefects' room was on the ground floor, and so was the Staff sitting-room. And though the Staff during this term made a good deal of use of the new roof-garden, the dormitories, once the bell for silence had rung, were usually left unguarded.

In what was known as Garden dormitory, this mattered less, for the heads there were Violet Allison and Ruth Wynyard, both excellent people to be in charge. But in Leafy, on the other side of the staircase, the head was Lieschen von Hoffman, a pretty gentle Viennese, who had gained her position by virtue of her age, and who was easily overruled by anyone. Her second was Luise von Starken, a harum-scarum, who was hand-in-glove with most of the wicked spirits, so Lieschen had none too easy a time. Other members of the dormitory were Biddy O'Ryan, Alixe von Elsen, and Mary Shaw, three sinners who loved wickedness for its own sake, and were not devoid of originality.

One hot afternoon, when even the younger middles felt disinclined to rush about in their usual way, Biddy, by way of passing a quiet hour under the trees, began to tell some of her own gang Irish folk-stories. They were delicate, graceful stories, and took the fancy of the girls, for Biddy possessed the soft County Kerry voice, with its persuasive intonations, and told her tales well. So the girls thrilled to the account of the Fairy Fithir, who is allowed to come to earth from her captor husband's fairy realms once a year to seek someone who will succour her soul. Then Biddy made them all feel choky with the exquisite tale of Coreena the Dancing Girl, who, so the old legends say, gave the first shamrock to Ireland.

'I say, you *can* tell tales, Biddy!' said Alixe idly, as she lay on the pine-needles, fanning her hot face with her hat. 'Why have you not told us before?'

'When'd I be getting the time?' protested Biddy, with the faint touch of brogue that made her speech so fascinating to her hearers. 'Sure, aren't we always an' always at work?—without it's hot like this?'

'You could tell them after we've gone to bed,' suggested Mercy Barbour, usually a quiet little puss.

'I reckon she just could!—Do you hear, Biddy? You're to yarn to us after silence-bell has gone!' exclaimed Mary Shaw, coming to life at this moment— she had been lying flat on her back in an attitude reminiscent of one who has died from over-eating— and sitting up. 'I reckon that's just the cutest idea you ever had, Mercy!'

'It's a fine fuss there'll be, an' we caught!' protested Biddy.

'We won't be caught. We'll have a sentry,' declared Mary.

'An' who's to be it?' demanded Biddy, with point.

There was no answer to this for a moment, for nobody wanted to miss the stories. And, equally, nobody wanted to run the risk of being caught out of her dormitory during unlawful hours without a legitimate excuse. Alixe finally settled it. 'We must take it in turns. And whoever is sentry shall have a piece of chocolate—we must pool all we have.'

'And where do I come in?' demanded Biddy. 'If I tell the stories, and amuse the rest of you, what do I get out of it?'

'You shall have chocolate, too,' suggested Alixe. 'Does everyone agree to that?'

'But that leaves *us* out,' complained Enid Sothern, who was with them as usual. 'Can't you manage to take the dormies turn about, Biddy? And come to us one night, and the Leafies the next?'

'I can *not*,' said Biddy with emphasis. 'If you're wanting stories all that bad, you can just come to the Leafy dorm. Sorra a foot will I stir out av ut afther the silence-bell. Ye all know what happened last term with Joyce and the rest.'

Joyce flushed up. ' I wish you'd give me a rest and talk about someone else's misdeeds for a change ! ' she said petulantly. ' It's not fair—always raking up that wretched feast. Anyway, I paid for it all right.'

' I'll tell the world you did,' agreed Mary. ' I hadn't too good a time of it myself, but you held the baby all right that time.'

' Then leave it alone ! '

' O.K.! No one is to say another thing about that feast of Joyce's,' ordered Mary firmly. ' And as for Biddy coming to you every other night, Enid, do you really think Vi and Ruth would stand for it ? You must be batty ! '

' Well, I want to hear the stories, too,' grumbled Enid.

' Then do as Biddy says—come to us ! ' retorted Mary. ' If you're all that keen, you can risk being caught, if you think it's worth it.'

They were disturbed next moment by Marie von Eschenau, who came to inform them that as a little breeze had sprung up which was cooling the atmosphere, cricket was to begin, and they must come to the nets. After that, they were kept busy till Kaffee und Kuchen, and no one had time for anything but batting, fielding, and bowling. Marie was a conscientious captain, and saw to it that everyone had her full ten minutes at the wicket, as well as five overs of bowling. The middles might grumble at having to work so hard in the heat ; but they enjoyed it, all the same.

On the tennis-courts, the seniors were hard at work,

too. The first week in June would see their away match against St Scholastika's, the school at the other side of the lake, and they knew that they must work hard to beat the 'Saints,' as they were always called at the Chalet.

Kaffee und Kuchen took place in the gardens as usual, and when the meal was cleared away, some of the elder girls went off to work, while the others settled down with letters and books and sewing. The breeze had died away again, and it was hotter than ever, with a sultriness that left everyone limp. In the garden of the Chalet itself, Mademoiselle was chatting with two or three of the Staff who were taking things easily for the time being.

'Seems to me there's a storm brewing,' said Miss Wilson after a little. 'I don't like this abnormally hot weather we're having. It oughtn't to come before the middle of June at soonest; and here we are, sweltering at the end of May.'

Her great friend, Miss Stewart, turned to glance at the northern sky, for storms in the Tyrol frequently come from the north. 'Not much sign of a storm there,' she said, laughing. 'The sky's as clear as possible. Nell, you're a fusser!'

'Just you look to the south,' retorted Miss Wilson.

The mistresses turned with one accord, and looked south. They saw a brassily blue sky with two or three wisps of white cloud drifting across it.

'But I don't see anything there, either,' said Miss Annersley in bewildered tones.

'Don't see those clouds coming up? Hilda! Are you blind?'

'Of course I see them. But they're quite light—there's no rain there.'

' No ; but there's a promise of rain to come, or I don't know my weather-signs,' returned Miss Wilson seriously. ' Those little rags of cloud mean a wind somewhere, and when it comes it will bring storm with it—which is what I said. I never mentioned wind, I'll admit. All the same,' she added, ' I fully expect rain—*and* thunder too.'

' You'd better warn them at Le Petit Chalet—I mean, St Agnes',' said Miss Stewart. ' *We* know, of course. And Hilda and Mademoiselle will see to it that the Chalet isn't flooded out.'

' I'll run across later and tell Miss Norman,' agreed her friend. ' And I'll tell you what, Con,' she added, ' you might find Miss Nalder and tell her to warn Marie that there is a chance of rain, and all the nets should be lowered right down, and no balls or racquets left lying about outside.'

' Do you think it will come through the night, chérie ? ' asked Mademoiselle nervously.

' If not, it will to-morrow—early to-morrow too,' replied Miss Wilson. ' Well, I must go and do a spot of work. I have to interview our one and only Corney, and find out why she didn't condescend to prepare geography for me last night.—Coming, Hilda ? '

' I suppose I must. But this weather is so tiring. I wish it *would* end, though I must say I should prefer no storms.'

Laughing, the two mistresses went off towards the school, while Miss Stewart went to seek Miss Nalder and pass on the warning about the nets and other games paraphernalia.

The evening passed quietly. At twenty o'clock Marie went the rounds, accompanied by Louise Redfield, to see that nothing spoilable had been left outside. Then the two parted, and while Louise ran off to Abendessen at Ste Thérèse's, Marie made her way slowly to St Clare's, rather wondering what rebuke she would receive for being so late. For once, however, nothing was said. Matron was rather subdued, these days. Mademoiselle had spoken to her most severely, informing her that if trouble were to continue, then the school could do very well without Matron Besly's services. Matron did not want to leave like this, and she was beginning to be very sorry that she had not taken the advice everyone had given her, and had held the reins more slackly. Above all, she wished that she had let the prefects alone. She hated them, and especially Jo Bettany ; but she took pains not to let it be seen. After all, Jo and her compeers were leaving at the end of term. If only she could get through the few weeks that remained without further trouble, Matron had a feeling that she might manage better in future.

' Why all the fuss about the games things ? ' demanded Jo of Marie, as she sat down beside Frieda. ' You aren't usually so particular.'

' Miss Wilson thinks that a bad storm is coming up,' explained Marie, helping herself to a sandwich. ' Miss Nalder told me, and she asked me to see that nothing was left lying about, and that all the nets were dropped as far as they would go. You know yourself what happened last summer when we had a storm, and someone had left the net on Number Three court wound tightly up.'

' I do—it snapped, and we had to get a fresh wire-rope for it,' said Jo. ' But listen to this, you people. I've had a letter from my sister—Hansi brought it down—and she says that Margot is much better. She's up now, and sitting out in the garden, and Jem thinks that all danger of nervous breakdown is at an end. Isn't that splendid?'

'Oh, I am so glad!' cried Frieda. Then she stopped. 'But, Jo, won't the storm, if it comes, be bad for her?'

'After living in Queensland?' asked Jo derisively. 'They get awful storms there, sometimes.'

'Is there a storm coming?' asked Matron, who had overheard all this.

'Miss Wilson thinks so,' said Marie.

'Oh!' Matron looked unhappy, but she said no more. She detested thunder, and she had an idea—which was quite correct—that the storms of the Tyrol are not trifles.

'It may not come during the night,' said Jo thoughtfully. 'Quite possibly it won't come till to-morrow.'

'It may even blow over,' added Frieda. 'What shall we do about the windows, Jo? If it should rain heavily against them, and we have the lattices open, I am afraid we might have floods indoors.'

'We'd better not have them too wide,' agreed Jo reluctantly. 'When it rains here, it does rain.'

'Gee! I hope it won't be like the storm we had my first summer term here,' said Evadne. 'Do you remember, Jo? The thunderbolt fell into the playing-field, and everything was like tinder. Only the hail came, and put out the fire, so it was all right, after all.'

'What was that?' asked Matron sharply.

'It's a storm we had two or three years ago,' said Jo civilly. 'It isn't likely that such a thing will occur again, though. Besides, don't they say that thunderbolts never fall twice in the same place ? '

' You are thinking of the old idea that lightning never strikes twice in the same place,' said Miss Wilson's voice from the doorway. ' When you have finished, girls, please go to bed. I'm very much afraid that storm will come up during the night, and you'd better get all the sleep you can early in case you are disturbed.'

' We'll be likely to be disturbed ! ' murmured Cornelia to her compatriot. ' Some of those babes will just yell their heads off if we get a real bad storm, I guess. They always do ! '

' I'm sleepy,' yawned Jo. ' I don't mind how soon I go to bed. But I haven't finished my prep yet, Miss Wilson.'

' Never mind. I don't suppose you will be the only one,' said Miss Wilson soothingly. ' And everyone is off to bed as soon as Abendessen is over. Mademoiselle has just rung me up to tell me. Goodnight, you people. If it comes through the night and you wake up, you'd better stay where you are. Matron and Miss Stewart and Miss Nalder and I will have quite enough to do to see to the middles.'

' Yes, Miss Wilson ; good-night, Miss Wilson,' chorused the eight.

' Bill ' nodded to them, and left the room. Matron waited impatiently until Marie had finished her meal, and then rustled off after her. The eight people left behind looked at each other for a moment.

' Matron is upset,' said Frieda at length. ' I think perhaps she hates storms.'

' I can't say that I exactly love them myself,' said Jo. ' Well, I suppose we'd better perform the whole duty of prefects, and then get off to bed. Whose turn is it to see to the windows down here ? '

' Mine,' said Simone, getting up. ' Are you going to lock *all* the doors, Joey ? '

' I suppose so. We'd better carry on as we always do. In any case, with a storm of the kind Bill seems to anticipate in the offing, no one is likely to be paying visits to-night.' And Jo, following her friend's example, got up, and pushed her chair back into its place. The others did the same ; and the four seniors, after bidding the prefects good-night, retired to bed.

Simone ran away to see to the closing and fastening of all windows on the ground-floor, while Jo attended to the outer doors, and Frieda saw to it that the rooms had been left tidy. Marie slipped upstairs to peep into the dormitories and make sure that everyone was all right. Her coming caused great consternation to the members of the Leafy dormitory when their scout arrived with the news that she was coming. They had barely time to pull close their curtains before she was in the room. Biddy was left sitting up with a sentence half-finished on her tongue, and if Marie had been inquisitive enough to go right round, she would have found more than one girl highly flushed, and far from sleepy. As it was, beyond noticing a billowing of some of the curtains— a fact which she set down to the windows and door being open, though why she should have done that when there was not a breath of air stirring, it is hard to say—everything was normal. Cautiously she entered those cubicles where the windows were, to draw the lattices to more closely, and nearly causing Mercy Barbour to suffocate, for that young lady,

having a guilty conscience, was convinced that the
prefect suspected something, and lay holding her
breath until Marie was safely out of the cubicle.

However, nothing happened after all, and having
decided that the only thing left for her to do was to
run up to the roof-garden and close the skylights,
Marie departed, unaware of Mercy's predicament.

'What did she want, at all at all?' demanded
Biddy, after the shutting of the skylight over their
heads had given them a second horrid shock.

'She has closed the windows nearly shut,' said
Jeanne le Cadoulec, severe censure in her tones.
'That is very wrong. And she has shut the skylight
altogether. The room will have no air.'

'P'r'aps it's going to rain,' suggested Mary Shaw,
sitting up in bed and hugging her knees. 'Anyway,
she's gone now. I heard her door shut.—Go on
with the story, Biddy: it's a regular screamer!'

'You're sure she won't come back?' asked Biddy
cautiously.

'Of course she won't. I tell you I heard her bedroom door shut!' Mary sounded exasperated. 'Do
get on, and don't be such a 'fraid-cat!'

Thus urged, Biddy consented to finish the truly
hair-raising history of the Banshee of the O'Connells,
and the rest drew back their curtains once more, and
listened to the mysterious half-whisper with which
she sent agreeable shudders down their spines.

When the story ended—very tragically, of course
—Biddy insisted that the séance was over for the
night. Though they did not know it as yet, it was
over for ever, so far as bed-time tales were concerned.
That being hidden in the future, they settled themselves comfortably and went to sleep.

Meanwhile, the prefects finished their work, retired to bed with all speed, and Frieda, Marie, and Simone soon were sleeping as soundly as their juniors. Jo, more sensitive and highly-strung, and generally affected by thunder, found it harder. She twisted and turned, and wished the storm would hurry up and come. She heard the Staff come upstairs and retire to their rooms, not long after the domestic staff had clumped their way up to the top of the house. Then she sat up, and saw that over at the school all lights were out. She got out of bed, moving cautiously for fear of waking anyone else, and leaning out of her window contrived to get a view of Le Petit Chalet—now St Agnes'—and noted that they, too, were in darkness. Evidently everyone was following Mademoiselle's advice, and getting what sleep they could before the storm came.

Jo went back and proceeded to remake her bed. Then she lay down and began to repeat the prayers of the Rosary. She had a rosary given her by Frieda, and she knew how to use it. Often she had found that the repetition of the office soothed her to sleep if she were wakeful, so she resorted to it this night, and it soon had its usual effect. With the beads slipping from her lax fingers, Joey was sound asleep at last.

It must have been after midnight when the entire house at St Clare's was wakened most dramatically by a long eerie wail that echoed through the hushed corridors in a truly ghostly manner. It woke Frieda, who had been sleeping sweetly ; it woke every member of the three dormitories, who promptly and thoroughly buried their united heads under the bed-clothes, as another of those eldritch shrieks echoed again through the house ; it woke Marie and Simone, who, scared and nervy, began to repeat their prayers as fast as they could, sure that something unpleasant was close at hand. Matron, cowering at the bottom of her bed, was certain that it must be the beginning of the storm, and prayed incoherently that it might soon be over. The Staff, roused up so unceremoniously, switched on lights and began to seek dressing-gowns and bedroom-slippers to go and investigate. Finally, it woke the maids, who added to the awful sounds coming up from the floor below by their screams ; and Jo Bettany, who, heedless as usual, leapt out of bed and made for the door to see what was happening.

Jo certainly got a shock when she opened her door. Standing in the heavy gloom, she could see faintly a small white figure, from which those horrible wails were issuing at regular intervals. At almost the same time a flash of lightning tore across the black skies, and Jo was able to see a slender figure with long light hair flowing over its shoulders, and wide-open, unseeing eyes fixed on her.

Jo had gone to sleep in an overwrought condition ; she had been wakened from vaguely horrible dreams ; and this was the last straw. With a choking sound she fainted away, going to the floor with a thud that brought Miss Wilson, who was just coming, to her end of the corridor, at a run. She found Jo stretched out full-length in her pyjamas, while Alixe von Elsen, obviously walking in her sleep, was uttering wail after wail in a way that would have turned any properly constituted Banshee green with envy.

It was a good thing that Bill was remarkably level-headed. She knew that those awful cries must have

roused the whole house ; and she also knew that
Alixe must not be wakened suddenly. But Jo's need
seemed the greatest at the moment. Calling softly
to Miss Stewart, who had followed her, to come and
take Alixe back to bed, she bent over the Head Girl,
real anxiety in her face. Jo had been a very delicate
child ; and though she was now far stronger than
anyone had ever hoped she would be, she was
not a robust girl, and her stillness frightened the
mistress.

' Miss Stewart, take Alixe back to bed, and stay
with her ! ' she called. ' And send someone for
Matron at once ! '

' I 'll go ! ' And little Miss Nalder, the games
mistress, slipped past and into Matron's room.

Miss Stewart took Alixe's hand, feeling rather
nervy herself at sight of those wide-open, unseeing
eyes, and led her back to the Leafy dormitory, where
she was startled to find all the occupants completely
out of sight, only humps under the bedclothes showing that anyone was there. Alixe was her first care.
But once she had got the child safely back into bed
again, she said cheerily, ' Now then, babies ! It 's
only Alixe walking in her sleep.—Luise, get up
and switch on that light. You 'll all feel better
then.'

At the unexpected sound of her voice, a series of
muffled screams came from the beds ; and Alixe,
disturbed by the noise, woke up with a wild yell, and
clung madly to the mistress, gasping in her own
tongue, ' Oh, the Banshee—the Banshee ! She 's
at the window—she 's after me ! Save me—save
me ! '

' Alixe, you silly child ! ' cried Miss Stewart, speak-

ing in German, too. 'What nonsense is this? Wake
up and don't be so foolish! And do, for goodness'
sake, stop pinching me! I shall be all black and blue
to-morrow.' And she unloosed Alixe's gripping hand
more firmly than gently, which helped to bring the
child to her senses.

By this time, also, Luise had managed to pull herself together, and had got up and switched on the
lights. Alixe opened her eyes cautiously, and when
she saw the blessedly matter-of-fact Miss Stewart,
with her curly, red-gold hair tumbling about her
shoulders, and her eyes full of amazement, she
released her hold, and gave a little sob. 'Oh, Miss
Stewart! I have had such nasty dreams!'

'You've been reading some awful rubbish or other,
just before you went to bed,' said Miss Stewart in
her uncompromisingly downright manner. 'Girls!
Come out from under those bedclothes, and stop being
so silly!—Lieschen, you come here and sit with Alixe
till I come back. I want to see what's happening outside.—And the rest of you, stay in your
beds.'

'Oh, please, Miss Stewart, can't we draw the curtains?' pleaded Mercy Barbour. 'The lightning is
so horrid!'

'Draw them, by all means. Shut the jalousies,
too, or I'm afraid you won't find the curtains much
use to you.—Come along, Lieschen!' And Miss
Stewart got up, giving her place to Lieschen, and
went off to see what was happening.

She found that Marie and Frieda were already
with the members of the other two dormitories, and
Miss Wilson and Simone, with some help from a very
scared Cornelia and Ilonka, had got Jo back to her

own room, where they had succeeded in bringing her round, though she was still very shaky.

'And where's Matron in all this?' demanded Miss Stewart when she got her colleague to herself for a moment.

'Bill' turned a disgusted face on her. 'Having hysterics in her own room! Nally's with her, threatening to shake her, I believe! Hallo! Here comes the thunder! And here's the rain,' she added, shouting at the top of her voice to make herself heard above the artillery-like roar of the thunder. 'Get that window shut quickly, Con, or we shall have a young flood in here!'

'I say! I've left my *Forsyte Saga* on the ottoman at the window,' remarked a feeble voice from the bed. 'I hope it hasn't got wet?'

'You lie still and don't try to talk,' said Miss Wilson sternly, as she left her friend to see to both book and window, and crossed over to her invalid. 'Here—drink this! Yes; I know it's not pleasant. But people who scare other folks as you've scared us deserve unpleasant things to drink. Down with it, Jo, all of it, and don't argue!'

Seeing no help for it, Jo 'downed with' the brandy Miss Wilson was holding to her lips. She felt better almost at once, and then memory returned. 'That *awful* thing I saw! Oh, Bill, what was it?'

Refraining from reminding her that to call a mistress by a nickname to her face was not done, Miss Wilson answered, 'It was only Alixe von Elsen walking in her sleep. How *could* you be so silly, Jo? I admit that the sight was not a nice one; but to faint because you see a child sleep-walking, is scarcely what I should have expected from a girl like you!'

Bill's stinging speech brought Jo to herself in a hurry. She had been feeling rather sorry for herself—trust 'Bill' to recognise that!—for fainting is a most unpleasant sensation; but this remark removed from her all idea of self-pity.

'I—I didn't think,' she murmured ashamedly.

'Evidently not, or you would scarcely have paraded out on the corridor without putting on your dressing-gown and bedroom-slippers. However, it's done with now. But another time, my dear girl, do try to use your common sense! Now, do you feel all right?' Miss Wilson's tone was carefully casual, but inwardly she felt very anxious as she scanned the Head Girl's white face.

'I'm all right now,' said Jo sturdily. 'Sorry I gave you a scare. I don't mind saying I had rather a nasty one myself—what on earth is that?' she asked, interrupting herself suddenly.

'Only the rain,' said Miss Wilson. 'Ah, here's Miss Stewart come to report!—Well, Miss Stewart?'

'All windows closed, and only a tiny flood in one of the bathrooms which got overlooked,' said Miss Stewart. 'Karin has gone downstairs to make coffee for everyone, and she has marched the entire staff of domestics down with her to butter rolls. No one has a chance to be frightened, she's keeping them so busy. Really, Miss Wilson, that woman is worth her weight in gold!'

'Coffee?' Jo's voice was growing stronger every minute. 'Oh, I could drink some coffee!'

'I must go and see to things.' Miss Wilson got up

from the bed where she had been sitting. 'Miss
Stewart will stay with you, Jo.'

'I'm all right, thanks,' began Jo ; but Miss Wilson
was already out of earshot.

'Yes ; you look better,' agreed Miss Stewart,
inspecting her. 'I hope you don't think this affair
will get you out of lessons to-morrow, Jo, for I can
assure you that it's most unlikely.'

Jo went red, and said nothing. The Staff at the
Chalet School were wise in their generation. If they
had petted her, she would certainly have made the
most of her attack ; but their matter-of-fact way of
taking it convinced her that she had made an idiot
of herself.

It was nearly four o'clock before the house finally
settled down to rest again. By that time the storm,
which had been raging furiously for nearly four
hours, had worked itself out, and all that remained
was the thunder growling in the distance, and the
crash of the rain as it fell in torrents. Jo, and Alixe,
and most of the School were asleep. Matron had
recovered from her attack of hysterics, and was
feeling bitterly ashamed of herself. The maids were
all upstairs again, dragooned to bed by the redoubt-
able Karin ; and Miss Wilson, having rung up Mademoiselle and given her a brief résumé of the events
of the night, also retired to bed, hoping wearily that
this would prove the last of the night's alarms ; and
certainly the last of the term's adventures ; she had
had enough !

She was nearly asleep when she suddenly roused,
sat up in bed, and exclaimed aloud, ' Now what has
that wretched child, Biddy O'Ryan, been doing with
her Irish spooks ? She's at the bottom of this fuss,

as sure as my name is Helena Margaret Wilson!
Well, I'll settle *her* finally in the morning!'

Then she lay down again, and fell into such a heavy
sleep that it was only by sound shaking that Miss
Stewart and Miss Nalder were able to wake her at all,
next morning.

CHAPTER XV

THE BAND AT THE NEW HOUSE

'BRIDGET, I should like to speak to you after Frühstück in the Staff room.'

Biddy O'Ryan looked up, dismay in her face. What was coming now ? 'Bill' didn't seem to be angry exactly, but you could never judge by that, and her face and voice were both serious. With a thoroughly guilty conscience Biddy O'Ryan felt apprehensive of what was to follow, and certainly did not enjoy her breakfast. Alixe von Elsen, looking rather pale after last night's experiences, and Jo Bettany, with heavy shadows under her eyes, were inclined to trifle with their food also. Matron was looking painfully subdued. As for her own clan, Mary, and the two or three others who had heard Miss Wilson's quiet remark, glanced at each other in horror.

' What does Bill know ? ' asked Mary in a frantic whisper of Biddy, as they took their seats at table after Grace had been said.

' Sure, Oi couldn't be tellin' ye that, at all at all ! ' replied Biddy, becoming richly Irish in her agitation. ' It's mesilf was wondherin' that same, just now.'

' I think she knows too much,' said Jeanne le Cadoulec, who sat between them. ' Oh, Biddy, ma pauvre, I greatly fear you will be scolded.'

' I reckon that's on the mat, too,' agreed Mary. ' Well, they can't say much to you, Biddy. After all, no one ever said we weren't to tell each other stories after lights out.'

' No ; but the rule says no talkin' after silence-bell,' rejoined Biddy dismally. ' It's throuble's before me, gerrils ! Oi can fale it in me bones ! '

' If you talk like that, it certainly is,' said Evadne, who was going back to her seat from the buttery hatch, and had caught this remark. ' And what, under the canopy, were you little boneheads doing last night to give us all such a scare ? I know it *was* you, for Alixe von Elsen is in your dormy. It's a wonder my hair's not white this morning, after listening to the awful noises she made.'

' *You* can't talk about language, anyhow,' muttered Mary. ' I reckon your own's an eye-opener any day of the week. Biddy couldn't produce anything to beat that ! '

Evadne went on in dignified manner. She considered that she would lose less dignity by ignoring these remarks than by squashing the maker of them.

After breakfast, Biddy, escorted as far as they dared by her own crowd, went quakingly to the Staff room.

' You tell Bill it was our faults as well,' Mary ordered her. ' If you don't, we'll have to do it our-selves—if that's what she wants you for, that is.'

' Indade, Oi'll be tellin' no tales ! ' flared Biddy. ' So ye naden't be expectin' it ! '

Then she left them, and entered the room, where a sternly judicial Miss Wilson was awaiting her.

' Come in, Bridget,' she said, ' and shut that door after you. Now come here. What stories have you been telling the girls in Leafy dormitory ? I know that it *is* you, for they were Irish stories. Alixe talked about banshees, and they are a peculiarly Irish form of the supernatural.'

Not understanding this last remark, Biddy stared at the mistress in silence. She vaguely wondered if an insult to her beloved country were intended ; but as she was not sure, she said nothing.

' Well,' said Miss Wilson when the silence threatened to become oppressive, ' I should be glad of an answer to my question. What stories have you been telling the middles in your dormitory ? '

Biddy considered. ' The Fairy Fithir was wan,' she said in her soft voice. ' An' the story of Coreena an' the shamrocks was another.'

' Is there anything about banshees in either ? ' asked Miss Wilson. ' I 'm afraid I don't know them.'

' There is not,' said Biddy.

' Then what else—and hurry up and tell me ! I don't want to have to drag it out of you a word at a time.'

' Sure, Oi tould them av the Banshee at Castle Rathdearg—where Miss Honora lived, that me ma was maid to,' said Biddy in a hurry.

' I see. And don't speak like that,' added Miss Wilson. ' Your English is good enough when it suits you. Any others ? '

Biddy shook her head. ' No, Miss Wilson. That was the only one.'

' And when—at what time, I mean—did you tell this tale to the others ? '

Biddy gave it up with a sigh of despair. ' Bill ' meant to have an answer, she knew. She might as well tell her and get it over. ' Afther—after, I ma—mean, silence-bell,' she said resignedly.

' Quite so. Well, Bridget, you have succeeded in

upsetting two girls very badly, to say nothing of being the worst cause of last night's disturbance. That sort of thing cannot go on. I shall tell Matron to set up a camp-bed in my room, and you will sleep there for a week. Perhaps, by the time it is over, you will realise that telling ghost-stories when you are supposed to be sleeping is not the correct thing. You are, for various reasons, much freer here than you were at Ste Thérèse's. That means that we trust you girls implicitly. You have not shown yourself worthy of the trust, so you will be punished accordingly. Now you may go, and send the other members of your dormitory to me. I don't suppose for a moment that you insisted on telling the tales. I know quite well that they encouraged you. Run along.'

Biddy went, weeping like her own beloved skies, and gave the others, who had been waiting for her in the common-room, ' Bill's ' message. Then she departed upstairs to make her bed, still weeping. It was bad enough to have to sleep with ' Bill ' for a week. Biddy shook in her shoes at the bare thought. But to be told that she was untrustworthy nearly broke her heart.

Jo met her on the stairs as she toiled up, the tears streaming down her cheeks, and her loud sobs attracting the Head Girl long before she met the little sinner.

' What's up, Biddy ? ' asked Jo, a hand on the small girl's heaving shoulders.

' Bill says Oi'm not trustworthy—an' Oi'm to slape with her for a week on end,' sobbed Biddy, ending with a low howl.

' What on earth for ? ' Jo was puzzled. So far,

she had not connected Biddy especially with last night's disturbances.

' Bekase Oi tould the others about the Banshee av Castle Rathdearg, an' Alixe thried to *be* it ! ' wailed Biddy.

' I—see ! ' Jo was dying to laugh. She thought that Miss Wilson's punishment was highly original, and would certainly prove effective. Besides, the idea of Alixe of the saintly face as a banshee was too funny for anything. But discipline must be maintained, so she merely said, ' Well, the person *I* '*m* sorry for is Miss Wilson, if you really want to know. Do stop howling like a lost dog, and go and wash your face, child ! You 've deserved it all, you know.' Then she left Biddy to carry out her commands, and retired to the prefects' room, where she chuckled over the story as she gathered together the books she would need that morning.

' But oh ! what a term we are having ! ' she thought, as she sat up in her chair and tried to put her hair tidy. 'Nothing but alarms and excursions ! Let 's hope that storm has cleared the air in more senses than one, and we get a little peace after all this ! '

Peace, however, was the last thing that was likely to come to St Clare's yet, though what happened next was something that no one had ever anticipated in their wildest moments.

On the Saturday following the storm, Mr Flower paid a flying visit to the school, and carried off Cornelia and Evadne for the week-end. He was staying with the Lannises in their pretty home in Salzburg, and he decreed that they should all have a royal time together. The girls were overjoyed, and went away in high glee. If he had come the next week-end, they must have missed the excursion to the Zillerthal, for it had been decided to make it then. But, as Cornelia said, to have a week-end with her father, and still have that to look forward to, was something too thrilling for words.

They came home early on Monday afternoon, when the School at large was at drawing, singing, or needle-work. The storm having cooled the atmosphere, work had been resumed as usual, until the heat should come again. Matron was in her own room, where she spent most of her time these days. Her foolish behaviour during the storm had sealed her fate, and she was leaving at the end of the term, though the girls did not know it. Miss Wilson welcomed the pair, who arrived just before she left for the Sonnalpe, whither she was going to discuss various matters appertaining to the school with Mrs Russell. Mr Flower insisted on taking her up in his car, and as it would save her the somewhat arduous climb by the path opposite the Tiern See, 'Bill' consented. She told the girls to go up to their rooms and change, and then get over to school in time for their sewing-class, which came twenty minutes later.

They said, 'Yes, Miss Wilson,' with becoming meekness, considering that the pair of them detested the very sight of a needle, and then she got into the car and was driven off—Mr Flower had taken leave of the girls previously.

Left alone, the two grabbed the handles of a wooden chest they had secreted in the bushes by the prefects' room window, and carried it upstairs between them, setting it safely under Evadne's bed.

'Better here than with you,' panted Evadne when it was safe. 'You live too near Matron for safety.'

'I guess I know all about that,' was the rueful reply. 'Well, I'd better hustle if we've to be over there in time for sewing—*ugh*!' And with a hideous grimace she went off.

Of course, everyone wanted to know how Evvy and Corney had enjoyed themselves, and what they had done. Frau Mieders, who was responsible for the domestic economy side of the school curriculum, was an amiable creature, and as they were only doing mending to-day, she agreed to shut up the book they usually had read, and let them talk. Cornelia and Evadne seemed to have had a very full time from their own account, and they kept the entire class amused until the bell rang for the end of the afternoon and Kaffee und Kuchen.

But when they were sitting in one select group in the garden, with no one in authority near enough to hear them, Margia Stevens tackled the pair. 'What else have you been doing?' she demanded.

'What d'you mean?' asked Evadne in injured tones. 'I guess we did a plenty in the time.'

'Oh, rubbish! I didn't mean that, and you know it, Evvy Lannis! You and Corney have been up to something while you were away! What is it? Come on! I mean to know!'

'Then I'm sorry, but I'm afraid you can't,' retorted Cornelia. 'We *did* transact a little business while we were away, but it's house business, and we can't talk about it.'

'Oh? Sorry I asked,' said Margia haughtily. 'Have another cake, Gill, won't you?' and she turned to Gillian Linton, who had been listening, with her eyes opened to their widest extent.

Meanwhile Ilonka, Maria, Giovanna Donati, Stacie

Benson, and Kitty Burnett, who were all in this select group, were staring at the pair as if they couldn't believe their ears. As soon as they could, they dragged Cornelia and Evadne away from the rest into a corner by some bushes, and begged eagerly to be told what was happening.

' What's on for to-night ? ' asked Evadne cautiously.

' Cricket and tennis till nineteen o'clock. Then Abendessen—that's all,' Kitty assured them. ' What on earth have you two been up to ? '

Evadne glanced round. ' This is too public, I guess,' she said. ' Come on ! Let's go to the field and sit in the middle of it. Then we'll see any little snoopers stretching their long ears to hear what isn't meant for them.'

An indignant snort from behind the rhododendron bushes near which they were standing gave point to her remark, but she refused to let her clan administer justice as they wished.

' I guess it isn't worth while,' she said. ' What those long ears have heard won't do them a mite of good, and won't hurt *us* any. Come on to the field.'

They followed her obediently, collecting one or two others on their way. Evadne chose with discrimination. She summoned Joyce Linton, and rejected Mary Shaw with decision. ' I guess we don't want *infants* in this stunt ! ' she said scornfully.

Emmie Linders, Ruth Wynyard, and Faith Barbour were added to their crowd. The rest were sent off with the contemptuous remark, ' This isn't a crèche, thank you ! '

By the time they had reached the playing-field, there were eleven of them. Evadne surveyed them, and then said, ' Someone—you, Ruth—go and fetch Vi Allison, and tell her to say nothing. Hurry ! There's reams to discuss, and we can't take too long over it, for we'll be wanted for games, and no one must hear of this till we're quite ready.' Which cryptic remark drove her band nearly crazy with curiosity.

Ruth ran off, and returned presently with Violet, a quiet girl, who yet had a good deal of influence among her own peers. Meanwhile the rest had progressed to the centre of the field, where they would be safe from eavesdroppers. They had to go slowly because of Stacie Benson.

Nearly eighteen months before, she had met with an accident which had laid her on her back for a long period. Indeed, at one time the doctors at the Sonnalpe had been afraid that she might be crippled for life. But by slow degrees the wrenched and torn muscles healed, and now she was able to move about, though she had to be very careful lest any exertion should retard the mending process that was still going on.

' Come along,' said Cornelia, as Violet and Ruth neared them. ' Here, Stacie, come over here, and lean back-to-back with me. That'll be better for you than sitting over there in a heap. Comfy ? Good-oh ! Then I guess it's up to Evvy to spout, for it's her plan.'

' Oh well, you helped it,' said Evadne, wriggling into a comfortable position. ' If it hadn't been for your pop, we couldn't have done it.'

' Pop's a good sport, I'll tell the world,' agreed his daughter. ' But you thought of it, so you ought to tell it.'

'Well,' said Evadne, 'it's just that I thought we ought to do something as a house.'

'But already we are to play Ste Thérèse's at cricket and tennis,' protested Emmie. 'Then we shall see which is the better house.'

'I know that. But Ste Thérèse's has the Library—all except one case of books, that is—and the Hobbies club is held there, and all the big stunts seem to go on there. I thought *we* ought to have one of our own. So I asked Poppa for some cash, and Corney asked hers, and Mr Flower told us to go ahead and get what we wanted, and he'd fix the bill.'

'But what is it?' asked Kitty Burnett, who was an impatient young person.

'Why,' drawled Evadne, 'I just thought it would be a good notion if we had a band of our own.'

For a moment or two they were stunned into silence at the magnitude of the idea. Then the comments flew fast and furious, and in two or three languages at once. But there could be no mistake about it. Everyone was thrilled at the idea.

Evadne listened as long as she could. Then she broke in. 'Say, I guess you can leave all that alone. What I want to know is how many of you can play anything?—Emmie, you have a 'cello, I know; and Kitty plays the fiddle.—What about the rest of you?'

As it happened, the rest all learned the piano, with the exception of Joyce Linton and Stacie Benson. Evadne nodded her curly head. 'I guessed as much,' she said. 'Well, you'll all have to buck up and work. We've got heaps of things to play, and everyone has to learn something. Then we'll learn pieces, and give a concert. And if Ste Thérèse's isn't green with envy, well, I miss my guess—that's all.'

'But what are the instruments?' asked Stacie. 'The only thing I can do in music is singing.'

'You can learn one of ours,' said Evadne. 'Here's the list. I'll read it out, and you can choose what you'll have. And don't all try to choose the same thing, either,' she added severely.

'Here you are,' said Cornelia, handing over the list in Evadne's unexpectedly pretty handwriting. 'I've bagged the saxophone. We've only got one of him, he was so expensive.'

'Just like you to bag the best, Corney Flower!' cried Kitty.

'There are plenty more things,' said Evadne. 'And you've got your fiddle, anyway, so what are *you* fussing about?'

The instruments were certainly varied. They included jews'-harps, ukuleles, mouth-organs, whistles, a drum, a tambourine, castanets, cymbals, a bugle, and a zither. Most parents would have fainted on beholding the bill, but both Mr Lannis and Mr Flower were wealthy men, and spoiled their only children outrageously. Luckily, the various squashings administered at school helped to counteract any spoiling they might get at home, and both girls were level-headed young persons on the whole.

Kitty and Emmie were out of it, having their own instruments already. Joyce swooped down on one jew's-harp, and Faith put in a word for the other. Stacie, by common consent, was awarded the zither, though she made wild protests. Evadne herself had claimed a ukulele, and the other came to Giovanna Donati after a fierce argument between her and

Violet Allison, who had ambitions that way. Violet was soothed by being offered the cymbals, tambourine, and castanets. The drum went to Ilonka, and the other pair of castanets to Ruth, who was *not* musical. The three whistles were distributed between Ilonka—who complained that you couldn't drum all the time—and two additional members they decided to co-opt—Lilli van Huysen, a Dutch girl, and Greta Macdonald, a very shy Highlander, who was Violet's great chum.

'You tell Greta, Vi, and I'll see to Lilli myself,' said Evadne. 'Now everything's arranged. I'll give out the things to-morrow, and we must practise as hard as we can.'

'But where?' demanded Stacie with point. 'We can't practise anywhere where people are likely to hear us, or it'll be no surprise to anyone. Some of those juniors couldn't keep their tongues still if they were paid for it, and Ste Thérèse's would hear all about it in half no time.'

'That's so. Well, we'll just have to get up early and practise in the woods. Let me know as soon as you can do something with whatever you've got, and then we'll see about pieces. Now we'd better go, or Jo will be yelling for us.'

CHAPTER XVI

A JOLLY EXPEDITION

JO was sprawled in a deck-chair in the garden at St Clare's, nominally studying French grammar, when sounds attracted her attention from her work, and she looked up. Cornelia and Giovanna were stealing out of the side-door, each carrying something.

'I wonder,' mused the Head Girl, 'what those imps are doing now. I can't imagine them getting up so early for any good purposes. It can't be seven yet.' She looked at her watch. 'No; ten to. Now, what are they doing? I must see into this.'

She got up from her chair, laid her book on it, and stood watching the pair as they made their way across the playing-field to the wicket-gate at the far end.

'The woods!' said Jo to herself with satisfaction. 'Hallo! Here come some more of them. I'd better not be seen, for find out what they are up to, I simply must!' She dropped on the grass, aware that the low bushes round the garden would hide her from sight, and watched while a small procession of girls —each carrying something—left by the side-door, and all followed the direction the leaders had taken.

'Violet — Ruth — Lonny — Evvy. There's certainly something doing. And it's almost as certainly something they shouldn't, or they wouldn't be going about it like this.'

'Jo! What in the world are you on the grass for? Have you forgotten how heavy the dews are still?'

Jo jumped. She had not seen Frieda come out of the front entrance, books under her arm, so intent had she been on the middles.

'Do get up!' continued Frieda. 'Your dress will be in such a mess!'

At this reminder, Jo got to her feet in a hurry, and stood looking down at her skirt, where long green stains told all too plainly that the dews *were* heavy.

'Oh, gemini!' she ejaculated in dismay. 'What a mess!'

'Well, but why were you kneeling on the grass?' persisted Frieda. 'No; don't try to rub it; you will only make it worse!'

'Will it come out with washing?' asked Jo hopefully.

'Not with washing. You must send it to the good Sisters. They may be able to take it out with their laundry.'

'Oh, bother—bother—*bother*! And I'm nearly broke as it is! Well, I must change before Frühstück, I suppose. Meantime, my child, you and I must do a spot of detective work.'

'Why?' asked Frieda.

'Because the middles—some of them, at least—are up to mischief, or I'm a Dutchman. Six of them, including Evvy and Corney, of course, have just streaked across to the woods, all carrying something. You know as well as I do that it usually takes an earthquake to get Evvy out of bed before the bell rings. And it's fairly safe to assume that they're doing something they oughtn't. Come along!

They 've had plenty of time to get out of sight now, and we shall soon find them. That gang all talk like magpies once they get together. Their voices will soon guide us to them.'

Frieda dropped her books on top of Jo's. ' Very well. I agree that it must be something strange to bring Evvy out of bed early.'

Together the two prefects strolled through the garden and into the playing-field, where they were rewarded by the sight of Joyce Linton coming out of a side-door, carrying some small article in her hand.

' Grüss Gott, Joyce ! ' called Joey, giving her the pretty old Tyrolean greeting. ' You 're down early this morning.'

' Ye-yes,' stammered Joyce, rather taken aback at the sight of Jo and Frieda. ' I thought I would—er—have a stroll in the woods before Frühstück.'

' What a funny coincidence ! ' Jo's eyes were twinkling wickedly, but Joyce was too confused to look up at her face. ' Frieda and I thought *we* would have a matutinal stroll, too.'

' Oh ? ' stammered Joyce, not knowing in the least what ' matutinal ' meant.

' Yes ; you can come with us, and we 'll enjoy it together.'

Joyce looked like anything but enjoyment as she fell in with the two elder girls. Her fair little face was flushed, and there was a worried look in the forget-me-not blue eyes she turned on the dark woods that clothe the lower mountain slopes round the Tiern See. But she dared not contradict Jo, so she could only go with them, hoping devoutly that the musicians had got well away, and would not be found. What was Jo doing out at this time of day ? It was really too bad of her ! Frieda, too !

Quite aware of Joyce's feelings, Jo strolled on, one hand through Frieda's arm, the other in the pocket of her blazer. 'Isn't it a glorious morning ? ' she said conversationally. 'I love this soft air. It's considerably better than that awful heat we had last month.'

'It is certainly possible to work better now,' assented Frieda.

'What have you got there, Joyce ? ' asked Jo, with a glance at the thing in Joyce's hand.

'Oh, just a—a toy,' said Joyce, slipping her jew's-harp into her blazer-pocket, and wishing she had put it there in the beginning.

'Rather big for toys, aren't you ? ' commented Jo unfeelingly.

Joyce flushed again, but said nothing ; and the three went on in comparative silence. They reached the gate, and Joyce held it open for the two grandees to pass through. But when she would have followed with some wild idea of making a dash for it and coming up with the others before Jo and Frieda could reach them, the Head Girl turned on her a look as hard as a diamond. 'No, Joyce. You can stay here and amuse yourself in the field. Do you understand ? You are not to leave it, unless you go back to the house.'

Wildly stuttering, Joyce began to protest ; but Jo was adamant. She had to stay on the other side of the fence and see the prefects go marching gaily off to the woods. The beautiful secret Evvy and Corney had provided was going to be discovered !

Joyce stamped her foot rebelliously at the thought. But for all that, she obeyed the Head Girl.

Meanwhile Jo and Frieda were talking as they crossed over the strip of wild meadow-land, up which the cattle were coming, their bells sounding sweetly on the summer air.

'Joyce is wild with me,' said Jo cheerfully. 'All the same, she's a little idiot, and she's not going to get into any trouble that I can keep her out of.'

Frieda laughed. 'I wonder what it was she had. I do not see how they could get into mischief with toys, Joey.'

'I don't myself,' agreed Jo. 'All the same, I'm not going to take any risks. Joyce got into trouble last term. She's not going to do anything mad this.'

'But a good deal of that was Thekla's fault,' argued Frieda. 'I have always thought that she would never have been so bad if Thekla had not encouraged her.'

Jo gave her a startled look. 'Do you know, I'd nearly forgotten about Thekla. Of course, after what Mademoiselle said, no one has ever mentioned her that I've heard. Poor little ass! She paid all right for her sins!'

Frieda nodded. 'She deserved it,' she said—and coming from gentle Frieda, the speech was a strange one. 'She was the first girl who has ever merited expulsion here, Joey, and I hope she will be the last. I know Joyce would never have been so silly if she hadn't urged her on—Gott in Himmel! What is that?'

She might well ask!

As they began to climb up the narrow path leading

through the woods, a burst of sound reached them which was only comparable to the dying efforts of an elderly bull. At the same time a wild squeaking arose from their left, and the tang-tang of two ukuleles played by people who seemed to know very little about their instruments came from the right.

'Good Heavens! Who is being murdered?' exclaimed Jo. She pushed up through the black tree-trunks, and came upon a touching vision—Cornelia standing in a little clearing, an enormous saxophone set to her lips, while, with distended cheeks, she was bringing from its trumpet the remarkable sounds which had first startled them. At a little distance stood Ruth with a mouth-organ, though this they had not heard at once. The squeaking of a tin whistle sounded much worse here, and Jo jumped to the right conclusion at once.

'Great Cæsar's bath-mat! *Frieda!* D' you understand? These babes are starting an orchestra, if you please! And a jazz one at that, if one can judge by the sounds! There's enterprise for you!'

Frieda collapsed on the ground, and rocked with laughter. 'Oh, Joey! How I wish I had my camera with me! I *should* so like a snap of Corney looking like that!'

'You shall have one, my love! Not a word to anyone! You stay here and keep guard, and I'll scoot back and fetch it. I'd bring my own, only I used the last film yesterday. Corney hasn't seen us, luckily. Lie flat, and don't make a sound. I'll be as quick as I can.'

With this, she slipped off again, and ten minutes later she was back, flushed and panting with the speed she had made.

' Here ! ' she gasped, holding out the kodak. ' I
was as quick as I could be. Joyce is still wandering
round, looking as though she had lost her pet canary !
Be quick, now ! '

Frieda took the kodak, opened it, and pulled it out
to its fullest extent, while her friend dropped noiselessly down on the pine-needles, and mopped her
streaming brow. Carefully the younger girl focused
the unconscious Cornelia, who was still standing
blowing, looking as if she were about to break a blood-
vessel, and producing sounds that none of the
banshees Ireland ever produced could have hoped to
rival. There was a moment's pause, and then Frieda
snapped the player. Just in time, too, for at that
moment Cornelia took her instrument from her lips
and surveyed it gravely. The prefect dropped at
once, while the middle shook her saxophone with a
professional air. Jo was nearly strangling in her
efforts to keep from laughing, and Frieda herself was
very little better. Finally, having made up her mind
that the instrument was all right, Cornelia applied
herself to it again, making sounds which, as Jo truly
declared, were enough to bring the bell-swinging herd
wending its way slowly along the banks of the stream
below them to inquire if a member of their family
were expiring.

The prefects took advantage of her preoccupation
to crawl cautiously away on all fours. ' For she
simply *mustn't* see us ! ' explained Jo, when at length
they were sufficiently hidden by the trees to stand
up and progress in a more usual way. ' Well ! So
this is the middles' latest ? I shan't worry about
this, I can tell you ! '

Frieda leant against a convenient tree-trunk and

laughed till the tears rolled down her cheeks. 'Oh, Jo! Shall you ever forget Corney's face? She looked ready to burst!'

'I thought she looked more like a fit of apoplexy,' returned Jo, mopping her eyes. 'I suppose Joyce's "toy" is another instrument. I wonder what? It isn't a saxophone, that's certain. It was too small.'

'It is as well, I think,' replied Frieda, as the melancholy sounds pursued them downhill. 'And the squeakings, they must have been a pipe of some kind.'

'More likely a tin whistle. I wonder how they got hold of the things. Saxophones are expensive belongings, I believe.'

'What are you going to do about Joyce?'

'Oh, forbid her to say anything to the others, of course. And tell her to go ahead.'

Accordingly, when they reached the fields, Jo raised her clear voice in a long call of 'Joy-oy-ce,' which brought that young lady running.

'It's all right,' said Jo. 'I know what you're up to, but I shan't say anything, and neither will Frieda. Only I want your word of honour that you won't mention to any of your crowd that we know. Will you give it?'

Joyce's face had cleared. 'Oh, rather!' she said eagerly. 'Can I go?'

'You mean, "May I"?' said Jo, wickedly quoting Miss Annersley, who was death on the misuse of this particular phrase. 'Yes; off with you. I must go and gulp down some more French grammar.—Coming, Frieda?'

Frieda nodded; and the two prefects went off, leaving Joyce to bound happily across the field and vanish into the woods, where Cornelia, warming thoroughly to her work, was producing some most complicated notes which were enough to frighten most people away.

The ' band ' kept those of the middles who were in it pleasantly occupied for the rest of the week.   Jo warned off the prefects, saying that she and Frieda knew all about it, and it was all right.   So they practised in peace, greatly to their relief.   As for the others, Biddy's and Alixe's exploits had sobered them for the time being, and they gave their minds to games, much to the contentment of all in charge of them.

Finally, Saturday morning arrived, and the School was astir at a very early hour.   The first part of the journey would be made in the queer little mountain railway that runs from Spärtz up to the Tiernthal. At Spärtz they would catch the train that runs down the Zillerthal to Mayrhofen, a journey of nearly two hours.   The juniors were left waving farewell at the head of the mountain railway, for, as their expedition was a much shorter one, there was no need for them to set off so early as their elders.

' Juliet, it's topping having you and Grizel with us again ! ' said Jo, as she squeezed in beside Juliet Carrick, the Head of the Annexe, and an old girl of the Chalet School.

' Glad you think so,' smiled Juliet, as she sat down after waving to her small charges, who were all with the juniors from St Agnes'.   ' I've been looking forward to to-day.'

' It's rotten though that 'Veta can't come,' put in Evadne, who was just behind them.   ' What on earth did she want to go and get measles for just now ?'

'Poor Elisaveta!' laughed Miss Wilson from the other side of the little carriage. 'I expect she's very miserable about it all.'

'I should think she is!' agreed Jo. 'I know she was looking forward to this, and now she'll miss it.'

'And miss trying to find gold in the Ziller, also,' added Frieda, with a provoking glance at Margia.

'That was years ago,' returned Margia calmly. 'We were only babes at that time.'

'You are so elderly now!' said Jo sarcastically. 'Well, we'll have a jolly good time, anyway.—How far are we going, Miss Wilson?'

'Up to Mayrhofen. How much farther do you want to go?' demanded 'Bill.'

'Oh, that will do me nicely, thank you. But I know the railway goes farther on, and I wondered if we were to go to the terminus.'

'No, thank you! There isn't a prettier part of the Zillerthal than the country round Mayrhofen. And we'll follow up the river's course through the gorge, and to the farm where we got milk that time.'

'Good!' Jo sat back with a sigh of contentment.

The journey down to Spärtz was accomplished without any mishap, though half-way down Jo was moved to wonder aloud what would happen if the cables broke and the train slipped.

'It would go bang into the station,' she said with relish. 'What a crash that would be!'

'Indeed, it would do nothing of the kind!' said Frieda. 'It would leave the rails altogether, and plunge over the side there, among the trees. What horrid things you imagine, Joey!'

Jo laughed. 'Well, I never do come down by it without wondering.'

'Then keep your horrible imaginings to yourself,' said Miss Wilson. 'You're making Miss Leslie look quite white and wan.'

'That's a libel,' declared Miss Leslie, the mathematics mistress. 'The only thing that ever makes *me* white and wan, is Jo's ideas on maths!'

Everyone laughed at this. Jo was notoriously poor at mathematics, and many were the battles royal she and Miss Leslie had had over them.

At Spärtz they left the train, and waited ten minutes or so before the train from Mayrhofen came puffing in. Then, when the few passengers had got out, the girls poured into the carriages, filling them fuller than they usually were at this time of year. The season for the Zillerthal towns opens at the end of June, as a rule, and lasts till September. During that time the little railway is busy, but at other seasons of the year it is very quiet.

'Take care of the baskets!' cried Mademoiselle, as the girls crowded in. 'Remember that there are grapes and apricots in one of them, and I cannot remember which.'

They handled the baskets with considerably more care after that. The fruit this year was very ripe and juicy, and no one wanted to spend the day with a stained frock if she could help it. Finally they were all settled, and a minute or two later, with portentous puffings and much loud screeching of her whistle, the train was jerked out of the station, and they were off.

The journey up the Ziller valley is very beautiful, though very different from that up the Tiern valley. Here, they were in a wide plain with great fields sown with grain which waved in the slight breeze. Past great farm-houses they went, where the walls were decorated with gay frescoes, and white-headed children came running to wave to them as they passed. Presently they left the fields, and ran through woods, where the sunlight, dancing between the leafy boughs, dappled the earth with a golden chequering. They stopped at little, primitive stations—Fügen, and Ried, and Zell-am-Ziller, which is a great tourist centre, and where the railroad swerves to the east. And at last they saw through the trees the steep roofs, and the gilded spire of a church, and knew that they had reached Mayrhofen.

'Out you tumble!' cried Miss Annersley. 'Go over there by the gate, and wait till we come to you. —Mind that basket, Jo. It has the mugs and plates in it.'

'But they're all unbreakable, anyhow,' murmured Jo to Simone, as she swung the basket down to the ground. 'Now then, is that all? Where's that one that has the rolls in? I suppose we *could* buy bread if we had to, but I can't say I'm anxious to waste my money that way.'

'Here it is, Joey! I have it!' cried Gillian Linton, carefully putting back the big white napkin she had just lifted to peep at the contents.

'Then that's all, I believe.' Jo swung herself down to the ground, and surveyed the baskets with a puzzled frown.

'What is the matter?' asked Frieda.

'I could have sworn there were eight baskets; but there seem to be only seven. Oh well, I suppose I made a mistake.' And having thus settled the matter in her usual happy-go-lucky fashion, Jo forgot all about it, and ranged up with the others, waiting till Mademoiselle appeared with the railway tickets, and they were permitted to pass through the wide gate and out into the village street.

The largest town in the Zillerthal is Fügen, though Zell has come to be regarded as the chief. But Mayrhofen is as charming as any, with its six hotels, several pensions, and its picturesque private houses. There are two or three shops, where it is possible to buy most necessaries, and a beautiful little church stands in the centre of the little town.

But the girls were not specially interested in it. Their main idea was to get to the woods, which surround the little place, and have Mittagessen.

'Why?' demanded Miss Annersley. 'It's only eleven-ten now. You can't be hungry as early as this.'

'It isn't that,' said Jo plaintively, 'but these baskets are heavy. I'd rather carry them empty as full, any day.'

'Jo—Jo! Don't be so lazy,' said the English mistress, laughing. 'However, we'll set off, if that's how you all feel. Mademoiselle is staying here for Mittagessen with Stacie, as the walk may be too long for her; and Violet and Ruth are staying with them, too. So pick up your burdens and come along.'

They did as she told them, and set off, chattering merrily, and watched curiously by most of the population.

'Poor old Stacie!' said Juliet, who was with Jo, Frieda, and Simone. 'She's having a long time of it!'

'All the same, when I think what Jem and the rest were afraid of last year,' said Jo, 'it seems wonderful that she can do as much as she does.'

' If ever a girl paid for silliness, Stacie has,' added
Frieda. ' And she has been so brave about it,
too. Oh, here are the woods. How beautiful they
are ! '

' Jo—Jo ! Miss Annersley wants to know if you
have the basket with the fruit ? ' called Marie, running
up the long line from the back where she had been
talking with Miss Annersley.

Jo shook her head. ' I 've no idea. Half a minute,
and I 'll look.' She set her basket down on the grass,
and cautiously unpacked one end of the napkin that
covered it. ' No ; this is little pies. Why does she
want to know, Marie ? '

' Because we can't find it,' said Marie. ' She
thought that Evvy and Corney were carrying it ; but
they have the mugs and plates. And Sophie has the
rolls. Elsie has one basket of cakes, and Vanna has
the other. I was sure I had seen you take it. Oh
dear ! Where can it be ? '

' There are two other baskets,' suggested Jo.
' Who has them ? '

' Well, Bill is carrying the smaller one, which has
sweets and chocolate, I know, for I saw her packing
it myself. Maria Marani has the other, but *it* can't
be fruit, because it is small, too.'

Jo dropped the corner of the napkin she had been
about to tuck in. ' Oh, I say ! Do you mean that
we 've left the fruit behind ? I say ! What a mess ! '
she exclaimed. ' Go and see what it is Maria *has* got,
Marie ! If it isn't the fruit, then some of us must go
back and buy more.'

Marie sped back to Maria Marani, only to find that
that young lady's basket contained some hard-boiled
eggs which had been put in for those who preferred

them to pies. There could be no doubt about it—
the basket with all the fruit was missing.

There was an instant outcry. The girls were
thirsty, and had been looking forward to their fruit.
Besides, as the mistresses supposed it to be there,
they had brought nothing to drink, for they knew
that the girls would get milk at a certain farm, some
little way up the river.

'Oh *dear*!' exclaimed Miss Annersley when the
sad news had been broken to her. 'What are we
going to do?'

'Go without until we reach the farm,' said Miss
Wilson. 'It won't kill the girls to wait that long.
—No, Joey. None of you may go back for more
fruit. The only thing I hope is that we haven't lost
it altogether. It may be at home. I can't say that
I thought much about it till Miss Annersley spoke of
it just now, and Marie said she didn't know where it
was.'

'It's as bad as that first picnic to the Mondscheinspitze!' said Jo, with a chuckle. 'We left all the
lemonade behind that time. Oh well, I suppose we
shan't die if we don't get anything to drink for an
hour or so. We'd better get on, I suppose?'

Miss Wilson agreed; but this mishap cast rather
a gloom over the proceedings. Naturally, a good
many people at once began to find out that they were
thirsty, and to complain because they were forbidden
to drink of the river water.

'Certainly not!' said Miss Annersley firmly, when
Cornelia and Ilonka came to her with a request to be
allowed to go down to the bank and get a drink.
'We have had very hot weather lately, and the
river is reduced by half. You aren't going to run

any risks of imbibing fever germs by drinking from it.'

And she held to this. Mercifully, when they reached their chosen glade and had settled down to their picnic, it was found that the meat in the little pies was embedded in rich jelly, which took the edge off their thirst. But no one wanted sweets or cakes, and they had to be put back into their baskets until after the girls had had something to drink. When they had eaten their pies, therefore, and rested a little, Miss Annersley called to them to get up, and they would go on to the farm.

' It's to be hoped it's still there,' said Joey pessimistically. ' It's three years since we were here.'

' It'll be there all right,' said Miss Wilson briskly. ' Remember, *I* was here last summer, with Miss Stewart, and we found the farm safely enough then. Get on, Jo, and don't grouch ! '

Thus admonished, Jo led the way with her three friends, and the rest followed behind, laughing and chatting, and every now and then breaking into snatches of song. They met nobody, so the mistresses let them do as they chose.

At first the Ziller winds its way between the forested banks which, in the thaws and the autumn, are frequently flooded. But after a little the forest ends, the banks become steeper, and the grass vanishes, giving place to bare soil, strewn with rocks and stones. Here the river rushes down, foaming over its stony bed, leaping up round the boulders in the stream, and filling the air with the music of running water. The path is wide enough on the right bank, though on the left there is a low cliff, which overhangs it. The girls went along, enjoying the fresh, sweet air and the beauty of the scene, which quickly became wilder and wilder. Presently the low rock wall on the other side of the path began to rise, till they were walking at the foot of a craggy hill. Here the bed seems to have fallen, for from the path to the water it is a depth of between fifteen and twenty feet, with the river, now a torrent, tearing along towards the Inn. At this point, too, a tunnel has been cut through the living rock, since the hillside becomes one with the bank. At the far end of the tunnel is a plank bridge, roughly and strongly made, with steeply-sloping roof to protect the bridge from the winter snows and avalanches. At this point the scenery is magnificent, though on a small scale. The river swirls and thunders down, forming strong-flowing rapids, and tossing its spray high in the air. The girls hung over the stout hand-rail of the bridge, admiring the effects of the rainbows formed in the air, and comparing it with similar scenes they had visited.

At length, Miss Annersley insisted on their moving on. They wanted to get to the farm and have their milk; and then they must walk back, and be in time to catch the train, or they would lose the last train up from the Innthal to the Tiernthal, and that would mean walking. And a climb up the mountain-path at the end of a long day was something none of the mistresses wished for their charges.

'Isn't there a legend about this place, Frieda?' asked Jo, with a backward nod to it as they went forward.

Frieda shook her head. 'I have never heard of one, Jo. But I can tell you about the building of the Maria-rastkapelle at Hainzenberg, if you like.'

'Oh yes; do!' cried Marie. 'I love all the legends of the Tyrol, and I am sure this one must be new.'

'It is; *I've* never heard of it,' said Jo with emphasis.

'Then it *is* new,' said Simone. 'I believe collecting legends of the Tyrol is one of your hobbies, my Jo. Do you intend to make a book of them some day?'

Jo went darkly red. All unwitting, Simone had lighted on one of her cherished ambitions. However, she only said, 'Oh, never mind me.—Get on with the story, Frieda.'

Thus encouraged, Frieda began at once. 'In the olden days, when the men of the Tyrol worshipped heathen gods and goddesses, there was one who was called Hulda, a beautiful nymph, whose glittering home lay beneath the blue waters of a lake, and who loved all lakes and streams. It was said that at midday she could be seen, bathing, and then disappearing.

'But Christianity came to the Tyrol, and to the Zillerthal as to other places. Near Hainzenberg there is a little, clear brook, and near the brook there stood a patriarchal oak which was sacred to Hulda. When the people of the Zillerthal became Christian they had this oak hewn down, and then they decided to build there a chapel to Our Lady. It is said that when the tree crashed to the ground, a loud cry from Hulda was heard; and it is certain that nevermore was she seen in that place.

'The people began to collect together materials for their chapel. All day they laboured, and did not stop until the sunset painted the sky with marvellous colours. Then they left their heaps of stones and baulks of wood, and went home to eat and sleep, intending to come back next day and add to the piles.

' But when they returned the following morning it was to find that all the materials had been carried away to a neighbouring spot. They could not understand it ; and while some brought back what had been gathered, others went to seek more. But the next morning the same thing had occurred ; and the next ; and the next. Finally a daring youth vowed to remain beside their work through the night, to frighten away anyone who might be playing tricks on them.

' When his friends returned next morning they found the heaps removed as before, and he himself was kneeling by them, praying. When he saw the men of his village, he sprang up and came running to meet them with his tale. He told them that throughout the night ravens had come, and had carried off the stones and the timber, and brought them to the place where they were now found. Nor had all his shouting hindered them.

' The people took this story to the priest, and when he had heard it he said, " Then it is evident that Heaven means that place shall not be used which was profaned by the worship of Hulda. Therefore, my children, let us build our chapel on the site chosen by the ravens."

' So it was done. And there the chapel stands to this day,' finished Frieda.

By this time they had left the wild gorge behind, and were once more walking through a green field ; while over the brow of a hill they could see the chimneys and roof of the farm-house for which they were making. They were soon there, and the farmer's wife, when appealed to for milk, promised it gladly. She brought it forth in two big pans, into which they dipped their mugs, and everyone drank thirstily.

'I remember this one,' said the woman, as Jo paused near her. 'It is some years ago, but I could not forget the pointed face, and the black eyes and hair, so strange to see.—Am I not right, mein Fräulein ? You were here then, nicht wahr ? '

Fluent as Jo was, she found some difficulty in following the broad patois, but Frieda helped to interpret it, and Jo nodded at once. 'But yes, meine Frau. I was here ; and this, and this, and this ! ' And she indicated her friends, as well as pointing out Juliet and Grizel, who were with Miss Wilson.

The woman gave them all hearty welcome, and insisted on their coming in and partaking of a huge bowl of the sweet wild strawberries which her boys had brought home earlier in the day. As a substitute for the grapes and apricots they were without peer, and the girls feasted rapturously. They were very loth to go ; but Miss Annersley and Miss Wilson were determined not to miss the train ; so after many expressions of thanks and goodwill, they picked up their baskets and set off again, along the banks of the stream, through the woods, and finally reached Mayrhofen, where they were greeted by Mademoiselle and her three charges, who had had a quiet but pleasant time.

It was late when they finally reached the Chalet School, and some of the younger ones could scarcely keep awake long enough to get their Abendessen. But Miss Stewart and Miss Nalder attended to them.

' Bill,' Miss Annersley, and the four prefects had been detained at Seespitz, the tiny hamlet at the foot of the lake, by the man who was in charge of the little railway cabin.

Raising a large basket, he held it out to them, saying, ' Bitte, meine Fräulein, is this yours ? It was lying on the path here when the train had gone this morning, and I locked him into my cabin.'

It was the missing fruit !

Miss Annersley claimed it, and gave it to the girls to carry, while she and Miss Wilson presented the man with Trinkgeld in return for his kindness.

' You must share it for Abendessen, mes enfants,' said Mademoiselle, when she had heard the story.

Jo's comment was peculiarly Jo-ian. ' Better late than never ! ' she remarked, as she set her teeth into the luscious flesh of a pinky-golden apricot.

CHAPTER XVII

THE FINAL WEEKS' EXPLOITS

THE weeks of the term flew fast after that expedition. The following week-end, Joey Bettany, with mournful eyes, was found counting the days till the end of term on the common-room calendar.

'But, Joey! What are you doing?' cried Marie, who had caught her.

Jo lifted black eyes which were wells of sorrow. 'Do you realise that we have only thirty-two more days of school-life?' she demanded. '*Thirty*-two days! And then we're finished with school!'

'But not with the Chalet School,' returned Marie, slipping an arm through her friend's. 'Do hang up that calendar, Jo, and don't look so miserable. I have something to tell you. Will you come down to the stream with me?'

'Something to tell me?' Jo hung up the calendar, and ceased to look as if she were mourning her entire family. 'What is it?'

'If you will come, you will be told,' said Marie, flushing. 'Frieda and Simone have already gone on, and I came for you.'

Jo made no more remarks, but went with her chum out into the garden, and down to the stream, where the other two were awaiting them. Marie, with one arm through Frieda's and the other through Jo's, and with the faithful Simone on Jo's other side, drew them along to a place where the steep banks were covered with grass which was starred with wild pansies, marguerite daisies, and many other flowers. Here she sat down, and the other three sat down with her.

'Well, what is it?' demanded Jo, plucking a daisy and tossing it into the little stream which babbled along over its pebbly bed.

Marie said nothing, and the Head Girl twisted round to stare at her. 'Marie von Eschenau!' she exclaimed, 'what have you been doing?'

The other two were staring, too, and it is little wonder that Marie was red as a peony. However, she lifted her head and faced them bravely.

'It—it is that Eugen von und zu Wertheimer has spoken to Papa—about me,' she said, with a little catch in her throat. 'We will do nothing till I have left school; but I am eighteen now, and he thought it well to ask Papa if he would agree if—if I did.'

The girls said nothing for a moment. Naturally, ever since last year's boat-race against St Scholastika's, when they had seen how much the young Baron was attracted to the prettiest girl in the Chalet, they had guessed how it would end. But to have it in as concrete a form as this robbed them of speech for the moment.

Characteristically, Jo was the first to recover herself. 'Well, I be *gum-swizzled*!' she ejaculated.

'Josephine! What language! I am ashamed of you!'

Then all the girls sprang to their feet, for the voice was the voice of Madge Russell, and they had seen next to nothing of her that term.

'Madge!' cried Joey, flinging her arms round her

beloved sister. 'When did you come? Why wasn't
I told? Where's Sybil? Oh, and just listen to
this! Marie is engaged—actually *engaged*, if you
please! And she's still just a babe at school!'

Poor Marie went scarlet, and the other two began
to laugh, while Mrs Russell herself gasped.

'Let me sit down, girls. And let me recover my
breath after this shock.—Why weren't you told,
Joey? Because I didn't know myself till just about
an hour ago. Sybil is at the Chalet with Mademoiselle. And now, what is this wild news you have
just sprung on me?—Marie, is Jo romancing, or is
it true?'

'It's true, Madame, though not *quite* as Joey says,'
stammered Marie. 'Eugen has spoken to Papa;
but, of course, we shall not be properly betrothed
until I have left school.'

Madge Russell put out a slim hand, and pulled the
girl to her, and kissed her. 'Marie, dear, I am very
glad. I think we all like the Baron.'

'Yes; and the beauty of it is that she'll be quite
near us,' added Jo. 'Wertheimershof isn't so fearfully far from here, and as the Baron has a car, she'll
be able to come and see us often. When will the
wedding be, Marie?'

'Joey!' cried the confused Marie. 'We are not
yet betrothed, even!'

'No; but you soon will be,' returned Jo sagely.

Marie turned to her former Head Mistress. 'I
had Papa's letter this morning; and also one from
Mamma. They are very pleased about it, Madame,
for they like Eugen so much. And, yes; Joey is
right. We shall be betrothed early in August, I
think. And I want you three,' and she turned to

her friends with a lovely smile, ' to be at my verlobt feast.'

' But I shall be in Paris ! ' wailed Simone. ' How can I come so far ? '

' It will not be in Wien,' said Marie, using the Austrian name for Vienna. ' It will be held at Wanda's house in Salzburg. Mamma is always ill now, when the hot weather comes to Wien, and she and Papa and Wolfram will spend the summer with Wanda and Friedel. Besides, Wanda herself could not come so far just now, and I must have my sister there. So it will be at Salzburg ; and perhaps you could stay here, Simone, until then. It would not be more than a month.'

' Of course she will ! ' declared Mrs Russell, with a reassuring smile at Simone. ' She will come to us for the first fortnight. And then, perhaps, Mademoiselle will be back at Briesau by that time, and she can come down here if she has no other invitation.'

' Simone will spend the remaining fortnight with us,' said Frieda quietly. ' I know Mamma would be so glad, Simone.'

' There you are, then, my dear girl. No need to worry, after all, you see.'

Simone drew a long breath of relief. ' Oh, I am so glad ! I should have been so sorry to miss the betrothal of the first of our set.'

' And how long will it be before you are married ? ' asked Jo.

' That, I do not know,' replied Marie, who had recovered a little from her embarrassment. ' But I know that Eugen does not wish us to wait too long. I think it will probably be at Christmas time.'

'Then have it just before term begins,' suggested Jo. 'Then the School can come to it, as we did to Bernhilda's.'

Marie laughed. 'Nothing is really arranged yet, Joey. And please, you must say nothing to anyone about it. I had to tell you three because we are friends. And Madame had to know; and perhaps she would tell Mademoiselle. But I think no one else ought to hear until we have left school.'

'Oh, but Bill—you'll tell Bill!' protested Jo.

'Well, perhaps she might know. But there must be no one else.'

'I quite agree,' said Madge. 'If this got round the school there would be so much excitement that nobody would do another stroke of proper work this term. So we'll let Mademoiselle and Miss Wilson— I wish you people would try to remember that in term-time, at any rate, it is not the thing to call any mistress by a nickname before me!—know about it; and then we'll say nothing more. You have not quite a month left of your school-life; and you must make the most of it. After it is over will be time enough to think of grown-up things.'

They agreed with her. But she was interested to note that even Jo, usually so rebellious about anything that seemed to hint that her childhood was ending, accepted this latest affair quite happily.

'I am glad of this,' thought the elder sister. 'Joey is beginning to grow up, and to grow up happily. This past year has done much for her. The child has given way to the girl; and the girl will be lost in the woman, and Joey will be happy and contented.'

They chatted for a while about school matters, and then Mrs Russell got up. 'I must go now. My daughter will be crying for me. Do you want to see her? Then come along, and you shall have a peep before Guides.'

'We aren't having parade this morning,' said Frieda, as they fell in step with her. 'It has been so hot; and there is the cricket-match against St Scholastika's this afternoon. So none of the team go to Guides; and Miss Wilson has not been well, and Miss Stewart is very busy with examination-papers—she said so—so we have no Guides to-day.'

'Oh, I see. What is wrong with Miss Wilson?'

'I don't know.' It was Jo who answered this. 'She hasn't looked too fit for the last week or so. I thought she seemed better last Saturday when we were up the Zillerthal; but on Sunday she was in bed nearly all day. And though she's taken her lessons as usual this week, she *hasn't* been really fit.'

'I'm sorry to hear that.' Mrs Russell looked grave. 'I must go and see her as soon as I have attended to the needs of my daughter.'

They had reached the bridge across the ditch by this time, and they went up the garden-path and in at the front door. Mademoiselle was in her study, and they could hear soft gurglings and cooings from Baby Sybil. Mrs Russell opened the door and went in, to find her daughter rolling on the low, broad couch, where she was well fenced in by cushions. Jo darted forward, and caught her up.

'There! Isn't she getting on?' she said proudly. 'Do you notice the ginger locks?—and Jem calls them *chestnut*!'

'So they are!' declared the baby's mother indignantly. 'They're not ginger in the least—they are much too dark for that. Give me my baby, Joey Bettany, and take yourself off! You don't deserve to be allowed to have anything to do with her!'

Joey resigned her niece, and then listened while the other three poured out exclamations of delight and admiration. Jo to the contrary, the thick curls that adorned the baby's head were deep chestnut in hue. She had eyes of the same deep sapphire that helped to make Gillian Linton such a pretty girl; and her small face was coloured like a wild-rose.

'That schoolgirl complexion!' pointed out Jo. 'I must say her skin and eyes are lovely, even though she *is* my niece!'

'Now you've all seen her,' said her mother, 'so you'd better go away and leave me to see to her. We are staying till Monday, so you'll have plenty of chances to play with her.'

'Just a moment, Madge!' implored Jo. 'How is David? Why didn't you bring him down, too?'

'Because Sybil is enough for one person to manage at present. Besides, I knew that if I brought David it would mean bringing Primula Mary. They are inseparable these days. And then Peggy and Rix would have demanded to come, too. And schools are *not* places for babies.'

'Just one more question, and then we'll go. How is Margot?'

'Much better! Jem says that she is recovering tone in every way, and will soon be fit as ever. She sent her love to you and Frieda, and she is longing to see you both again. She is out in the garden all day and every day; and she's actually got a little colour in her cheeks now, and is beginning to lose those awful dips and hollows in her face.'

' Oh, I am so glad, Madame ! ' cried Frieda.

Mrs Russell smiled. Then she glanced at Mademoiselle and raised her eyebrows. ' What do you think, Mademoiselle ? Shall we tell them ? '

Mademoiselle laughed. ' But of course, if you wish it, ma chérie. But they must promise to say nothing to the others.'

' Oh, what is it ? ' asked Simone eagerly.

Mrs Russell nodded to Mademoiselle. ' You tell them. It 's your business, after all.'

Mademoiselle smiled at the eager faces. ' Well, mes enfants, it is that when the term ends, Matron Besly leaves us. And in her place we shall have Mrs Venables.'

' What ? Margot coming down as Matron at St Clare's ? ' gasped Jo. ' Why, it 'll be enough to give her nervous breakdown, after all—unless the middles reform at one bang,' she added.

Mademoiselle shook her head. ' Mrs Venables will manage very well. She, we feel sure, will not try to keep you all within very narrow limits. I regret having to say it, but much of Matron Besly's troubles have been her own fault.'

After this Mrs Russell chased them off, and they went away, having promised faithfully that they would tell no one the news.

' That means two enormous secrets to keep ! ' sighed Joey. ' I can see myself having to go dumb for the rest of the term.'

However, there was no need for that. For just as they were promenading down the path, a wildly-shrieking Cornelia came tearing up to find someone to bring to Elsie and Margia, who had got stuck half-way up one of the tall pines in the forest and were able to move neither up nor down. Jo set off at her best pace, the rest following at her heels, and presently they reached the place, where Elsie, having looked down, had turned giddy; and Margia, in trying to go to her help, had got hooked on to a broken bough.

Getting them down was a difficult matter, and in the end Jo had to send for the tall ladders which were used when the houses were refrescoed every spring, before she could loosen Margia. Elsie was helped down, and the pair reached earth to fall into the tender mercies of an irate Mademoiselle, who lectured them severely, and then issued an edict that no one was to climb any of the pines in the future.

After that came the match with St Scholastika's, when the Chalet School were beaten by five runs after a heated fight, in which Marie carried her bat for 47; Frieda achieved 33; and Jo, Margia, and Elsie were ignominiously out for ducks. However, Jo managed to bowl two of the St Scholastika men in one innings; and Elsie, at coverpoint, made a catch that had looked impossible, and certainly saved the School from a much worse beating than they got. So everyone felt that honour was salved; and no one was too much cast down at St Scholastika's victory.

The match ended, the two Schools met for supper, where they had a royal time, singing songs, and making speeches.

Sunday was a quiet day, only broken by attendance at the services; and with Monday came the round of ordinary work. Exams were now looming ahead, so most people were thankful to settle down and study hard. On the exam results depended largely the

removes for the coming year, so that even the middles,
scared lest they should be left down, were to be found
with books in their hands.

'I'm sick of French, German, Italian, Spanish,
history, geography——'

A cushion cut short Jo's diatribe on the Thursday
evening of that week.

'You aren't nearly as sick of them as we are of
your voice!' Anne Seymour assured her. 'Go and
put your head in a bag! If you don't want to work,
other people do!'

Simone, who was trying to cover a year's work in
one week, heaved a sigh of relief, stuck her fingers
more firmly into her ears, and glued her attention
to her *Histoire de l'Europe*. Vanna and Carla,
struggling with the plays of Molière, never even
looked up. Only Marie and Frieda smiled sym-
pathetically at Jo, as she tossed the cushion aside,
rose with much dignity, and left the prefects' room
where they were all working.

'Jo is annoyed, Anne,' said Sophie Hamel.

'Can't help it if she is,' retorted Anne. 'It's all
very well for her. She leaves at the end of this term.
But I simply *must* have a decent showing!'

Later, however, when she had forgotten all about
the little contretemps, she was startled to find that
a pleasant remark of hers was snubbed by the
Head Girl. Anne had merely said, looking at the
sunset, 'Alpenglueh to-night! That means rain
to-morrow. Well, the courts can do with it, Jo, can't
they? They're beginning to crack all over with the
heat.'

'Indeed?' was Jo's only comment, as she moved
away.

Anne stared after her in amazement. 'What on earth's the matter with Jo now?' she demanded of the company present.

'She's mad because of what you did and said before Abendessen,' said Louise Redfield.

'Jo mad for a little thing like that! Oh, don't be stupid!'

'At the same time,' said Frieda quietly, 'it was not quite the thing from a sub-prefect to the Head Girl, Anne. If I were you, I would ask pardon for it.'

'I'll do no such thing!' retorted Anne, up in arms at once. 'If Jo Bettany likes to be such a baby about a little joke, she can just carry on! *I'm* not going to do anything about it.'

What Frieda knew, though she had no intention of saying it, was that Jo was feeling rather unhappy at leaving school. As she had truly said, for most of the others there was definite work to do. Frieda herself was to go up to the Sonnalpe to help her sister-in-law, once Gisela Marani; for a little sister had come for small Natalie only a week ago, and Gisela's hands would be full. Marie had her betrothal coming; Simone was going to the Sorbonne at the next semestre; Carla, Vanna, Sophie, Eva von Heiling, all had something awaiting them. Carla was to take up singing and go to Florence to study; Vanna, the only child of an invalid mother, would have plenty to do at home; Sophie had two small sisters to whom she was to act governess for the next two years; and Eva had announced her intention of going to England to train as a kennel-maid, thus turning to advantage her undoubted influence over animals. Only Jo would find little to do. Her sister had an excellent nurse, and was engaging a young girl to take charge of the Bettany twins until they were old enough for school. There was her singing, of course ; and her writing. But Jo felt that she would have no settled duties, and after the full, busy life she had led at school, she found the prospect very dull.

Anne could not be expected to understand this. While Jo was perfectly friendly, as a rule, with all the girls in her form, she was reserved with all save her three great friends. They knew how she was feeling ; but none of the others could.

Anne, disgustedly proclaiming that she would never have believed that Jo Bettany could be such a baby, refused to make any advances, and Jo herself became chilly, and built up a wall of icy courtesy between herself and the sub-prefect that even her chums dared not try to break down.

Things remained in this unpleasant condition for two days, during which the entire prefects' room seemed to be under a cloud. Then something happened which ended it all in a hurry.

It seemed good to Frau Mieders, the domestic economy mistress, to ask Mademoiselle to grant a half-holiday on the coming Monday, so that the girls could go and gather wild strawberries for jam. They were very plentiful this year, and just at their best. She proposed that all the middles and seniors should take Kaffee und Kuchen with them, as well as big baskets, and spend the afternoon gathering, having a picnic up on the mountain-side, and not coming down till dusk.

' Where do you wish to take them ? ' asked Mademoiselle.

' To the Mondscheinspitze, Mademoiselle,' said

Frau Mieders in her pleasant voice. 'Herr Denny tells me that the strawberries grow most luxuriantly there, and that it will be easy to fill our baskets soon. Then we can climb up to the alm, and ask the herdsmen for milk, and make our Kaffee there, and have a pleasant time with the English picnic. We could also stem the berries up there, and thus have them all ready for the jam-making next day.

Mademoiselle considered this. It struck her as a good plan. The examinations would begin on Wednesday of that week, and this little expedition would give the girls a much-needed rest. She consented to it, and on the Saturday night informed the School at large what was in store.

Most of the girls were overjoyed, though one or two looked rather worried at the thought of the time lost from cramming. But Mademoiselle was wise in her generation. She knew that many of them had been trying to do too much lately, and the result was fratchety tempers and bickering, which she detested. She went a step further.

'To-morrow no one may read unless it be a story-book,' she said. 'I myself will go the rounds of all lockers to see that all lesson-books are safely put away. Then we will lock them up, and you will take a complete rest from work. There will be the usual services to-morrow; and in the evening we shall take a long walk.'

Several people—notably Evadne, Cornelia, and some of the younger middles—pulled long faces at this. How were they to do decently in the exams if they were to be docked of cramming-time like this ? However, they dared not argue, and Mademoiselle carried out her intention. Accompanied by the Staff, she made the rounds of all lockers that night, and when any book was found missing, the girl to whom it belonged was promptly called upon to account for it. It was easy enough, for all girls were required to keep a correct list of text-books and exercise-books pinned on the door of the locker, as well as a time-table. Mademoiselle made some surprising discoveries during her search, and sundry books which had been ' missing ' for weeks turned up in the most unexpected places. But at last it was finished, and nothing was left but story-books for them.

Next day was spent as usual until the evening, when the three divisions of the school set off for different walks. Miss Edwards and Miss Norman, with pleasant little Mademoiselle Lachenais, the modern language mistress, set off up the valley to the foot of the Mondscheinspitze. The middles were taken off to the far side of the lake for a walk to Scholastika, the village at the head of the lake. They had with them Miss Leslie, Miss Nalder, Miss Annersley, and Frau Mieders. Miss Wilson and Miss Stewart took the seniors up to the Bärenbad Alpe, whence they intended to strike across by the narrow isthmus, through the valley of flowers, and so to Mechthau, the little village on the neighbouring alpe, and down to the great Tiern Pass. Mademoiselle, who was middle-aged and growing stout, though as yet she needed no glasses, and could dance half the evening with the girls, elected to stay at home with Stacie Benson, who must not risk the exertion, though she was much better than at the beginning of the term, and two or three of the very small ones. She promised to read aloud to them, so they were quite happy, and made no complaints.

The seniors duly set off, led by Jo and Frieda, for they must form a ' crocodile ' as long as they were in Briesau. There were many visitors there now, and both Schools had to behave with great circumspection until they were away from these aliens. As it happened, Anne came next with her other self, Louise Redfield, Marie and Simone having elected to walk with Miss Stewart, while Miss Wilson was escorted by Vanna and Carla.

The way up to the Bärenbad was thronged with people who were coming down after having Kaffee and wild strawberries and cream at the little Gasthaus on the alpe; so the girls walked very properly, speaking in low tones, and generally behaving as if, to quote Miss Wilson later on, they were unfledged angels.

In their white frocks, big shady hats, with twist of yellow silk round the crowns, and brown sandals, they looked all they ought to look. The two mistresses in charge felt very proud of them as they went. They reached the Bärenbad, but instead of going straight ahead to the Gasthaus, which stands a little way back from the head of the path, they climbed up over the green hummocky ground, until they were right at the top of it, and then turned left, making their way to the narrow isthmus of land that joins this alpe with the next. Here they were freed from the visitors, who, as a rule, preferred to rest at the Gasthaus, and then return as they came. Once they were assured of solitude, the girls broke rank, and straggled along in twos and threes. Simone and Marie joined Frieda and Jo; and Anne and Louise co-opted big Thora Helgersen. The rest wandered on as they chose, so long as they kept in front of the two mistresses, who strolled after them, chatting idly.

It was a beautiful evening. Down beneath them gleamed the sapphire waters of the Tiern See, a blue jewel in a white setting. Across from them they could see, at the other side of the lake, the Sonnalpe, with its great Sanatorium, its clusters of gay chalets, the two churches, and the hotel. To the north lay the great mass of the Tiernjoch peaks, to which they were crossing, since Mechthau lies along one of the shelves of the easier slopes.

'Be careful in crossing, girls,' called Miss Wilson. 'I don't want to take anyone home all bits and pieces.'

They went on carefully, for though the path is never less than six feet in width, the grass was slippery with the baking heat of the sun, and if they had fallen, they must have rolled down among bushes and thorns, which would be unpleasant though it could not be fatal.

From the isthmus they went on over a rough pasturage, with pines growing here and there, and so came to the valley of flowers. They knew of it some time before they reached it, for the faint breeze blowing up here carried to them the perfume of a thousand scented things, and as they neared it they could hear the faint 'tinkle-tinkle' of the little brook that runs through it.

'It must be gorgeous now,' said Marie. 'I do hope Bill lets us stop to gather some flowers. It was wonderful last September, so what must it be like in June?'

Her expectations were not disappointed. The whole of the little wedge-shaped valley was starred with flowers; and the air was heavy with the scent of narcissi, wild-roses, pansies, and other blossoms.

' Ten minutes for picking, girls!' called Miss Wilson. 'Don't take too many, for most of you will have nothing with which to tie them, and I hate to see flowers dying by the roadside, dropped from careless hands.'

The girls obeyed her. Each gathered only a handful, and Jo hunted about till she found a broad-leaved plant with which she swathed the stems of her bunch, so that the heat of her hands might not wither the flowers. The others followed her example, and then they were ready to go on.

Unfortunately, Anne was seized with a brilliant idea. If she could wet her flowers, they would be so much fresher when she got home. Only she couldn't put them into the stream, because it was a wild little brook, and its fury might dash the blossoms to pieces. She must go to the rock wall which hemmed in the valley at the eastern side, and try to dabble them in the pool which she had noticed the water had made for itself just at the edge. Accordingly, she left the others and crossed to where the water swirled into the tiny basin, seeming to pause a moment before it hurled itself over to the rock beneath. It was not a safe thing to do, for the splashing of the water had made the rocks slippery, and there was a sheer drop of seventy or eighty feet below. But Anne recked nothing of that. She climbed up, and then bent down, clinging to the tiny parapet with one hand. She knew that if she were caught she would get into trouble, so this may have accounted for what happened. Or it may have been that she was wearing new sandals. However it came about, her foot suddenly slipped. She shrieked, and clutched at the parapet ; but it, like her foothold, was slippery, and her clutching fingers slid off it. With another wild cry, echoed by one a little behind her, she fell. Mercifully, a fir-tree a little way down had found root-hold, and she crashed against its trunk. Grimly she grabbed it, and just succeeded in staying her fall. Meanwhile she screamed again and again for help. The tree was a young one, and she was not sure how its roots would bear the strain of her weight, for she was a well-built girl.

But help was at hand. Jo Bettany had heard her first scream, and, dropping her flowers, she rushed to the edge, and kneeling down, looked over.

' Hold on, Anne ! ' she called. ' I 'm coming ! '

Before anyone had quite realised what had happened, she had wrenched off her sandals, and was standing on the slippery parapet, her toes gripping the tiny rough edges of the rock with the prehensile grip of a monkey. Cautiously she lowered herself to another projection just below ; and then, clinging with one hand and both knees and toes, she stooped down.

' Stretch up ! ' she called. ' You can reach my hand, and help will be here soon.'

Anne had recovered her head now. Moving cautiously in case she overbalanced, she reached up and her fingers met Joey's, and clung with the firm ' sailor's grip.'

By this time the mistresses were beside them, and Miss Stewart had an arm flung round Joey's waist, while Frieda held her, and Simone held Frieda. Miss Wilson was looking round for something that could be used as a rope, for the girls were stockingless, and none of them wore belts.

It fell to Marie to make a practicable suggestion. Stripping off her white frock, she wriggled out of her petticoat, and several of the others snatched at the idea. The petticoats were knotted together by the shoulder-straps with reef-knots, and at length a rope, frail enough, but better than nothing, was ready.

While this was going on, Evadne, fleet of foot as 'silver-footed Thetis,' had turned and sped back to the Gasthaus. But it was a good distance away, and Miss Wilson could see, though the girls could not, that the little fir was beginning to wrench itself away from the rock wall. It would not hold much longer, and then, not only Anne, but Joey too, must be flung to a ledge far beneath.

'Bill's' face was white as she realised this; but she said nothing.

Dropping the 'rope' over the low wall, she called down, 'Anne, can you possibly get this round yourself?'

For reply, Anne let go of her agonised hold of the tree for a moment and gripped the fine, jersey silk of the petticoat. Joey held on like grim death; and Miss Stewart, leaning perilously over the parapet, held on to her. More of the girls were now helping to form the living rope, and 'Bill' considered an instant. Then she said sharply, 'Thora, come here and stand by Frieda. Now grip Miss Stewart round the waist.—Louise, you come, too.—Move carefully, girls.—Sophie, Carla, and Vanna, come to the rope.— The rest of you link up.'

They obeyed her implicitly. Then, still quaking inwardly at thought of what failure must mean, she said, 'Now, when I say "Heave!" we four on the rope will haul, while Miss Stewart will raise Joey, and the rest of you will try to help her to pull in.'

She paused after that, to get her feet firmly planted against the rock wall, and to let Elsie Carr slip two more petticoats under the rope to save it from chafing, though the water had worn away most of the rough edges of the rock just here. Then, with a final, ' Hold tight ! ' she gave the word, ' *Heave!* '

It was well for all concerned that most of the girls had been well drilled into instantaneous obedience. On the word, they all heaved, while Miss Stewart, putting forth an effort of which she had never deemed herself capable, swung Joey up, so that her knees were on the top of the parapet again. At the same moment the rope was dragged upwards, and Anne was raised to Jo's projection, which she slowly passed, being hauled upwards with many a swing and bang against the rock.

It seemed hours to everyone concerned, but actually it was barely minutes, before Anne herself was dragged in across the top of the parapet, and safely landed among the flowers. She was white and gasping, and the blood was trickling down her face from a nasty cut on her cheek. Her dress was torn and soiled, and her hands were all torn ; but she was safe. As for Joey, beyond looking very white, she was much as usual, though her feet were badly cut on the soles. The worst off was Miss Stewart, who had wrenched herself when she made that mighty effort, and who was crouching against the wall, white and sick with pain.

CHAPTER XVIII

THE VERY LAST DAY

' JOEY, Mademoiselle wants you ! '

Jo Bettany, wandering round the ground floor of St Clare's, started. ' Goodness, Corney ! What a shock you gave me ! Mademoiselle, did you say ? Where is she ? '

' In the Staff room.'

' All right.' And Jo, with a deep sigh, left the prefects' room, and went slowly across the passage to the Staff room, where Miss Wilson and Mademoiselle Lepâttre were waiting for her. Miss Stewart was still unable to do much, for the wrenched muscles of her shoulders were healing slowly, and she had not quite recovered from the shock of the whole appalling adventure of three weeks before. So St Clare's had been minus its second mistress for that time, though the doctors said that she would be quite all right by the time the new term began.

' Come in, Joey,' said Mademoiselle, as the Head Girl appeared at the door and made her curtsey. ' We wish to know what you know of this ? ' And she held out to the startled Jo a sheet of paper, decorated with drawings of various musical instruments.

Jo took it, and began to read, a delighted grin slowly illuminating her face as she read. ' Oh ! ' she exclaimed when she reached the end. ' What a priceless joke ! '

'But what is it all about?' demanded Miss Wilson. 'What is this St Clare's Orchestra? *I* haven't heard anything about it.'

For reply, Jo slipped her hand into the pocket of her white drill tennis-frock and produced a snapshot. This she held out to the mistresses. They took it, and gazed at it. The next moment they both collapsed in fits of laughter.

'Jo!' cried 'Bill,' first to recover herself, as might have been expected. 'Where *did* you get this?'

'That,' said Jo, 'is a photograph of Corney practising the saxophone. Frieda took it—one morning when we tracked them to the woods before Frühstück. So far as I've been able to gather, Corney and Evvy decided that St Clare's ought to have an orchestra. The only thing is, their tastes are apt to lean towards jazz, and they've got jazz instruments. They doled them out among their own gang, and they've all been practising the things hard. But I didn't know they were well enough on to give a concert,' she added, scanning again the invitation which had been thrust at her.

'ST CLARE'S ORCHESTRAL SOCIETY.'

The above Society request the pleasure of the Company of Mademoiselle Lepâttre, and the Staff and Members of Ste Thérèse's, on the last day of school at 18.30, at

A GRAND CONCERT OF MUSIC

to be given by the aforesaid Orchestra in the Common-room at St Clare's.

ALL SEATS FREE. COME AND ENJOY YOURSELVES!'

'What a nerve those kids have got!' she murmured.

'But why wasn't I informed of this?' demanded Miss Wilson.

'Well,' said Jo, 'it seemed quite a harmless way for them to spend their spare time. I didn't think they'd get as far as a concert in the time; and what with one thing and another, I suppose I forgot it.'

Miss Wilson laughed. 'Well, but they haven't asked for the use of the common-room yet; and before they have their concert, they must do that.—Come in! Yes, Miss Nalder?'

Little Miss Nalder waved a sheet, similar to the one Jo held, at her superiors. 'We have an invitation,' she said solemnly. Then she saw the other one. 'Good gracious! Do you mean to say that our enterprising musicians have invited Ste Thérèse's?'

'Not only that, but they have also invited St Agnes',' said Mademoiselle. 'I came over to ask when this orchestra had begun, and as Miss Wilson knew nothing about it we sent for Jo, who tells us that it is the affair of the middles solely.'

'It was news to me, I assure you,' said Miss Wilson. 'Well, Joey, you may tell Cornelia and Evadne to come to me, and we'll settle the question of the common-room before they go any further with their "Concert."'

'Yes, Miss Wilson,' said Jo. Then she paused. 'I say, you'll let them have it, won't you?' she pleaded. 'It really ought to be the joke of the season, for I'm prepared to swear that none of them know much about their instruments. I wonder if they are giving us solos or symphonies?' she added.

Miss Wilson laughed again. 'Oh yes; they may have the room, of course—after I have told them that it was not courteous to proclaim such a public

use of the common-room without asking permission
first. Like you, I think it will be very funny. And
it *is* the last day of term.'

' Yes ; you can't count to-morrow,' assented Miss
Nalder. 'Considering that twenty or so of them
are off by the seven train in the morning, and most
of the others will be gone before ten, to-morrow is
not a day.'

' Then go and send them, Joey,' ordered Miss
Wilson. 'But say nothing to them. Oh, by the
way, may I keep this ? '

' Oh yes,' said Jo. ' I 've got an enlargement of
it—Frieda had three done.' Then she went off,
chuckling, for what she was telling no one was the
fact that one of the enlargements had been entrusted
to Stacie Benson, so that it might be included in
next term's magazine. Jo's only complaint about
this was that she wouldn't be there to see Cornelia's
face when she found it out !

She found the pair, and sent them off to Miss
Wilson, merely telling them ' Miss Wilson wants to
see you two for a minute.'

As, for once in a way, they had fairly clear con-
sciences, they went quite cheerfully, and were greatly
taken aback when they were called to account for
their lack of courtesy in not notifying their house-
mistress of the formation of the ' Orchestra,' and for
calmly assuming they could use the common-room
as they chose. However, as she relented at the end
of her few biting comments, and gave them leave,
they were not unduly downcast, and they went off
to collect the rest of their clan and make final
arrangements.

The next event happened that evening when the

common-room was packed with girls and Staff to its limits. The light, movable platform, which was kept in a shed, had been brought in and set up by the two men who worked on the estate, and it was very prettily draped with golden and brown draperies, and adorned with bowls and jars of flowers. The piano stood at one side of it; and there were three music-stands and two chairs set at the back. The middles had worked hard that afternoon.

Seated in a wicker chair between Simone and Marie, Jo was preparing to enjoy herself to her heart's content, when Evadne, the master of the ceremonies, stalked on to the platform and proceeded to electrify the company with the information that the concert would open with a solo by ' Miss Josephine Bettany.'

Jo leapt to her feet indignantly. She was not prepared for this! Really, Evvy's cheek was illimitable, and she was going to tell her so! But before she could open her mouth, Cornelia was at her elbow with a selection of songs, and whispering urgently, ' You can't argue now. This is for St Clare's. Choose your song, and Lonny will play for you.'

' I 'll wring all your young necks when the visitors have gone! ' retorted Jo in an undertone, for she realised that the wily middles had cornered her. She could *not* argue about it just then. She selected Roger Quilter's setting of ' Sigh no More, Ladies,' and went up on to the platform, looking somewhat flushed with her mixed feelings, and waited while Ilonka played the short prelude. Then she opened her mouth and sang.

Jo had a lovely voice, sweet and effortless as any boy-chorister's, with something in it that no boy's voice ever has. She had been carefully trained, and, as she herself said later on, she could have sung *that* particular song backwards. Of course she was encored. It would have been the same thing if she had elected to sing exercises. She glanced over her songs—what impudence to rifle her music-case !— and finally chose a favourite of her own, Schubert's ' Gretchen am Spinnrädchen ' [' Margaret at her Spinning-wheel ']. Then she spoke, ' You can't play this, Lonny. We 'll have to ask Miss Denny.'

' I am glad ! ' said Ilonka sincerely. She turned to the front row of seats, and went to where good-hearted Miss Denny sat. ' Please, Miss Denny, Jo wishes will you play for her ? ' she asked, muddling her English in her shyness.

Miss Denny looked surprised. However, she was too good-natured to refuse, so she came and played the accompaniment, while Jo gave full rein to her vocal and dramatic powers in the song.

When the applause had ceased, and Miss Denny and Jo had gone back to their seats, Evadne once more mounted the platform and announced, ' A mouth-organ duet by Miss Joyce Linton and Miss Faith Barbour.'

Looking rather scared the performers got on to the platform, sat down facing each other, and began. The ' duet ' was supposed to be ' Annie Laurie,' but after the first two or three bars no one would have recognised it for any known tune. Mr Denny, the singing-master, and an exceptionally musical man, put his hands over his ears and groaned loudly, his feelings completely overcoming his manners. The girls leaned against each other and shrieked with laughter. And the Staff, all their dignity forgotten, were mopping their eyes and holding their sides.

Unmoved by all this the instrumentalists continued to the bitter end, and then looked round gravely at the overcome audience.

'But why are you laughing?' demanded Joyce, her fair face suddenly flushing. 'It—it's a *love*-song. There's nothing *funny* about it!'

It was impossible for anyone to laugh any more. But Margia and Elsie slipped off their chairs on to the floor, and held each other up; and Miss Nalder uttered a positive squeak. The puzzled pair glared round, and then marched off the platform, thoroughly indignant.

Evadne got up again, and gave out a violin and 'cello duet by Miss Kitty Burnett and Miss Emmie Linders. She sounded rather choked, and she got down again as quickly as possible. Kitty and Emmie, both very scarlet, climbed up and arranged their music, and then embarked on a classical affair of the seventeenth century. Mercifully, there was nothing special to mark this performance, and the audience gradually revived and sat up.

The next item on the programme was a zither solo by Stacie, who had wisely chosen something very simple and well within her powers. She got quite a little ovation when she ended, and had to come back and bow. She refused to give an encore, saying truthfully that that was the one thing she could manage yet.

But the cream of the whole affair came next. Anxious to show the powers of her orchestra, Evadne had decided that they must have a concerted piece, if it was the only one. Unfortunately she couldn't get anything that would do. So she had finally arranged that each girl should play two or three bars of the thing selected—and of all things, she had chosen ' Land of Hope and Glory,' from Sir Edward Elgar's march ' Pomp and Circumstance ' !

Evadne opened it herself on the ukulele—and the effect can better be imagined than described !—and was followed by Kitty on the violin. Stacie managed two bars on her zither, and Greta Macdonald piped about three correct notes on her C major pipe. The mouth-organs followed with many halts and false notes, and then came a shock, for the mouth-organ experts suddenly discarded those instruments, and essayed to play the next bars on jews'-harps ! The audience, of course, was almost incapable of following anything by this time ; but they sat up at the next sounds—both literally and metaphorically. For Cornelia came in next with her saxophone, and produced some sounds that transcended anything that had gone before.

Jo was hanging over her chair, sobbing with laughter. Frieda and Marie had tears streaming down their faces. Simone was almost hysterical, and the Staff and other girls were in no better case. Even Anne, who had been exceedingly subdued since her silly adventure, was sitting back in her chair and shouting with laughter.

It was just as well that here it had been decided to give the drum, castanets, tambourine, and cymbals a chance—of which they certainly made the most !— or what might have happened next there is no saying. When they had ended, Giovanna Donati plucked the tune from the strings of her ukulele; but that was bearable after what had gone before. Finally, Cornelia suddenly dropped her instrument, jumped to her feet, opened her mouth, and began to sing the grand chorus. Cornelia's voice was not to be compared with Jo's, but she had a very sweet little pipe of her own, and before she had sung three words the rest of the orchestra had joined in, and were singing it with might and main. Naturally the rest of the School joined in by degrees, and by the time they had sung it three times they were all more or less normal.

That ended St Clare's concert, although, as Evadne and Cornelia calmly informed their own prefects later, they had intended calling on Frieda for a harp solo, and Marie for her violin. Simone, not being musical, learned nothing, so was exempt from this. However, they thought they had better bring the affair to a close with the chorus ; and when it had ended, Evadne got on to a chair and informed the audience that the concert was finished ; but next term, when they should all have had time to practise more, St Clare's orchestra hoped to give another.

After that, Mademoiselle Lepâttre rose and thanked the orchestra for the unexpected—here she paused before she went on—treat. She knew that everyone wished St Clare's orchestra every success in the future. And now Abendessen for everyone would be ready at Ste Thérèse's, so she thought they had better go over.

There were cheers then, both for St Clare's and Ste Thérèse's, and finally the girls formed into line and marched across to the original house, where a gorgeous supper, beginning with chicken sandwiches and ending with ices, awaited them.

When it had ended they were sent off to bed, for most of them must be up very early. Only the prefects remained, and the Staff, the two Matrons of

St Agnes' and St Clare's undertaking to see the girls to bed.

'Well, Joey,' said Mademoiselle, turning to the Head Girl, 'I hope it has been a happy last day for you, and for all who leave us to-morrow.'

'Oh, it has!' cried Joey. 'I shall never, never forget that concert, and I only hope that all of us here may hear more concerts from St Clare's orchestra in the future.'

They all applauded her speech. Then, as it was getting late, Mademoiselle bade them 'Gute Nacht,' and they parted. Jo and her friends walked over to St Clare's, pausing now and then to look round them.

'Thank goodness, *we* haven't to get off at dawn to-morrow,' said Jo, as she opened the wicket-gate between the two gardens.

'I agree,' said Marie. She looked round at her friends as they stood there—Jo, tall and dark, and with that something about her that told of a great gift; Simone, little, and dark, and keen; Frieda, pretty as a picture in her white frock, with the coronal of plaits swung round her head. 'Oh,' she said, her voice quivering with the intensity of her feelings, 'we have had beautiful school-days here, we four. And we have had a beautiful friendship. Let us try to keep it always like this, even though other things come to us!'

'Whatever comes to us, nothing can alter our friendship,' said Jo sturdily. '*You* won't change, just because you are going to marry Eugen. Simone won't change because she's going to the Sorbonne. And Frieda and I won't change, even though nothing much comes our way. We'll always be friends, and we'll always remember our school-days.'

' Yes,' said Frieda softly. ' All of them have been happy—and especially this last term, for we four have been so much closer.'

' That 's thanks to St Clare's,' said Joey, with a quick glance at emotional Simone, who had tears in her eyes. ' So I say, bless the whole Chalet School. But a special blessing on our new house. May St Clare's always go forward ; and may the girls there be as close friends as we four have always been.'

And with full hearts the other three replied : ' St Clare's for friendship ! May God bless St Clare's ! '